Curve

Carrie Brennan

Yellow Rose Books

Nederland, Texas

ISBN 1-932300-41-4

First Printing 2005

9 8 7 6 5 4 3 2 1

Cover design by Donna Pawlowski

Published by:

Yellow Rose Books
PMB 210, 8691 9th Avenue
Port Arthur, Texas 77642-8025

Find us on the World Wide Web at
http://www.regalcrest.biz

Printed in the United States of America

Acknowledgments

So many people deserve thanks for offering advice, support, encouragement, and therapy during the writing of this novel, from its infancy in bits and scraps online to the finished product you hold in your hands (or maybe you've propped it on your stomach — my advice to you: cut back on the Krispy Kremes).

I can't begin to thank you all, even those who have threatened to never speak to me again if I don't thank them here (OK, OK, thanks, Jane). But I do need to offer thanks for above-and-beyond the call of friendship to Pat, my personal Moocher. And of course, big hugs and kisses to the love of my life, Shaun, who has joined me on the true love ride for more years than some of you have been alive. I love you, babe.

Cheers everyone!

Prologue:
The Elevator

TWO WOMEN SQUEEZED between the rapidly closing elevator doors, one's overstuffed briefcase nudging the other's uniformed knee. The old courthouse had only one elevator, and both women knew if they missed it, it would take ages for the car to deliver its passengers to the five floors and return to the lobby.

After exchanging embarrassed grins and mumbled apologies, they studiously ignored each other while contemplating what they'd seen.

Way too cute to be a cop, the taller woman mused. *Surely a gorgeous woman like that could find a better career, like a teacher or librarian or personal masseuse to a rising young attorney. Well, maybe not that last job.* The officer's dark blue uniform did contrast nicely with her eyes, she noticed. They were the most amazing color — sea green, just like the crayon.

Strangely enough, the young officer was also thinking about eyes. The blue eyes of the tall, dark-haired woman beside her reminded her of blue raspberry Slurpees. It actually wasn't uncommon for her to think about food and gorgeous women at the same time.

Well, she's got a briefcase jammed with files and a laptop in the other hand, she considered. *Could be a lawyer. Expensive silk shirt and tailored suit, so she sure isn't from the DA's office or a public defender.*

The two women, simultaneously, thought about saying something to the other. But reasons for staying silent quickly clamored for attention.

I'm on duty.
I'm late.
I shouldn't.
She wouldn't.

The old elevator lurched to a stop on the third floor and pinged to announce its arrival. The tall woman got out and turned to the left, walking down the hallway without looking back. The redhead sighed and, for a dizzying moment, felt profound regret as the elevator doors slowly closed.

Why didn't I say something? Maggie groaned, as she leaned back against the elevator wall.

Why didn't I say something? Anne asked herself, shaking her head as she entered the courtroom.

Chapter One

"PLEASE STEP TO the side."

The metal detector's annoying buzz drowned out Anne's sigh. She moved where the guard directed and lifted her arms as the officer passed the wand over her body. They were both used to this, and knew that Anne's cell phone had set off the alarm. She'd accidentally left it in her jacket pocket, just as she had the hundreds of other times before. It was some kind of cosmic joke that it only happened when she was late.

"I swear this is the last time," Anne said with a rueful chuckle. Officer Schmidt smiled, but focused on passing the detection wand over every inch of Anne's anatomy.

"OK, you're clear," he announced after a few long seconds. "Have a nice day, Ms. Doyle."

Anne rolled her eyes but smiled pleasantly. As she hurried away, her heels clicking against the polished floors, she checked her watch. She'd make it to the courtroom if she didn't have to wait for the elevator. She turned the corner, watched the elevator doors close the last inch, and muttered a curse under her breath. Then she smiled. She'd seen a flash of red hair and amazing sea green eyes just before the doors had closed.

In the two weeks since she'd literally run into the redheaded cop, Anne hadn't managed to speak to the woman. In fact, she'd never gotten as close as she had been that first afternoon in the elevator. But she did manage fleeting glimpses now and then, as they passed down intersecting corridors or stood in different places in line waiting to pass through the metal detector. Once, Anne had finished a long and impassioned speech to a bored judge and had turned around to see green eyes peering at her from the back of the courtroom. Her client had claimed her attention, and when she turned back, the cop was gone.

This has got to stop, Anne mused as she tapped her foot impatiently—frustrated by the elusive woman as much as the elevator. *I'm an adult woman who is attracted to another adult woman. I just need to talk to her, find out if she's gay, and then ask her out. Simple.*

Anne frowned as she thought about it some more. There was the talking part. That was always difficult. And then the finding out if someone was gay part. Often complicated. And the asking out...*oh, Jesus.*

Five minutes later, the elevator returned and the doors jerked opened. Anne tried to think about what excuse she'd make for being late. That diverted her attention for about thirty seconds, before Judge Ramirez's face was replaced in her mind by one with a scattering of freckles across her nose.

"Hi, I'm Anne and I think you're cute and I'm gay and I hope you are and would you like to go out for a coffee and if you're allergic to coffee or you're not gay or you don't like women named Anne then forget I said anything and have a nice day."

Had she said that out loud? She looked at the two other people in the elevator and decided, since they weren't staring at her with open mouths, that she hadn't.

"I'm late because I've been thinking obsessively about this beautiful woman that I ran into in the elevator a couple of weeks ago. Oh, and my car wouldn't start."

She hadn't said that out loud either, she decided. She then decided that she needed to work on both speeches. They were a little rough around the edges.

Anne was still practicing her excuses when she entered the courtroom, but quickly discovered that the judge's tardiness made her speech moot. He arrived frazzled and grumpy, mumbling his own excuses, which involved cars but not gorgeous women. Anne set aside her obsessive thoughts and began to arrange her notes, preparing for the day's case.

"OFFICER MARY MARGARET Monahan."

Maggie was thinking about the woman again—the woman with the long obsidian hair and clear blue eyes, the woman she'd had the wonderful fortune of seeing again that morning. Maggie had been thinking about the woman for two weeks and wondering why she hadn't said anything that afternoon in the elevator, metaphorically kicking herself over and over until she had metaphorical bruises.

"Officer Mary Margaret Monahan?"

Maggie wondered why people in the courtroom were murmuring so loudly. Then she wondered why everyone's heads were swinging toward her. She stopped wondering both things when she felt Moocher's sharp elbow jabbing her in the ribs.

"That's you, doofus," Moocher hissed.

"I heard," Maggie hissed back at her partner, then tried to look cool and professional as she scrambled toward the witness box. She hit the corner of the lawyer's table as she passed, jabbing her handcuffs painfully into her hip and sending the defense attorney's palm pilot sliding off the other edge. He caught it in mid-air and glared at her.

As Maggie swore to tell the truth, the whole truth, and nothing but the truth, she watched the angry attorney stride toward her. His eyes held a predatory gleam, and she tried not to feel like a rabbit caught in a snare.

"Officer Monahan, I want to take you back to the morning of March 13th, 2000."

Maggie took a deep breath and nodded as if reliving the details of arresting a low-life scum who put his cigarette out on his girlfriend's cheek was what she wanted to do more than anything in the world. Her dad had always said that court appearances were the worst part of police work.

"Always look 'em straight in the eye," Connor Monahan had advised his daughter when she was getting ready for her first court appearance, "and never tell them more than they ask."

Maggie never had trouble looking people straight in the eye, even when they looked like they wanted to eat her for lunch. Telling people more than they asked was something altogether different. She had a habit of burbling when she was nervous, as if a constantly moving mouth would eventually blurt out something that would save her from the awkward situation. It never did—only made matters worse. She'd end up either sounding like a gibbering idiot or saying the wrong thing.

Which is why I have to figure out exactly what I'm going to say to Blue Eyes next time I see her, Maggie thought. *Something memorable and witty and...*

"Officer Monahan, did you understand the question?"

Maggie's mind returned from its brief flight around the courtroom and resettled in her skull. She could see Moocher's rolling eyes out of the corner of her own.

"Could you repeat the question, please?"

It was going to be a long morning.

THE CUSTODY CASE that Anne was working on was routine and uneventful. The only details left to iron out involved child support. Agreeing to visitation rights had been a breeze, but when it came time to discuss the monetary side of the

divorce, both parties were inflexible. By the time they broke for
lunch, Anne had a headache the size of the San Francisco Bay
and if she heard "*how* much for a pair of shoes?" one more time,
she was going to throw her own black pump at someone's head.

The lights of the courthouse cafeteria were old, flickering
fluorescents, and they made her eyes sting and her head throb.
She scanned the large room for a dark, quiet corner as she
ordered her salad and bottled water. The sight of familiar red
hair and green eyes standing near the back of the line brought a
smile to her face. The cafeteria worker winked back at her and
she fumbled for her change, dropping it all in the tip jar before
grabbing her tray and moving toward the corner she'd mentally
staked out.

Anne didn't look behind her, playing it cool as she
frantically recalled her prepared speech. What was it again?
Something about coffee and names and sexual orientation...and
would this be the chance she'd actually get to say the words, or
would they die on her lips once again?

MAGGIE SPOTTED THE tall lawyer leaving the line with
her food tray and grabbed frantically at her partner. "Oh, my
God, Moocher, there she is. Look, look, heading toward the
corner."

"Maggie, you're gonna leave a bruise if you squeeze my arm
any harder." Despite her friend's plea, Moocher's eyes were
firmly fixed on the ass of the woman in line in front of them.

"It's her," Maggie said, digging her fingers in a little harder.
"It's the woman with the eyes. The one I ran into two weeks ago
in the elevator."

"And the one you've been stalking ever since?" Moocher
looked where Maggie had indicated, watching as the tall
brunette moved through the cafeteria toward an empty table.
"Ooh, she's a looker all right."

"Don't look at her; don't let her see us staring."

"First she says 'look,' then she says 'don't look.' " Moocher
shook her head. "You know, her eyes do resemble blue
raspberry Slurpees."

"Oh, my God, did she notice us?" Maggie tried to look
across the room without moving her head. She wondered if it
was possible to sprain eyeball muscles.

"And by the way, how do they have the nerve to call them
'raspberry'? They're just frozen high-fructose corn syrup with
blue coloring. And why fluorescent blue? A raspberry isn't
fluorescent blue. Nothing in nature is fluorescent blue."

"Moocher, would you focus, please? The woman of my dreams is walking across the Alameda County courthouse cafeteria carrying a salad and bottled water."

"And your point is?"

Maggie looked at Moocher and tried to remember; it was something about focusing.

"Oh, for God's sake," Moocher said. "Just go up and talk to her."

"And say what?"

"That you want to have hot monkey sex with her?" Moocher suggested.

"Ha fucking ha."

"Just find out her name and phone number. How's that for a start?"

"I don't know what to say." Maggie knew she was whining. She didn't want to whine. She hated whining.

"You are so pathetic," Moocher said with a disgusted snort. "All right, I'll do it."

Maggie grinned and decided whining wasn't so bad when it helped you get what you wanted. "Thanks, partner. I owe you."

"Good." Moocher walked a few paces, then turned back. "Get me a pastrami on rye."

"You know, I'm constantly reminded why your nickname is Moocher."

"Leave me alone, I'm making a love connection."

"HI, EXCUSE ME, I'm officer Michelle Bryan—Moocher for short. I may be wrong, but didn't we meet a few weeks ago at a reading at Mama Bear's?"

Anne had almost made it to her corner without looking behind her, without spilling her food, and without coming up with an intelligent word to say—should she get up the nerve to talk to the cute cop. The sudden voice startled her so much that she nearly dropped the tray, thereby ruining her three-for-three record. She turned around to answer and found a pair of twinkling brown eyes staring back at her.

"I don't think so," Anne replied in a distracted voice, wondering why she wasn't talking to the cute cop. "I'm Anne Doyle. Pleased to meet you."

Anne balanced her tray in one hand and held her hand out to the unexpected woman, who was dressed in the uniform of the Berkeley police, just like the redhead. That's where the similarity ended. The redhead was compact, her obvious strength softened by delicate, almost child-like features and a hint of baby fat. Moocher's power, on the other hand, was more obvious. She was a few inches shorter than Anne, maybe five-eight, and she moved with a confident swagger. Her brown eyes held a constant light—a flickering sparkle of amusement—as if laughing at a world that found her intimidating.

"Hmm," Moocher mused, still pretending to recognize Anne. "Maybe it was at a Habitat for Humanity job site. My partner and I were working on a house with the East Bay Gay Officers Association last month."

"No, I haven't ever done that. I've always meant to." *Partner?* Anne tried not to twitch. *Did she mean "partner" as in fellow officer or "partner" as in "lover, wife, lifelong companion"?*

"OK, to be honest, my partner—that's her over there, the cop in line—ran into you in the elevator a couple of weeks ago." Moocher pointed and Anne glanced over without making eye contact, and then quickly looked back. "She'd really like to buy you a drink or something."

"Really? Um..." *OK, can't be that kind of partner...unless they have a really open relationship.*

"If you're straight, that's cool. We're not recruiting or anything."

Anne thought there might have been an invitation in there somewhere. "OK," she said, hoping she was right.

" 'OK' you're straight or 'OK' you're willing to consider going out with my partner?"

"OK, nothing like this has ever happened to me and I'm not sure what to say. Except that you're a very good friend."

It was at that moment in the conversation that Anne realized her speech, the one she'd been writing and rewriting and practicing and re-practicing for two weeks, was suddenly redundant. The going out part was covered, the gay part was a done deal, and even her name had been thrown in there. Life was good.

"Look, let me get her over here and you can talk to her," Moocher said with a sigh. "This love-connection crap is exhausting."

Moocher looked toward her partner, and Anne finally allowed her own gaze to focus directly on Maggie, who had purchased lunch and was standing in the corner, looking at the napkins and condiments as if they held the secret to the universe.

"Hang on a minute," Moocher said to Anne. She made the trek back across the cafeteria.

Anne watched as the two women exchanged a few words. She smiled as Moocher took the tray of food and physically pushed Maggie toward the center of the room. Anne decided it was rude to stand still, so moved to meet the redhead. They reached each other by a window, underneath a tall rubber plant.

"Hi, I'm Maggie. I'm really embarrassed. My partner is insane, by the way."

"I'm Anne Doyle, pleased to meet you. So, was everything she said a lie?"

"Um, depends on what she said."

"That you wanted to buy me a drink or something."

"No. I mean yes. I want to buy you a drink or something. I mean, coffee or whatever."

"Sounds good. I'll call you?"

"Good. Great. Yeah."

"Uh, your number?"

"Oh, duh. Yeah, here's my card."

"Mary Margaret Monahan?"

"I know. Irish much."

"Mmm."

"What?"

"Your initials, mmm."

"I thought you were making a yummy noise."

"That too. Here's my card, in case...well, anyway, I'll call you."

"OK. Great. I'll see you."

ANNE HAD READ the same paragraph at least a dozen times. She wasn't sure of the number because she wasn't paying attention to that either. She finally stopped herself, and slammed the book closed. "Tea. I need tea," she announced to her little cubbyhole of an office.

She made her way through the old Victorian that held her law firm — Doyle, Smith and Goldstein — nodding at Smith and Goldstein, who were having a lively but good-natured argument. She made it to the kitchen without spotting Jill Doyle, the senior partner and her mother.

Anne had literally grown up in these offices in North Berkeley. Her mother had founded the practice, which specialized in family law, with two of her friends. All three had graduated together from Boalt Hall, UC Berkeley's law school. One of Anne's earliest memories was of lying on the rug in the entryway and watching dust motes float in a ray of sunlight. She had thought they were fairies.

That's what she looked like, Anne mused as she put a teabag in her mug and added boiling water. *Just like a fairy with red-gold hair and green eyes.*

It was twenty-six hours since she'd met Mary Margaret Monahan. Anne had placed Maggie's business card in her jacket pocket, and for the rest of the afternoon, she'd run her fingers over the embossed lettering. She'd deemed it too soon to call the night after they'd met, and too inconvenient to call her in the middle of the morning.

So when? she mused, feeling her nerves begin to crackle with panic. *Should I call her now? Tonight? Tomorrow? Should I already have called her and, since I didn't, would it now be a complete embarrassment to call her?*

She poked her finger into the mug and grabbed the corner of her tea bag, moving the bag through the water to make the tea brew faster. Her stomach was churning, joining the panic party, and she hoped the herbal tea would soothe everything. A hard jab to her ribs made her drop the bag and nearly the cup as well.

"Mother!" she squawked in protest, turning around to glare indignantly.

"Oh, my God, are you OK?" her mother exclaimed. "You're pale and sweaty. Are you sick? Did you eat something that didn't agree with you?"

"There's nothing wrong with me. I'm just making myself some tea."

"If you're not sick, did you see a ghost? I always said this place was haunted."

"I didn't see a ghost. I didn't eat anything bad. I'm not dying from the plague. I'm fine."

"You don't look fine." Jill peered into her daughter's baby blues.

"Mother." Anne tried to sound menacing, but it had no effect.

"So, if you didn't have an otherworldly experience, didn't eat too much cheese at lunch, and didn't have any encounters with rabid dogs, what *is* wrong with you?"

Anne tried to stare her mother out, but her eyes shifted minutely.

"Oh, my God," Jill whispered.

"What?" Anne asked innocently.

"You've met someone!" Jill shouted.

"I, uh, well."

"Who is she? When did you meet her? What does she do for a living? I want details."

Anne stuttered a few more minutes, and then pulled out the business card that was still tucked in her pocket.

"Officer Mary Margaret Monahan?" Now it was Jill's turn to

go a little pale. "A cop? You've fallen in love with a cop?"

"Now, Mom, the police are good," Anne said, as if speaking to a three-year-old. "This isn't the Sixties. Even then there were good cops; you know that."

"Of *course* there are good cops," Jill said. "They are wonderful people. Some of my best friends are cops. I just didn't expect my daughter to fall in love with one."

"OK, that's the second time you've mentioned the 'L' word," Anne interrupted. "I just met her and we clicked and I'd like to get to know her. That's all. And you need to get an attitude adjustment about the police."

"OK, OK, you're right. It's a new millennium and I need to open my mind."

"Yes, you do. But before you rush off to your therapist to talk about this, I need advice. I'm desperate." Anne took a sip of her tea before continuing. "So, I kind of told her that I'd call her. I think. And I'm just not sure if I should call her — I mean *when* I should call her — or whether it's already too late to call her."

"Oh, my poor innocent baby," Jill cooed sarcastically. "Aren't you just the cutest, most pathetic little thing?"

"Mother, if you don't treat me nice now, when you get old I'm going to put you in a really nasty nursing home and never visit you. One where everyone smells like chicken soup and pee."

"OK, I give, I give." Jill laughed. "Call her now and get it over with. If you stew about it any more, you'll probably throw up in the sink. And I'm not cleaning up after you."

"Are you sure I won't seem too desperate?" Anne asked, feeling about as desperate as a woman could. "Maybe I should just play it cool for a day."

"Give me a break with that macho shit. If you start thinking like that, your relationship is going nowhere. Just call her. Now." Jill pointed an imperious finger toward the kitchen door.

"OK, I'm going." Anne walked back to her office feeling like she was on her way to face a firing squad, and then decided it wasn't like that at all. *That would be a hell of a lot easier.*

"COFFEE. I NEED coffee." Maggie moaned, beating her head against the passenger seat's headrest.

"I hear ya," Moocher replied, patting her friend's knee. "We have to check the squad car back in by three, but we should have time to make a coffee run."

The two partners were normally officers for Berkeley's Bicycle Patrol Unit, working the late afternoon through evening shift, but they'd spent the past three weeks testifying in court for a case that had more postponements than an agnostic's baptism. After spending the morning sitting in the courthouse looking professionally dour, they'd been dismissed yet again while the judge and lawyers hashed out one more proposed plea bargain. Moocher was showing off her rustiness behind the wheel as they drove back across town.

"Jesus Christ, Moocher," Maggie shrieked, digging her fingernails into the dashboard. "You nearly killed that guy."

"Relax. He was totally at fault."

"I'll keep that in mind next time I'm flying through the windshield."

"You know, it seems to me that someone is a trifle on edge," Moocher mused.

"Shut up."

"And it occurs to me that someone might need a good lay," Moocher continued.

"I said, shut up." Maggie reached over and punched her friend in the thigh.

"Ow! Not while I'm driving."

Maggie decided to ignore her and pout for a while. She pulled out her cell phone and checked that it was on for the fourteenth time that afternoon.

"Yes, it's on," Moocher said, without looking at her partner.

"Shut up. I'm not talking to you." Maggie let out a tortured sigh and threw the cell phone onto the floor by her feet. "Could you call my cell and make sure it's working?"

"I thought you weren't talking to me," Moocher said in her best impression of a five-year-old.

"Please forgive me, dear sweet Moocher," Maggie crooned. "Please call my cell phone and make sure it's working."

"No. I did that half an hour ago. I refuse to become a part of your bizarro world. Your cell phone works fine. She just hasn't called yet. If you really want to talk to her, call her yourself."

"No. I don't want to look desperate."

"Newsflash: You are desperate. Call her."

"No." Maggie shook her head stubbornly. "I want her to make the first move. I think I—I mean, we—came on too strong."

"What the hell are you talking about?"

"Moocher, we friggin' tag-teamed her." Maggie sighed. "She didn't have a chance to say no. She probably thinks I'm a complete freak but couldn't say anything to my face. I want to give her a chance to run far, far away from me."

"First of all, you *are* a complete freak. But you are a

beautiful, intelligent, charming freak. And she will call you. Just be fucking patient and stop driving me insane."

"Buy me a large coffee and I'll consider it."

"And you call *me* Moocher?"

Maggie was about to reply with a scathingly witty retort, but a call on the radio caught her attention. "That's two blocks away." She flicked on the lights and siren without asking.

"Robbery suspect fleeing the scene." Moocher dodged through the heavy traffic. "Did they say blue or black Camry?"

"Black. You need your ears checked. Take the next right, and we should intercept him at Sacramento."

Maggie called Dispatch to tell them they were responding as Moocher drove swiftly through the narrow Berkeley streets. They listened to the calls reporting the driver's location and altered their course to keep up. Within a few minutes, they could see a black Camry at the top of the hill, heading down toward them. Moocher slowed and waited for him to turn. When he didn't, and passed the last opportunity to take a side street, Moocher gunned the engine and turned the car to the left, blocking the street.

"Moocher, are you sure this is a good idea?" Maggie wasn't exactly thrilled that her side was facing the oncoming car.

"Trust me." Moocher smirked.

It almost worked. As the driver approached, he momentarily sped up, looking as if he planned on ramming the squad car. Then, when his brain overrode his testosterone, he seemed to realize that what he was doing probably wouldn't ensure his escape — and might actually leave him dead. As the black car barreled toward her, Maggie imagined a mathematical equation which compared the size of the man's brain to the length of the block. His brakes squealed as he turned the wheel to the left, sideswiping a car parked nearby and smashing into the rear side panel of the squad car.

Brain smaller than block by a factor of twenty to the power of infinity, Maggie determined as the squad car was spun slightly by the impact. Their car wasn't moved enough to allow the Camry clear passage, even if the driver had been able to continue. Maggie peered at him through his cracked windshield and was reminded how much head wounds bleed. She did a quick self-assessment and then checked out Moocher, who was looking incredibly guilty, but whole.

"Trust you?" Maggie hissed.

"I'm sorry. I didn't... I mean he, um..."

"You don't need to apologize to me, Moocher. But, do you remember when you were an altar girl and the priest caught you drunk on the sacrificial wine? And you actually came up with a story that he believed?"

"Yeah."

"Well, I suggest you start thinking up your story for the lieutenant. You might get lucky again. But guess what? If you don't, your punishment won't be three Hail Mary's and a couple Our Father's."

Moocher groaned as the first of the other responding cars arrived. Maggie called for an ambulance and then got out of the squad car to inspect its damage. After a minute, she stuck her head back in.

"Call for a tow truck as well," she said. Moocher groaned louder.

While they waited, they endured the ribbing of their fellow officers. Moocher only managed to get in a few good comebacks. She was too busy thinking up her story for the lieutenant. When the tow truck arrived, they signed the appropriate paperwork and hitched a lift back to the station with one of the other guys.

Maggie sat in the backseat and leaned her head against the window. Then she quickly jerked back, realizing what sorts of things had previously been applied to the glass. She sighed and wished she had that cup of coffee as she watched the tow truck slowly pull their wrecked squad car down the street.

ANNE LISTENED TO the ring, waiting for Maggie to pick up. "Please answer," she murmured as the rings continued.

"Hi, this is Maggie Monahan," the recorded voice announced after the fifth ring.

"Oh, Jesus Christ, what the hell am I going to say?" Anne moaned as the greeting continued.

"I can't answer the phone right now. Please leave your name and number and I'll get back to you."

Anne waited for the beep, took a deep breath, and then launched into her message. "Hi. This is Anne. Anne Doyle. We, uh, met yesterday in the courthouse cafeteria." Anne tried to will the saliva to return to her mouth. "I was wondering, um, if you'd like to go out for a coffee...or whatever. Tomorrow night is good for me. How about you? Tomorrow night, I mean. And coffee. Is coffee good for you? It can be something else. Or some other time. I'm open. I mean free. Most of the time...well, a lot of the time in the next few days...um, so give me a call. 555-3174. OK? Great. Thanks. See ya. I hope."

Anne hung up the phone and buried her face in her hands.

"Please don't tell me I sounded as bad as I think I did," she mumbled between her fingers.

"You sounded as bad as you think you did," Jill called as she walked past the open office door.

"I didn't ask you!"

Chapter
Two

ANNE STOOD AGAINST the railing of the dock and looked toward the open bay. The fog had rolled in, as it did most warm afternoons, tucking itself into the nooks and crannies of the Berkeley hills, thick and grey like lint from a dryer. Out beyond the city and the Golden Gate Bridge, Anne could still see a strip of the blue sky of late afternoon. She watched as the patch of blue turned golden, glowing brighter and brighter until finally the sun blazed through the gap between fog and sea.

Anne loved this moment, when the sun seemed to scoff at the fog for its vain attempt to smother the world. The sun flared before its final descent, coating everything it touched in a patina of gold. The ugly became beautiful, and the beautiful became glorious.

"I see you found the place."

Anne turned quickly and smiled at Maggie, who stood before her bathed in sunlight.

Glorious.

"Near the wolf." Anne nodded her head toward the cast iron statue.

"Well, I guess there's only one statue of a wolf in Jack London Square. Should we grab some coffee? Then I'll tell you the story behind me not answering my cell phone."

Anne listened to Maggie's story as they walked to the little coffee shop, but she was more interested in the way in which Maggie spoke—the soft lilt of her speech, the way she caressed the air with her hands. Maggie's words ebbed and flowed, sometimes rapid and excited, sometimes slow and measured.

"So it took hours to process the paperwork for the accident and then we had to wait for the suspect to come back from the hospital, and in the middle of processing him I stood up and screamed, 'the cell phone!'"

"Did everyone look at you like you were insane?" Anne asked.

"No. No one even looked in my direction. They're all used to me doing stuff like that by now." Maggie laughed and Anne noticed that the bridge of her nose crinkled. It was quite possibly the most adorable thing Anne had ever seen.

"So Moocher, the bitch, refused to leave immediately for the garage," Maggie continued. "It was nearly three hours later when I got the phone back. You must have wondered if I was ever going to call back."

"No, of course not," Anne lied. "I just assumed you'd turned it off or didn't have it with you."

Actually, I assumed that you had come to your senses and didn't want to have anything to do with me.

"I think you're lying," Maggie said.

"Why do you say that?"

Oh, my God, I'm falling in love with a psychic. Oh, my God, again, I just said 'I'm falling in love.'

"Because when people lie, they try to remove all expression from their face. You know, the poker-face thing. The problem is, the very act of doing that is a clue that they're lying."

"Nice theory." Anne laughed. "I don't know if it would hold up in court, though." Anne continued to smile. She'd been in Maggie's presence for just under twenty minutes and she'd been smiling or laughing just about the whole time. The muscles in her face were actually beginning to ache.

"Do you know what you want?" Maggie asked. "We're almost up."

"Just a regular cup of coffee, I think."

"You've gotta be more specific than that," Maggie whispered, leaning toward Anne. "The guy behind the counter is kind of quirky. You have to order in just the right way or he'll go off on you or give you something that tastes like day-old dishwater. So what size do you want, which of the daily roasts do you want, and do you want any room left for the cream?"

Anne tried to answer, but the body leaning toward her distracted her. It was warm and smelled faintly of jasmine. It was nice. It was better than nice, it was...

"Anne, hurry, we're running out of time."

"Um, yeah, OK," Anne stuttered. "Large, Kenyan, no room."

"Right. I'll order. You just stand there and don't say a word. Just smile." Maggie inspected the woman beside her. "Let's see a test smile."

Anne blushed and responded with a self-conscious offering.

Maggie didn't say anything for a moment, staring back at her with wide eyes. "Um...yeah, that'll do."

When it was their turn, Maggie stepped up to the counter to

order.   Anne stayed beside her and turned on her smile,
wondering if the barista would look back at her the way Maggie
had.

"I'd like a large mocha with two shots of espresso, no froth
on top, but I'd love a petite dollop of whipped cream. My friend
will have a large cup of the Kenyan roast. She doesn't plan to
dilute it with any dairy product or non-dairy substitute, so fill it
right to the brim."

"Very good, ladies!" the man behind the counter proclaimed.
"I'll get that for you right away."

Anne felt the same way she had when she won the spelling
bee in second grade, but she forced herself not to high-five
Maggie. They still didn't have their drinks safely in hand. "That
was impressive," she whispered.

"Thanks. He hates it when you do the Starbucks thing. You
know, the 'half-caf dry soy' crap. He wants to know that you
share his passion for hot beverages."

Their drinks arrived quickly. In fact, they received them
before the person in line in front of them. *Must have ordered
wrong,* Anne mused.

"You want to walk?" Maggie asked.   "Or we can stay in
here."

"No, let's walk. It's a beautiful night."

They strolled in silence for a few minutes, looking out at the
blinking lights of Alameda across the water. The day had been
warm, but the temperature had dropped when the fog rolled in.
Both women had dressed for the cold night and didn't mind
walking along the waterfront.   They passed busy bars and
restaurants, walking until the sounds of people faded and were
replaced by the noises from the cranes on the docks and the buzz
of the freeway. When they reached the end of the wooden
boardwalk, they found a bench and sat down.

"Thanks for coming to Oakland," Maggie said.   "I love
Berkeley, but sometimes I hate hanging out in the same place I
work."

"That's understandable. Anyway, I like it here. We used to
come to Jack London Square when I was a kid and eat at The
Spaghetti Factory."

"So you grew up in the Bay Area?" Maggie chuckled ruefully
when Anne nodded. "OK, I guess now is the time we tell each
other all about our lives, our loves, our philosophies, our
families — you know, all the light topics."

"Oh, I hate that." Anne smiled back. "Where do you start?
Where do you finish? If you say too much, the other person
becomes overwhelmed with the details, not to mention probably

thinks you're looking for a therapist instead of a girlfriend."

"And if you don't say enough, she thinks you're a secretive bitch or just incredibly boring," Maggie added, playing along.

"So who goes first?"

Maggie thought a moment before answering. "Let's start by telling each other the one thing that we're most proud of."

"OK, let me think about that." Anne leaned back and took a sip of coffee before beginning her story.

"Well, I guess it would be the first case that I handled without help. It was a custody case. The parents were each fighting for sole custody, no visitation rights. They each accused the other of mental and physical abuse of the little girl. I represented the father. I really believed that he was telling the truth.

"The mother was a total nut case," Anne continued, "but she was really believable. Not to mention the fact that judges hardly ever grant sole custody to fathers. But we did it. We won."

"Wow, that's great." Maggie reached out and squeezed Anne's arm.

Anne felt a tingle shoot straight up her arm and into her heart, sending it into a skittering beat. "It's tough dealing with custody cases," she said, trying to calm her racing pulse. "It always reminds me how lucky I was. My parents had a really amicable divorce and they never argued about custody. It made things a lot easier for me, even though I wanted them to stay together and be happy. What about you? What are you most proud of?"

"I saved my brother's life when I was eight," Maggie replied without pausing to consider. "We were having dinner. Dad was working, so my oldest brother Patrick was in charge. He was about sixteen at the time. There were four boys and me: the baby of the family. Needless to say, we were loud and obnoxious and I barely noticed when Sean, who was sitting next to me, started choking. He kind of reached out and I finally saw what was going on."

Maggie's eyes filled with fear, as if she were back in the moment, sitting next to her brother. "We'd just learned about the Heimlich maneuver in school, so without thinking about it much, I got up and did it. The piece of hot dog he was choking on flew out of his mouth with so much force it hit my brother Michael in the cheek. It almost started a food fight."

"I bet Sean was grateful to you for saving his life." Anne mimicked Maggie's earlier gesture, reaching out and squeezing Maggie's arm. She could tell from the pulse under her fingertips that there were now two racing hearts.

"He acted like it was no big deal, but later that night he came into my room and thanked me. Since he normally gave me an Indian burn before bed, I knew he was serious."

"That's a great story." Anne smiled. "But what about your mom? Where was she during all this?"

"She died when I was three. Ovarian cancer," Maggie stated simply. She swallowed down the final gulp of her mocha.

"Sorry."

"Don't be. It wasn't your fault." Maggie smiled sadly.

"I know, but I still..."

Maggie held up her hand. "Remember the whole thing about wanting a therapist instead of a girlfriend?"

"Yeah?"

"Well, I want a girlfriend," Maggie announced decisively.

"You got anyone in particular in mind?" Anne teased.

"I think you'll do nicely," Maggie replied with a mischievous smile.

Anne imagined she was sitting in a symphony audience as the curtain rose on an orchestra ready to strike the first note. She could just about hear the tap of the maestro's baton.

Here we go.

"AND THEN I said, 'I think you'll do nicely.' "

"You didn't!" A carrot dropped off the fork poised halfway to Moocher's mouth.

It was Monday, three days after Maggie and Anne's first date, and as Maggie's best friend, Moocher had demanded a blow-by-blow description of the night. They met over lunch at The Big Salad Place before their shift began.

"Anyway, we just sat there for a long time and chatted about everything and nothing." Maggie shrugged her shoulders. She actually couldn't remember much of what she and Anne had talked about.

"And then you went to her place and had hot monkey sex?" Moocher guessed.

"No-o-o," Maggie drawled.

"Then you went to *your* place and had hot monkey sex?"

"No. There was no sex — heated, simian, or otherwise. We said good night and went home. Separately." Maggie speared a kidney bean and a piece of hard-boiled egg and popped them into her mouth.

"But before you left, you kissed good night, of course."

"No."

"Um, excuse me, I was munching too loudly. I thought you

said 'no.' As in, no, you didn't kiss her good night. But that would be so tragically wrong I must have heard incorrectly."

"You heard correctly." Maggie felt her ears burning. Moocher would notice. Time to initiate damage control. "It was just one of those things. She didn't yin when I yanged. It's no big deal."

"It's a very big deal," Moocher countered. "And you know it is. But I'm going to assume you rectified the situation. Did you talk to her the next day?"

"Yes, she called me the next morning."

"And..."

"And she told me that she'd had a wonderful time, and I told her that I'd had a wonderful time."

"And you made a date for that night and now it's Monday and you've had non-stop sex for thirty-six hours."

"No. Would you get off the sex thing?" Maggie felt the blush spreading down from her ears to her neck.

"OK, I'm sorry I mentioned s-e-x. What did you do on your second date, then?"

"Nothing," Maggie mumbled. She sorted through her salad, searching for a garbanzo bean.

"Um, Mary Margaret, can you explain what 'nothing' means?"

"She asked if I wanted to do something over the weekend," Maggie replied sheepishly. "And I told her that I had other plans and I'd call her." Maggie's blush conquered her cheeks, completing its military campaign across her face.

"No! No, no, no, no! I am not hearing this!" Moocher threw her fork down in her salad bowl and pressed her hands against her ears. Maggie continued her bean hunt. She hoped that if she just waited out her friend, Moocher might forget the entire thread of the conversation.

"Are you insane?" Moocher finally asked, holding very tightly to the thread. "Why am I asking? Of course you're insane. Maggie, she's gorgeous, she's intelligent, you connected. For God's sake, you told her you wanted her to be your girlfriend. Twelve hours later, you're uttering the dreaded 'I'll call you'?"

"You don't understand." Maggie moaned.

"No, I don't." Moocher took a deep breath as Maggie dropped her fork in frustration. "OK, OK, help me to understand."

"I just felt so weird and everything," Maggie said. "I felt like I was on an airplane and we had just hit an air pocket and dropped a thousand feet. I felt like I was stoned or drunk. I don't know... I felt like I was a sleeper."

"A sleeper?"

"You know, a brainwashed spy. You don't know you're a spy until someone whispers something like 'would you like horseradish with your roast beef?' And suddenly you're trying to assassinate the president."

"OK, first of all, your brain is a really scary place. Don't take me there again. Second of all, and more importantly, I know why you felt all of those things."

"Why?" Maggie gasped.

"Because you're in love, you doofus!"

Moocher's shout prompted everyone who hadn't already been eavesdropping to take a curious look. She lowered her voice a few decibels. "That's what love feels like—falling, drugged, and yes, even the brainwashed thing."

"That's impossible." Maggie shook her head like a life-sized bobble doll. "I hardly know her."

"You knew you were in love when you asked her to be your girlfriend, didn't you?"

"Yes. I mean, I didn't think it was... I mean, I don't want to push, uh..."

"Look, the first date is either a complete bust or a heady overdose of pheromone-driven lust," Moocher explained. "You were lucky. You hit the jackpot. Now, just don't think about it too much and you'll find that things will move fast and slow in a natural rhythm. But for fuck's sake, call her right away and right this horrible wrong that you've perpetrated."

"Now she probably thinks I'm a freak or a tease or something." Maggie buried her burning face in her hands.

"Of course she does. But, Mary Margaret Monahan, I am not going to let this go. She's the one. I can feel it. If you don't call her immediately, I'm going to make your life hell."

"You already do that without trying," Maggie mumbled into her palms.

"Go! Now!" Moocher commanded. Maggie thought she would have looked more imperious without the drop of ranch dressing on her chin.

"OK, I'm going." Maggie got up from the table and handed her friend a clean napkin. "I'll be outside making a call. Give me a few minutes, OK?"

"No problem. I'll go next door and grab a cup of java."

"And flirt with the barista? Sounds good." Maggie smiled at her friend's transparency, and then frowned, remembering the phone call she was about to make. "Damn, I wish I was at home hugging Ambassador Squiggles."

"You'll be fine without him," Moocher said as she led her

friend out of the restaurant. "But, Maggie, word of advice—when you eventually do have the hot monkey sex, ditch the teddy bear."

ON THE OTHER side of Berkeley, Anne delivered a flurry of punches, finishing with a roundhouse kick. Drops of sweat sprayed from her body with each impact. She bounced on the balls of her feet and dodged the imaginary responding attack.

"Hey, Rocky, you want to retire to the weight machines? That poor punching bag would be cowering in a corner if it had feet and could run away."

Anne took the clean towel from her best friend Roz, grunting her agreement.

"So, you want to talk about it?" Roz asked as she sat beside Anne on the exercise machines.

"Talk about what?" Anne tried to sound innocent, but knew she'd failed miserably.

"Talk about whatever's bothering you."

"What makes you think something's bothering me?" Anne asked between pulls of the lat machine, keeping up a steady rhythm.

"Because your neck is so stiff, you're gonna pull a muscle."

Anne was always amazed at how well Roz could read her moods. Roz was always patient, waiting for Anne to talk when she was ready, but knowing just the right thing to say when a little encouragement was called for. Anne let her neck muscles relax and began to order her thoughts.

"That's better," Roz said. "Straighten your back. You're tilted slightly to the left."

They continued in silence for ten reps, and then Anne said, "I met someone."

"Oh."

"What does 'Oh' mean?" Anne pulled harder, but kept her rhythm smooth.

" 'Oh' doesn't mean anything. If you want to tell me more, go ahead. If not, that's cool."

"Sorry. I'm just pissed and confused."

Anne continued her exercises in silence until she knew her anger wouldn't be directed toward her friend. "So, yeah, I met this girl. She's beautiful and sweet and funny. We went out for coffee on Friday night and we really connected. At least, I thought we did..." Anne's voice trailed off, unable to explain what had happened.

Her reps finished, she moved with Roz to the next machine,

adjusted the weight and settings, and then sat down and started to lift.

"I felt something Friday night that I never have before," Anne said. "When I hugged her good night, I held her in my arms and I felt...complete. And yes, I know that sounds absolutely trite, not to mention impossible. I mean, it was our first date, for God's sake."

"Love at first sight," Roz offered.

"Which I don't believe in."

"But it happened," Roz stated rather than asked.

Anne lifted for three reps without replying, staring at the wall and thinking about the warm body that seemed to meld so well against her.

"Yeah," she finally agreed. "It happened."

"And then what?"

"I called her the next morning and everything was great. I told her I'd had a great time. She said she'd had a great time. I tried to set up something for that night. I was just totally consumed with her and I wanted to be with her. I could barely stand the thought of spending the rest of the day away from her. I swear to God I never felt like that before."

Anne stood up again, using the towel to wipe her face, neck, and arms, which were covered in a sheen of sweat. She took a swig from her water bottle and pulled at her sports bra, snapping it into a more comfortable position, then sat down on the next machine and started her leg lifts.

"So what happened?" Roz asked.

"She said she was busy Saturday night. And Sunday."

"Well, you'd just gotten together. She probably had other plans and —"

"She said she'd call me," Anne interrupted, watching Roz's face as the words sunk in.

"She actually said, 'I'll call you'?"

"Yep." The disappointment still burned in her heart and now matched the burning in her leg muscles.

Anne watched as Roz considered the situation for a moment.

"What did your mom say about the whole thing?" Roz asked.

"What makes you think I told my mom about this?"

"Because you tell your mom everything and then you listen to her advice and usually ignore it completely. Funny thing is, she's a lot smarter than either of us and she's always right."

"She's sometimes right," Anne conceded. "She told me to be patient with Maggie and give her some space. She said maybe things were moving a little too fast for her."

"Well, that sounds reasonable to me," Roz ventured. "And

you must have thought so, too."

"Why do you say that?"

"Because you're carrying your cell phone with you. Thinking you may be getting a call from beautiful, sweet, funny Maggie?"

Anne blushed and then tried to look tough. She picked up the item in question and was about to deliver a stinging comeback when it rang. She was so stunned that she nearly dropped it, and then struggled to find the right button to push.

"Hello?" she answered carefully. A familiar voice answered.

"Hey, Maggie. What's up?"

The reply was long and confusing. Anne definitely heard an apology and might have heard something about being drugged. She was sure she misheard the word "horseradish."

"Just tell me one thing," Anne eventually blurted. "Do you want to go out for dinner tonight?"

They set up the date and Anne hung up.

"Well? What the hell did she say?" Roz asked.

"I'm not exactly sure, but the bottom line is, she wants to see me again. She has to work tonight, but we're doing breakfast tomorrow morning."

Roz smiled. "Well, now that all is right with the world again, can we call it quits for the day? I'm exhausted."

Anne nodded in agreement and then struck her forehead with her palm.

"Oh, shit," she cried, "I just remembered I have a client meeting tomorrow morning. I'll have to call Mom and ask her to take it for me."

"When you talk to her, you might want to thank her as well." Roz picked up their towels and water bottles.

"What for?"

"For giving you such good advice. Again." Roz smirked and headed to the showers.

Chapter
Three

MAGGIE WAS LATE. This wasn't an everyday occurrence, but it certainly wasn't uncommon. She was usually on time for everyday events — going to work, meeting up with Moocher for a drink or a bike ride — but when it came to important occasions, like going on a breakfast date with a beautiful woman, her internal clock mocked her. And the later she was, the more her own body fought against her.

When the phone rang, she was trying to put her head through the arm of her shirt while simultaneously fumbling with the zipper on her jeans, which had eaten a small fold of her underpants. She managed to find the right hole for the right appendage on her shirt, gave up on the zipper for the moment, and answered the phone.

"Hello?" She hoped it was Anne, calling to tell her that she was running late as well.

"Mary Margaret." Maggie's father always started his conversations with her name, as if reminding her of something she might have forgotten.

Oh, Jeez, I don't have time for this. "Hi, Dad."

"You busy?"

Maggie hesitated. The question appeared simple and conversational, but she knew her answer would be judged, no matter how trivial. "Actually, I was just getting ready to go out to meet a friend for breakfast," Maggie replied. *Friend. That was innocuous, wasn't it?*

"Boyfriend?"

Not innocuous enough, I guess. "No, Dad, just a friend-friend."

"Not that partner of yours?"

"No, not Michelle. I do have other friends, Dad."

I don't have many, actually, but this one is special. I'm falling in love with her. Christ, wouldn't that blow his head clean off?

"Well, I wanted to tell you about an interesting conversation I had yesterday with Bob Lockhart."

Why the hell does my dad have to know everyone in the police force throughout the greater Bay Area, including my boss?

"Oh?"

"We met up at Henry Lo's retirement bash. You remember old Henry, don't you? I was his training officer back in '73."

"Dad, I wasn't born yet."

Maggie started working on her zipper, knowing if her dad was going to start reminiscing about work, she'd be stuck on the phone for a while.

"Oh, yeah, that's right. Anyway, Bob and I were talking and he told me he just gave you a great performance review."

"He, um...yeah, it was pretty good."

Sharing a performance review with someone's father — is that even ethical?

"And I think it's about time you thought about putting in for a transfer. You can't stay in bike patrol forever, you know. You need to start thinking about your future, Mary Margaret."

"I do think about my future, Dad."

I'm thinking about it right now. It involves a gorgeous woman with black hair and the most amazing blue eyes. They look like a swimming pool on a hot summer afternoon. I want to dive into those eyes and sink slowly to the bottom.

"Well, look, let me take you out to dinner this weekend. I want to at least congratulate you on doing so well and making your family proud."

In other words, you want to work on me face to face, when you can more effectively push all of my buttons. "I'm not sure I'll be free this weekend, I'm..." *Hoping to have a follow-up date with Anne.*

"No problem, weekend after next then. I'll make reservations at Roma's for Saturday at seven. You can come pick me up around six-fifteen. There's a Giants game that afternoon, so I don't know what traffic will be like. If we're early, we can grab a drink."

You've got it all worked out. What a surprise.

"OK, Dad. I better get going or I'll be late."

"Right. See you a week from Saturday."

Maggie hung up the phone and quickly finished dressing, trying not to think about dinner with her father. Thinking about breakfast with Anne was stressful enough.

"I CAN'T BELIEVE you've never been here before," Maggie said as she and Anne were escorted to an empty booth in J.J.'s Diner.

"Nope. I've driven by loads of times. I just never..."

"Never what? Eat?" Maggie laughed.

Anne smiled back. She was pleased when Maggie scooted over in the big booth to sit to her right instead of across from her. Their legs brushed under the table.

Anne looked around the restaurant and noticed its unique feature. "Maggie, why are there phones at every booth?"

"Well, that's a good question. Moocher and I have been trying to figure that one out for years. I just picture someone on the phone saying, 'J.J.'s has a special on chicken-fried steak, get down here!'"

Anne laughed. She noticed that her face hurt, just as it had on their first date, from smiling and laughing at Maggie. It was a wonderful feeling.

"You're not even looking at the menu," Anne pointed out. "I suppose you know what you want?"

"Yep, I get the same thing every time. I'm inconsistent in nearly every aspect of my life except food." Maggie looked pensive for a moment. "Speaking of which, have I apologized yet for Saturday morning?"

"Yes. Once at my place and twice on the way over here."

"I really am sorry. I guess I just want you to understand that."

Anne reached out for Maggie's hand and was about to respond when the waitress interrupted. "Are you ladies ready to order?"

Maggie pulled her hand away quickly and grabbed the menu. "I'll have three scrambled eggs, hash browns, bacon, sourdough toast, and a short stack of pancakes. Oh, and a large orange juice."

Anne took a few seconds to let the enormity of Maggie's order sink in. Then she just shook her head and smiled. Again. "I'll have the oatmeal, an English muffin, and hot tea."

"That'll be right up." The waitress took their menus and headed toward the kitchen.

"Are you actually planning on eating what you just ordered?" Anne asked.

"I most certainly am," Maggie replied with mock indignation.

"This I've got to see. Although I might get sympathy indigestion just watching you."

"Well, I have a wonderful job that lets me ride a bike for hours on end. It's great for my figure."

"I'll have to agree with that." Anne looked at the figure in question. Her attention was drawn to Maggie's ears, which were turning crimson. "You're blushing," Anne whispered, leaning toward Maggie and watching in fascination as the blush progressed across her throat and cheeks.

"Yes, I'm blushing," Maggie whispered back, looking down shyly. "Trust me, I do it at the drop of a hat."

"I hear that people who blush easily are usually very ticklish."

"Oh, don't go there," Maggie warned.

Anne straightened up as the waitress delivered their drinks. "Your food will be up in a minute."

"Thanks," the two women chorused.

"So, changing the subject completely," Maggie continued, taking a sip of orange juice. "I was trying to apologize again and explain what happened."

"You already apologized and you already explained." Anne smiled. "Don't worry about it."

"Can you honestly tell me that you understood half of what I said on the phone yesterday? I know myself better than that. I blather incoherently when I'm nervous."

"It was a little confusing. Did you say something about being brainwashed?"

Maggie blushed again.

Damn, that has got to be the cutest thing in the world, Anne thought.

"It's just that I felt so strange and it overwhelmed me," Maggie said. "I've never felt that way before. I didn't know what was going on. Instead of telling you all of this, I panicked and shut you out. I can't imagine what you thought."

I was pissed and confused and wondering what kind of game you were playing. She decided that answer was a little too blunt. "Don't worry about it. I understand now what was going on and I accept your apology."

Anne peered into Maggie's sea green eyes. They were the color of the Pacific Ocean on a clear day. She reached out for Maggie's hand again, and noticed how small it was compared to hers. She turned it palm down, and with the tips of her fingers traced the unusual tan lines she found.

"They're from my riding gloves," Maggie said softly. They sat there for some time, lost in their closeness.

"Here we are, ladies," the waitress finally announced. Maggie once again withdrew her hand quickly and grabbed her knife and fork. A tiny kernel of disquiet invaded Anne's mind, but she brushed it away and watched with amusement as her friend slapped the bottom of the Tabasco bottle, sprinkling the hot red sauce over her eggs and hash browns.

"You are sick in the head." Anne laughed. "And soon to be sick in the stomach."

"Don't worry, ma'am, I'm a professional." Maggie put-on a TV announcer voice. "But Maggie's stomach is indestructible. Yours is not. Remember this. Do not try to imitate her."

Anne laughed and poured milk over her oatmeal. She took a bite and looked over at Maggie, who had gone very quiet. Anne soon became fascinated by the efficient speed with which Maggie ate. It was like watching a machine—pile on fork, put in mouth, bite, bite, bite, swallow, repeat.   Her pace never wavered.

"Um, Maggie," Anne finally said. "Is there a time limit that I'm not aware of?"

Maggie blushed and slowed down slightly to answer. "This is a real stereotype, but in my case it's true. When you're raised with a lot of brothers, you have to learn to eat fast or food tends to disappear from the table, and even sometimes from your own plate. I just can't break the habit."

"Don't be embarrassed. It's very impressive, actually."

"Are you sure you have enough?" Maggie's brow furrowed with concern. "Do you want some of my bacon?"

"No thanks. I don't eat meat." Anne took a large bite of her English muffin.

"What?" Maggie's knife and fork were poised above her plate, frozen in their tracks

"Don't look so shocked." Anne laughed. "My parents didn't eat meat when I was growing up. My mother still doesn't. I went through a period of rebellion when I was a teenager, eating McDonald's hamburgers in front of her, things like that. But I really don't like the taste of meat. Plus, I feel healthier when I don't eat it."

"Wow." Maggie slowly began to eat again. "I can't imagine how you can do it."

"It's not that hard when you live in the Bay Area. There are so many stores and restaurants that cater to vegetarians. It's just what I'm used to now."

Maggie shrugged and then turned back to her plate. Anne watched as her speed resumed, realizing that she was kind of pleased that Maggie's eating silenced her. It gave Anne an uninterrupted chance to examine the beautiful woman. And she was beautiful, Anne mused. Her hair was red with golden streaks. It fell loosely to her shoulders, where it curled up in a slight wave. She had a scattering of freckles on her nose, and more on her shoulders. Anne looked at the freckle pattern disappearing under the sleeveless blue cotton shirt, and wondered where else the freckles were. Her mouth watered at the thought, and she took a quick gulp of her tea.

She could see Maggie examining her as she sputtered over the hot tea. Maggie appeared to be considering something, and then a shadow passed across her face. Maggie stopped eating, a forkful of pancakes poised halfway to her mouth.

"Are you OK?"

"Yeah, yeah." Maggie put the food down and pushed the plate away slightly. "Just thinking."

Thinking you've made a horrible mistake?

"Hah," Anne said, stifling her sudden insecurity, "I knew you couldn't eat all that."

"I left one pancake. Besides, I'm used to Moocher mooching at least one strip of bacon and one piece of toast."

"Excuses, excuses." Anne smiled at her friend, who had gone still once again. This time she was looking across the diner. Maggie looked momentarily flustered, and then, after a moment, relieved. "What's up?"

"Nothing," Maggie answered quickly. "I thought I saw a guy I know from work."

Anne considered Maggie's answer and compared it to her behavior. Suddenly, the pieces of the puzzle were fitting together.

"Maggie," Anne said slowly, "can I ask you a personal question?"

"Um, sure," Maggie replied warily.

"Are you out?"

"Am I out? You mean, out-out?"

"Yes. Out. As in, well...out."

"Sort of."

Anne watched as a tiny muscle twitched under Maggie's left eye.

"What does 'sort of' mean? You can't just step out of the closet, wave a rainbow flag, and then jump back in hoping no one saw you."

"All of my friends know I'm gay, but I'm not out to my family. It would kill my dad. I know it would."

"What about work?" Anne tried to be patient and let Maggie explain.

"I think some people know I'm gay, but I don't advertise it. Moocher obviously is."

"Yeah, she is kind of..."

"Butch and proud of it," Maggie finished. "And a lot of people assumed we were a couple. But Moocher is very open around town when she's on a date. So when no one saw us cuddling or holding hands, a lot of them then assumed I wasn't gay."

"Why do you care? Surely being gay in the Berkeley Police Department isn't that big of a deal."

"No, it's not. Problem is, the police are like family. My dad knows everyone, even though he's retired. If I came out at work, it would get back to him."

Anne was silent. She hadn't expected Maggie to be in the closet, hadn't even considered that it was a possibility. She wasn't sure how she felt about it. Her brief musings were interrupted when she noticed Maggie's hands trembling.

"I'm sorry I lied to you." Maggie's voice was full of remorse. "I'm fucked up, I know I am. You don't need that."

"You're not fucked up, and you didn't lie to me." Anne took another sip of her tea, allowing herself more time to consider the situation. "I'm not going to pretend that this isn't a big deal to me. My own journey out of the closet was traumatic, and I don't plan on going back in again. I know I couldn't get used to sneaking around. I'm falling in love with you, and I want to hold your hand, put my arm around you, kiss you behind the ear, and anything else I feel like—all in full view of anyone and everyone who cares to look."

"You're falling in love with me?" Maggie squeaked.

Anne froze. *Did I say love? Yeah, I said love.* "Yes, Mary Margaret Monahan, I'm falling in love with you."

"Me, too," Maggie whispered. Tears pooled in the corners of her eyes, catching the light like sunlight dancing on the ocean waves.

"Are you ladies done? Can I get you anything else?" The waitress startled them and Maggie quickly took the opportunity to wipe at her eyes with her napkin.

"No, that'll do it," Anne managed to get out. The waitress, sensing something was up, grabbed the plates as quickly as possible, and moved away. *Big tip,* Anne decided.

"Maggie—"

"Please, Anne," Maggie interrupted. "I'll understand if you want to forget this whole thing. You don't need my fucking baggage. I don't... I've never... I mean..."

"Do you want me to forget this whole thing?" Anne's entire being willed Maggie to say "no."

"No."

Anne grinned, suppressing a huge sigh of relief.

The waitress returned with their check, and again beat a hasty retreat.

"Let me get that," Maggie offered, reaching for the bill.

"No." Anne quickly withdrew money from her wallet, placed it on the table, and stood up. "Come on, I want to finish this conversation outside."

Anne set off. She didn't look back but heard Maggie scramble to catch up to her. Anne didn't stop until she was out of the diner and in the parking lot, leaning against the front bumper of the car.

"Hey, why the rush?" Maggie stopped beside her.

Anne smiled and took a step closer to Maggie. "Because I wanted to do this." She leaned down and placed a soft kiss on Maggie's lips. For a moment, Maggie didn't return the kiss, her lips soft but lifeless. Anne was about to pull away when the lips beneath her woke, returning the warm pressure. After a few seconds of eternity, they moved backwards, holding on to each other's gaze.

"I didn't think you were ready for me to do that in the middle of J.J.'s diner." Anne smiled.

"If you had, I could have called someone and said, 'I'm kissing Anne Doyle, get down here!' "

They both laughed, and Anne reached out and pulled Maggie into her arms. She fit perfectly.

"Maggie, I don't know what's going to happen. I can't promise you a happy ending. But I say we follow our hearts, see where we end up. What do you think?"

"I think I'm happier than I've ever felt in my life." Maggie snuggled her head against Anne. "And more terrified than I've ever felt in my life. But most of all, I think I want to kiss you again."

And she did.

MAGGIE'S EUPHORIA FOLLOWING her breakfast with Anne gave way to doubt by the afternoon. Her mind was churning as she rode her patrol route. A few hours of the shift had passed when Moocher rode alongside.

"Break," Moocher said. Without uttering another word, she rode away, swerving between the cars that had backed up at a traffic light and pulling up in front of their favorite coffee shop.

Moocher didn't say anything until they had their coffees in hand and took a seat next to the door, where they could keep an eye on their bikes and leave quickly if they got a call. Their uniforms insured that they would be left alone, a buffer of empty tables purposely left around them despite the crowded coffee shop.

"OK," Moocher said, "what's wrong?"

"What do you mean, what's wrong?"

"Oh, Christ! You're not going to play dumb, are you?"

Moocher narrowed her eyes menacingly. "We only have fifteen minutes. Talk fast and don't give me any 'what do you mean, what's wrong?' bullshit."

"I'm a fucking freak," Maggie said morosely.

"Don't waste time with the obvious. Tell me about the breakfast date and then explain why you've been wearing a frown all afternoon. By the way, your face is gonna freeze like that and then what will you do?"

Maggie sighed and frowned some more, not caring about freezing faces.

"Thirteen minutes," Moocher warned.

"OK. Jesus. So the deal is that the date went really great but she found out that I'm sort of in the closet — well, with my family and at work and...stuff."

"And that pissed her off?"

"Surprised her more than anything, I think," Maggie replied. "Once she gave it some thought, she seemed to accept it. It's just...I don't know. In the middle of breakfast, it just hit me. What the hell am I doing? I feel like a kid pretending to be an adult. I just don't understand what she sees in me. She's just so beautiful and..."

"Hello-o-o?" Moocher waved her hand in front of Maggie's unfocused eyes. "Earth to Magpie."

"Sorry." Maggie blushed. "I just don't understand what someone so beautiful and smart and...everything...can see in me."

"Didn't we already have this conversation?"

"I guess." Maggie's shoulders sagged.

"There's something more, isn't there?"

Maggie shrugged. "I just don't know if I deserve this."

"Jesus Christ!" Moocher shouted. "You're on some goddamn Catholic guilt trip, aren't you? I should have fucking known."

"Moocher!" Maggie looked around the coffee shop, worried that they were being overheard. "Calm down."

"OK, OK. I'm calm, I'm calm." Moocher softened her voice. "So explain it to me."

"If I could explain it, I wouldn't think I was such a freak. Don't you understand?" Maggie's voice squeaked with frustration.

"I understand all right. I understand that the Catholic Church has a lot to answer for." Moocher's eyes narrowed in anger.

"I just don't want to fuck this up," Maggie said morosely, staring into the foam of her latte.

"You're not going to fuck it up. Why don't you just tell her how you're feeling, what you're freaked out about?"

"What?" Maggie's eyes widened and she shook her head. "No, this is my hang-up. I've got to get over it without dragging her into it."

"A problem shared is a problem..." Moocher scratched her head. "Shit, what is it?"

"Halved. Stop throwing proverbs at me. They don't apply in the real world."

"Sorry," Moocher growled, "but if you're going to need a pep talk after all of your dates with Anne, I'm inevitably going to run out of helpful hints."

"That was a pep talk?"

"Yeah, I think so." Moocher looked hopefully at Maggie. "Do you feel peppy?"

"No," Maggie replied, downing her latte. "But at least you distracted me from my misery for a little while."

"All in a day's work, ma'am. We live to serve and protect."

Maggie scowled at her partner.

"Mags, I really do think you should tell Anne what you're thinking. Tell her what's worrying you. You're not going to get anywhere with the relationship if you don't communicate."

"I will, but I can't just dump all of my phobias on her on the third date."

"OK, go for the fourth date," Moocher said. "The fourth date is definitely the 'let's reveal all of our hang-ups' date."

"Fourth date it is, then." Maggie nodded. *If I get that far.*

ANNE PACED THROUGH her small cottage. Since she'd been home from work, she'd vacuumed, dusted, and cleaned the bathroom. She still felt a frisson of nervous energy. It was the way she'd felt on the night of her high school graduation. A road lay open before her. One moment, she felt like running headlong down that road; the next moment, she wanted to stay in her nice safe bed and pull the covers over her head.

She looked out the window as the fog crawled up the hill toward her home. The last rays of the sun were struggling to shine through on the horizon, but they were fighting a losing battle. She felt the damp darkness closing in on her, and hiding on the bed was sounding more and more attractive.

How could I have been so happy all day and now feel so scared? As she gazed out the window, she noticed a light come on in the kitchen of the main house. Sometimes it was a pain to live so close to her mom, even though the rent was great. But at this moment, the light seemed to beckon to her. Jill's head appeared in the kitchen window, and she waved at her daughter, holding up a package of pasta and a jar of sauce and quirking her eyebrow in a silent question. Anne smiled and nodded, heading out of the cottage and through the back garden.

"I'll make the pasta if you get the salad together," Jill said when Anne entered the back door into the kitchen.

"OK." Anne rummaged through the bag of groceries on the counter and removed the salad ingredients.

"And while you do that, you can explain to me how you went from walking on air all afternoon at work to moping in your cottage and gazing tragically out the window."

"It's no big deal," Anne mumbled.

"Being in love is a very big deal, my dear heart. So tell me what's bothering you."

Anne sighed as she tore the lettuce into the salad spinner. "Things are wonderful. They really are. I don't know why I got so freaked."

"Darkness began to settle in and suddenly old demons came knocking?" Jill offered.

"Something like that." Anne washed and then spun the salad.

"Talk to me, Anne. Tell me what you're feeling."

"I guess I just... I mean she's not... We were... Ugh." Anne stopped, giving up on her attempt to put a sentence together.

"One thought at a time," Jill instructed. "I don't care about the order. Tell me the first thing that comes into your mind."

"She's not out," Anne blurted. She stopped the spinner and looked at her mom.

"OK, that's an issue. How do you feel about that?"

"Mom, if you start talking like a therapist, I'm out of here."

"Sorry." Jill snorted. "Sometimes there's a fine line between Mom-speak and therapist-speak. I'll try to be more careful. So tell me this: does the fact that Maggie isn't out make you want to give up on this relationship?"

"No," Anne replied firmly. "But it scares me. I don't want to sneak around and act like being gay is a crime. It's who I am and it should be who she is. She should be—"

"As out and proud as you? Well, she isn't. And that's not something you can just make her be. She has to learn a new behavior and feel safe in that new skin. You have to be patient and supportive while that happens."

Jill filled a pot with water and put it on to boil. Then she poured the sauce into a pan and put it on the stove, turning the burner on low.

"I know that." Anne nodded. "It's just that..."

"Maybe it's about time someone was patient and supportive with you?"

"Huh?"

"Anne, you're facing the first serious relationship since Simone."

"And I don't want to fuck this one up as badly as I did that one." Anne shivered, suddenly feeling even more miserable than she had before.

"You can't take all of the responsibility for past failed relationships on your own shoulders. It takes two people to make a couple and two people to 'fuck things up' — to use your own term. So you can't go into this relationship with Maggie thinking that the entire responsibility of whether or not it works rests solely on your shoulders. That's not being fair to Maggie or to yourself."

Anne let her mom's words sink in.

"Have you told Maggie about this?" Jill asked. "About what you're afraid of?"

"No. What do I say? 'Hey, I've had three failed relationships since high school. I'm really worried that I'll fuck up again, so could you just promise me that you won't screw me?'"

"You probably want to word it a little differently." Jill laughed. "But, yes, I do think you should tell her — and do it as soon as possible."

"I guess you're right." Anne didn't feel totally convinced.

"Sweetie, I know it's hard. But on the second date, she told you she wasn't out. Don't you think that was hard for her?"

Anne sighed and nodded. She concentrated on the cucumber she was slicing. Jill poured the pasta into the water that had finally decided to boil and stirred it, then turned the heat down slightly.

"Maybe it's a mistake to even pursue this thing with Maggie." Anne finished chopping the last of the vegetables and scattered them on the lettuce in the large bowl. "Maybe my fears are really my inner voice telling me this is all wrong."

"Inner voices aren't always right, you know," Jill warned.

"Why does this have to be so complicated?" Anne huffed, tossing the salad. "I mean, I thought I was dating a straightforward, tough-talking cop and I ended up with..."

"A human being instead?" Jill's eyes twinkled.

"Yeah, something like that." Anne snorted.

"Welcome to the wonderful world of true love. Please keep your hands inside the ride at all times."

"And what makes you so sure this is true love? I've had three relationships before. You never told me then I was on the true-love ride."

"First of all, I would never question your relationships."

"Mom, you told me that Diana was a selfish bitch who would dump me if I didn't bankroll her."

"Oh, that's right." Jill grinned sheepishly. "I forgot that little argument. But I didn't say anything about the other two. Not even Simone."

"True." Anne winced, thinking about her failed relationships. "Maybe you should have said something. It would have saved some heartache."

"This isn't like your other relationships, Anne."

"I just don't know..."

"Sweetheart, sometimes you meet someone and date them for awhile, and love matures slowly. It sneaks up on you. This time, love walked right up to you and smacked you upside the head."

"How can I be sure?" Anne asked plaintively.

"Don't second-guess this, Anne. Don't let logic come into this. Don't let anyone tell you otherwise. The only thing you should listen to is your heart."

"I told Maggie this morning that we should follow our hearts."

"You were right." Jill smiled. "When did you get so smart?"

"When I started listening to you, I guess." Anne returned the smile. She felt the tension melting away.

"Ooh, I'll have to start ordering you around more." Jill flashed an evil grin. "OK, wench, drain the pasta and add the sauce, grab the salad and some bread and let's eat."

"Oh, man," Anne moaned theatrically. "A slave's work is never done."

Chapter
Four

"OH, MY GOD, that was wonderful." Maggie moaned ecstatically, falling back in her chair. She clutched her full stomach and closed her eyes.

"It was just lasagna, you goof." Anne chuckled.

"*Homemade* lasagna," Maggie corrected. "When I suggested we eat in, I didn't expect you to go to so much trouble."

"I'm tempted to play on your sympathy and tell you that I slaved over a hot stove all day, but I have to admit that it wasn't that much trouble."

"Well, I don't care what you say; you went above and beyond. Thank you." Maggie rubbed her belly. "My tummy is very happy right now."

Anne watched Maggie's hand making slow circles. Her own fingers twitched with the desire to stroke the woman's stomach. Her libido was like a pit bull straining at the leash, and she struggled to control it. She didn't want to force Maggie to do anything she wasn't sure about.

It had been three days since their breakfast. This was the first time their schedules permitted them to get together. In the intervening time, they had spoken to each other on the phone in every free moment. Sometimes, they had long conversations when they shared all sorts of details about their lives—their favorite television shows, their favorite music, where they went to school. When there wasn't enough time for a long chat, they would just say "hi, thinking about you, bye."

Between phone calls, Anne fought to concentrate on anything other than Maggie. She found herself obsessing on different body parts—Maggie's shoulders, her wrists, her eyes. Now, sitting right next to the object of her desire, Anne struggled to focus on doing anything other than taking the woman into her arms and making slow, passionate love to her.

Anne swallowed and forced herself to focus. "So now that the beast is fed, it might let us have a conversation."

"Very funny. We have been having a very lovely conversation, and you know it."

"Yeah, you're right. Just teasing."

"We've been discussing your senior year in high school." Maggie reached for Anne's hand and gave it a squeeze.

Anne had decided to start slowly when it came to explaining her horrible track record with relationships, so she'd told the simplest story. Her first girlfriend had been Rachel, her best friend in high school. Rachel had been wooed by the captain of the lacrosse team, and suddenly she had no time for Anne and conveniently forgot about the kisses and touches they'd shared under the bleachers. But Rachel's betrayal hadn't ended there. Apparently to cover her tracks, she had told her boyfriend and several other friends that Anne had made the moves on her, trying to "turn her" into a lesbian.

"I'm glad you told me about Rachel and how it's shaped some of your fears," Maggie said. "You've got to believe that I could never hurt another human being like that, no matter what was going on in my own life."

"I know that, Maggie." Anne smiled at Maggie's look of righteous anger.

"It just makes me so mad," Maggie continued, still clutching Anne's hand. "If I knew you then, I would have beaten the shit out of Rachel."

"Well, if I knew you then I don't think I'd give her the time of day," Anne replied softly, stroking her thumb along Maggie's palm. Maggie shivered and Anne could see goose bumps racing up her arm and making the fine hair stand on end.

"You have electric fingers," Maggie murmured.

"Do I?" Anne murmured back.

Maggie simply nodded.

Slow, slow, go slow. Anne sighed and let go of Maggie's hand. "I guess I should start getting some of these dishes soaking. Why don't you put on a CD and have a seat on the sofa?"

"Oh, no." Maggie got up and grabbed their plates. "I'm helping you. It's the least I can do after that great meal."

"No, really. I don't have a dishwasher, so I'll just put a few things to soak and do them all later."

"Anne, I am a pro at doing dishes. I could get an Olympic medal in dishwashing."

"OK." Anne laughed. "Now I'm intrigued. Please show me your stuff, oh, dishwashing guru."

They cleared the table and Anne put the leftover lasagna into plastic containers. Maggie went to the kitchen sink and turned on the water.

"Step back, and prepare to be amazed." Maggie grabbed the dish soap and Anne pulled a towel out of a drawer and prepared to dry.

"So you really would have beaten up Rachel, huh?" Anne asked with a grin.

"Definitely. I was raised with four brothers. I learned how to fight at a very young age."

"I'm sure you had a mean right hook."

"Actually, my dad had a strict rule about hitting." Steam from the hot water in the sink rose up around Maggie as she washed the silverware. "Fighting was a real big thing to him. When we were little, we all wanted to be police officers like our dad. He would always tell us that we could never be cops if we acted on our anger by hitting people."

Anne thought she saw a shadow cross Maggie's eyes, but it was gone in an instant.

"So you never hit anyone?" Anne dried the silverware and placed each piece into the nearby drawer.

"Only once. In elementary school." Maggie carefully washed the wine glasses. "These kids were picking on my brother Sean at recess. I was seven and he was nine. I saw someone push Sean and the world just went red. I ran in there with fists flying."

Anne laughed at the mental image of a little Maggie, all red hair and temper, beating up the older kids. "What happened?"

"I was sent to the principal's office. He, in turn, called my dad, who had to come pick me up from school. I was absolutely mortified."

"Was your dad really mad?" Anne was suddenly concerned, feeling an overwhelming need to protect Maggie -- even the young Maggie of sixteen years before.

"No, I think he was proud of me. He tried to look serious, but I could see a little twitch at the corner of his mouth where he was suppressing a grin. When we got home, he must have realized he was facing a serious moral dilemma. So he told me that I should never hit anyone, but if I did hit someone, doing it to protect my family was a pretty damned good reason. He sent me to my room without dinner, but he let Sean sneak me a peanut butter and jelly sandwich later that night."

"Did any of your brothers become cops?" Anne put the glasses away, turning them upside down in the cupboard.

"Only my oldest brother Patrick. He's a sergeant in the LAPD."

Anne again saw a flicker of something cross Maggie's face.

"Wow, LAPD is pretty hard-core, isn't it?"

"Yeah, he's, um...a lot like my dad. The family's very proud of him."

Anne still wasn't sure what was going on behind those sea green eyes, but decided that changing the subject was a good option. "And what about your other brothers?"

"Liam is a stockbroker in the city." Maggie began washing the plates. "Michael is a car mechanic and still lives in Millbrae, less than a mile from where we grew up and where Dad still lives, and Sean works for the National Park Service. He's currently stationed at Alcatraz."

"That's cool. Does he do the prison tours and everything?"

"Yeah, the rangers trade off and do the prison tours, the nature tours, and work in the museum. I think it would be a neat place to work, but he's bored with it. He loves the forest, so he's trying to get transferred to Yosemite."

"I love Yosemite, but only if you get out of the crowded areas, into the backcountry."

"Oh, I know what you mean. Have you ever gone backpacking on the east side?" Maggie's eyes sparkled.

"Not for a few years, but I love it. We should go sometime." Anne smiled at her friend. She was overcome by an image of cuddling Maggie in a sleeping bag under a canopy of stars.

Maggie nodded excitedly and then turned to the sink, beginning to work on the big lasagna pan. She was totally focused on the task, and Anne was able to watch her freely. Maggie's forehead was furrowed in concentration, a little line running up between her eyebrows. Anne fought an urge to rub the line away, but kept drying the plate she was holding. Maggie's face was flushed from the steam, and Anne watched as she blew a breath upwards, causing a tendril of her hair to wave off her hot forehead. Anne blinked and saw a different image, one of a flushed face lying beneath her as Anne's fingers... She blinked again and her mouth went dry. *Oh, man, I am never going to make it through this night.*

"I think that's it," Maggie announced, putting the pan in the drainer.

"Yep," Anne croaked, putting her very dry plate away and grabbing the pan.

"Are you OK?"

"Yeah, just got something caught in my throat." Anne quickly dried the pan and put it away. When she turned back, she noticed a smudge of soap bubbles on Maggie's cheek. She paused and then slowly raised her hand and wiped it away gently with her thumb. She met Maggie's unblinking gaze, and then leaned down slowly and placed a soft kiss on Maggie's lips. Maggie reached out and Anne felt the wet warmth of a hand as it tenderly held her neck. Then she was overwhelmed with the kiss and Maggie's tongue, which was seeking permission to enter her mouth. She happily granted the request, and their tongues engaged in a sensual dance.

Anne finally pulled back, breathless. She smiled at the flush on Maggie's cheek, which this time wasn't caused by the steam.

"Anne, I—"

"Shh," Anne interrupted, cupping Maggie's cheek. "We don't have to do anything tonight. We can go as slow as you need to."

"I don't want to go slow," Maggie blurted out. "I've been obsessing about you for the last three days. I can't get you out of my head. I was writing up an arrest report and instead of writing 'resisted arrest' I wrote 'resisted cheekbones.'"

"I've been the same way," Anne admitted with a laugh. "I spent at least a solid hour thinking about your earlobes."

"What about my earlobes?" Maggie rubbed one shyly.

"How I wanted to...um." Anne decided to let her actions speak for her, and leaned down toward the free lobe. She tenderly took it in her lips and drew it into her mouth. She sucked it, listening to the soft groans of pleasure the action elicited. Maggie moved her hands around Anne and massaged her back. Anne's mouth moved lower, tasting the soft warm flesh under Maggie's jaw. She kissed, licked, and sucked on her journey down Maggie's neck, ending above her collarbone, feeling Maggie's pulse beating hard and fast. Anne's resolve was crumbling, but she used the last of her strength to pull away again.

"Let's go sit down," Anne suggested.

Maggie, breathing heavily, merely nodded and followed Anne out of the kitchen.

Anne put on a CD and turned the volume down low. She wanted to let Maggie decide where to sit. *If she wants distance, she'll sit on the chair.* When she turned away from the stereo, she found that Maggie had taken a seat on the small sofa. Maggie patted the cushion next to her, and Anne sat down on the spot. She took Maggie's hand, staring intently into her eyes. She noted with surprise that they were a deep forest green and realized it was because the pupils were dilated with desire.

"Maggie, I want our first time to be special. I want it to be what we both want, how we both want."

"So far, it's perfect." Maggie glanced up at Anne with concerned eyes and added hastily, "If you don't want this, I can go. Or we can just sit here and listen to music and talk."

"No." Anne gasped loudly, and then repeated more softly, "No. I want this. It's just that..."

"That you think you're pushing me into this?"

"Well, yes, sort of. I'm thinking you haven't had a lot of experience, and..."

"Oh." Maggie smiled. She nodded as if she'd solved a difficult brainteaser. "I get it. Now's the time I tell you that I've never really done it before, that I don't know how to make love to a woman, and I need time to think and be sure of what I want. That kind of thing?"

"Um." Anne was feeling slightly disoriented. Maggie was deviating from the script she had been practicing in her mind. She had no idea what her next line should be.

"Don't worry, sweetheart." Maggie smiled tenderly. "Your powers of deduction haven't left you. I have made love to a woman a total of once. It was actually quite pleasurable, if I remember correctly, but it's all a bit hazy. I was very drunk and my grand finale was throwing up in the sink. There's a longer story there that I'll share with you sometime."

Anne smiled and tried to focus on what Maggie was saying, but everything after "sweetheart" was a blur.

"Please don't think that you're pushing me into something that I don't want or that I'm not ready for," Maggie continued. "My body is thrumming with my need for you."

She looked up and Anne could see the desire sparking from her eyes.

"I just didn't want you to think that I'm calling all the shots."

"Anne, I want you to call some of the shots," Maggie replied in a seductive purr. "But I've got a loaded gun here, and I know how to use it."

"You're a real sharp shooter, huh?" Anne asked softly, reaching forward and pulling Maggie into a loose embrace.

"Oh, yeah." Maggie nestled her head under Anne's chin. "You'd be amazed at what I can do with my handgun."

"Well," Anne said, stroking Maggie's soft hair, "hit me with your best shot, officer Monahan."

Anne felt all of her nerve endings tingle. She wanted so much. She wanted to consume and be consumed. Her head swam with her desire. She moaned with pleasure as Maggie's lips explored beneath her shirt collar. When Maggie undid two buttons on her blouse and trailed kisses on the top of her breasts, Anne could feel her nipples pressing against the silk of her bra with so much force she wondered if they would rip through the fabric. Maggie brushed her lips lightly against them through the silk, and Anne could stand it no more. She needed her blouse and bra off, and she struggled to remove both as quickly as possible. Maggie kindly assisted her and then leaned down slowly, stopping a few centimeters from Anne's breast. Her warm breath made the nipples even more erect, and Anne moaned with desire. Maggie ended the torture and began to suck the nearest nipple.

Anne's fingers entwined themselves in Maggie's hair and she did her best to hold on. After only a few moments, her hips jerked upward, searching for contact. Maggie shifted a thigh between Anne's legs, and Anne rubbed against it. But there was too much denim in the way, and Anne frantically fumbled at her button fly.

Maggie gently pushed Anne's struggling hands away and began to undo the buttons of the jeans. Anne watched Maggie's face as she concentrated on the simple task. Maggie was flushed with desire and breathing heavily. Her eyes were sparkling and focused intently on what her hands were doing. When she reached the last button, she paused and looked up into Anne's face. Anne had never seen such a look of devotion. She felt as if she were being worshipped.

"I love you," Maggie whispered.

"I love you, too." Anne bent forward and captured Maggie's lips with hers. Their tongues danced once again, but this was no serene waltz. It was the dance of hot, sweaty bodies swaying together in the dark. It was a dance of dominance and submission, of possessing something and then letting it go.

Without breaking away from the kiss, Anne pulled her jeans down her long, slim legs, taking the shoes and socks with them. Once the garments were on the floor, Anne pulled away from the kiss.

"Please." Anne moaned, unable to put words to what she needed.

Maggie paused again, and then carefully reached out, caressing the soft skin of Anne's upper thighs. Finally, she found warm, moist skin. Her fingers stroked and teased.

"Please," Anne begged, more forcefully this time. She gasped as Maggie thrust a finger into her opening, immediately beginning to thrust against Maggie's hand. Maggie soon picked up the rhythm. Anne felt as if she was running toward something—as if her very life depended on her getting to that place. She felt Maggie take a breast in her mouth and suddenly she was running right off a cliff. Instead of falling, she soared. She cried out with the pure joy of it.

Maggie held on to her until Anne returned to earth, then

slowly withdrew her hand. She looked at Anne, suddenly shy and uncertain.

Anne felt raw hunger ripping through her soul.

"Lie back," she growled. She could feel Maggie's reaction beneath her hand—a single jolt ending in a trembling vibration of desire.

Anne slowly undressed her lover, removing shoes and socks, shirt and bra, jeans and briefs. Then she ran her fingers over all of the areas that she had been obsessed with for the past few days. Maggie's wrists were as soft as she imagined. Freckles covered her chest, but gave way to milky white skin on her breasts. Her nipples were small and pink. Their delicacy was contrasted with the power of her legs, which were corded with muscles.

Maggie was like a cherished Christmas gift. Wished for all year, written down in letters to Santa, and finally waiting under the tree. *This is mine,* Anne cried over and over in her head. Her joy turned to desire, and she lowered her mouth to Maggie's breast and began to feast.

Maggie groaned with pleasure as Anne trailed kisses down her firm stomach. Anne whispered through the soft curls and then darted her tongue into Maggie's folds. Maggie cried out and thrust her hips forward, then opened her legs wide. She tangled her fingers into Anne's hair and gently pushed Anne's head down. Anne didn't need the extra encouragement. She licked and sucked every inch of Maggie's velvet skin.

"Oh, God, oh, God!" Maggie cried.

Anne focused on Maggie's clit, toying with the sensitive nub. Soon, Maggie was trembling with pleasure. Anne drew back and dodged Maggie's thrusting hips.

"Please, please," Maggie begged.

Anne waited and then descended again, now sucking with just the right amount of force. Maggie's orgasm ripped through her, and Anne held onto the smaller woman's hips. She placed soft kisses on her abdomen, until she felt the tremors slowly calm. When their breaths finally evened out, she looked up and saw tears falling from Maggie's eyes.

"Don't cry, baby. Please don't cry," Anne said softly, reaching up and wiping the tears away with her thumb.

"I'm all right," Maggie reassured her, smiling through her tears. "It was just so... I feel so..."

"Shh."

"Just hold me." Maggie reached out and Anne enfolded her in strong arms. "Don't let go."

"I won't let go. I'll never let go."

MAGGIE COULD STILL feel Anne's skin beneath her fingers, still smell their mingled desire, two days later. She had known that making love to Anne would change her world, but the way she was feeling was...

"If you don't wipe that smug, 'I've been well and truly fucked' smile off your face this instant, I'll wipe it off for you," Moocher said, riding up beside her.

"Jealous much?" Maggie continued to smile. She sat astride her police-issued bicycle and surveyed the crowd at the "How Berkeley Can You Be?" festival. She had serious issues with a festival that set itself up as a challenge, but so far she and Moocher hadn't encountered many problems. It was a beautiful sunny afternoon, there were only three hours left to work, and she was seeing Anne again that evening. All was right with the world.

"I'm not jealous," Moocher protested. "I'm pissed off that you won't share one detail of your night of hedonistic pleasure."

Maggie ignored her partner as a large family passed them, the three boys taking a long look at the police officers and their bikes. The boys' baby sister waved from her stroller and shouted "Hi!" and Maggie grinned, waving her fingers back at all of them. The little girl was holding a cookie and her chubby cheek was marked by a smear of chocolate. Maggie watched as the children's mother stopped and pulled a tissue out of her bag, then kneeled down next to the stroller. The mother smiled at the toddler, whispering something that only the little girl could hear, and then softly wiped the stain away. It was a simple, everyday action, but it evoked a whisper of a memory for Maggie: her own mother and a sunny day just like this one.

"So tell me," Moocher leaned over so as not to be overheard by the family, "how many big O's did you guys experience? Reassure me that my record is still intact."

Maggie groaned and looked skyward as her special moment burst like a water balloon against her chest.

"Would you just drop it?" Maggie asked once the family had moved out of earshot.

"Drop it?"

"Yes, drop it."

"You want me to just drop it?"

"Yes, I want you to just drop it," Maggie replied evenly. She would not allow herself to scream at her best friend when on duty.

"Um..." Moocher tapped her lips with her index finger, as if seriously considering the request. "No."

Maggie huffed angrily.

"So tell me, how many?"

"We had a normal one each, if you must know. We did not approach your record of a baker's dozen—which I've never believed, by the way."

"I am not going to start that argument again. I'd rather hear details of your under-achieving encounter. Like who went first?"

"What?" Maggie yelped.

"It's a simple question. Who went first? Who licked and who went 'mmm'?"

"You need help."

"Please. I can't help it if I'm a voyeur."

"I've already told you way too much. My sex life is private, between Anne and me. My lips are sealed." Maggie mimed locking her lips with a little key and throwing it away.

Moocher grabbed Maggie's arm like a kid begging her mom for candy at the grocery store. "Please, Maggie, please."

Maggie kept her lips closed tight.

"Maggie, you have to share. I'm your best friend, for Christ's sake. I taught you everything you know."

"Where do you get that idea?" Maggie released her lips to let out an outraged guffaw.

"I gave you a copy of 'Best Erotic Lesbian Stories' for your birthday. Surely you picked up a few pointers from that."

"I picked up a few euphemisms from that."

"OK, euphemisms are good," Moocher said. "I can work with that. So, did you drink at her fountain of love?"

"Shut up, Moocher."

"Did you caress her shaft of desire?"

"Shut up, Moocher."

"Did you taste of her succulent forbidden fruit?"

"Shut up, Moocher." Maggie was relieved to hear her cell phone ring, and reached into her pack to answer it.

"Gee, I wonder who that could be." Moocher feigned innocence. Maggie scowled at her.

"Hello?" A smile spread across Maggie's face when Anne greeted her.

"Again with that fucking smile."

"What? No, that was Moocher," Maggie explained into the phone. "I think she's suffering from a serious hormone imbalance."

Moocher stuck her tongue out at her friend. Maggie ignored her and listened quietly to Anne for a few minutes. A blush colored her ears and made its inevitable journey down her neck and up to her cheeks.

"Hey, hey, hey," Moocher said, loud enough for Anne to hear, "you better stop that love talk or someone's going to mistake you for a stop light and cause an accident."

"I love you too, sweetheart," Maggie whispered, continuing to ignore her partner.

"I'm gonna barf."

"Well, I better go. I need to make sure my partner takes her medication."

Maggie expected to hear a smart comeback, but Moocher was silently gazing toward the festival crowd. Maggie followed Moocher's line of sight, ignoring a group of kids playing hacky sack and focusing on a teenager on a BMX bike. He was moving slowly around the edge of a group of people who were milling around the animal adoption booth. Something about the way the kid was moving set off Maggie's warning bells. Apparently, Moocher felt the same.

"Hey, baby," Maggie said into the phone, "I'll call you when I get off work. Love you." She replaced the phone in her pack, never taking her eyes off the boy. Their police instincts proved accurate when the kid suddenly reached forward and grabbed a woman's backpack, ripping it violently from her arm. He threw it over his own shoulder and set off quickly on his bike. Maggie and Moocher immediately followed, winding expertly through the crowd. Moocher clicked on her shoulder mike and informed Dispatch that they were in pursuit.

"He's heading to the high school!" Maggie shouted. She watched as the boy jumped the bike down a short flight of concrete steps.

"He thinks he's trying out for the fucking X-Games." Moocher sneered.

"Let's show him how the pros do it." Maggie grinned back. They both jumped the stairs as well, and began to gain on the kid. He headed for Berkeley High School, passing between two buildings and heading toward a construction area where a new gym was being built.

"Split!" Moocher cried, and headed down a path to the right. Maggie knew if Moocher was fast enough, her partner could circle one of the buildings and cut him off when he came through.

Maggie stayed directly behind the boy, slowly gaining on him. She looked up and saw the end of the path ahead. It passed the construction site and opened up to a busy street with fast-moving traffic. She realized that the kid might be desperate enough to try to dodge through the cars.

"Come on, Moocher," Maggie mumbled, still not seeing her

partner. She switched gears and pedaled harder, her legs burning with the effort. She was only a few feet behind the teenager now. He was nearing the street, and Maggie reached deep, urging her legs to pedal harder. She saw a large pile of dirt next to the path. *Now or never.* She lunged out to her right and grabbed hold of the boy's T-shirt. She launched herself off the bike and let their forward momentum carry them into the mound of dirt while the bikes went in the opposite direction. She twisted in mid-air so that the boy would land on top of her, sheltering his unprotected head from the impact of the fall.

Unfortunately, his unprotected head impacted her sternum, and she felt the air leave her lungs with a great whoosh. The boy tried to roll away, but Maggie somehow managed to keep her grip on his T-shirt. It wasn't difficult, since their arms and legs were hopelessly entangled.

Moocher arrived and took advantage of their predicament, cuffing the boy as he squirmed to extricate himself. She then pulled him up off her partner by his bound hands.

"Are you OK?" Moocher asked.

"Yeah," the teenager replied.

"Not you, idiot."

"I'm OK." Maggie wheezed, trying to pull air into her lungs.

"Not your most graceful move, Princess." Moocher smirked. She helped Maggie to her feet and dusted her off. She waited until Maggie's breath had evened out and then leaned down to whisper in her ear. "When you tackled Anne like that, I hope you showed a little more coordination."

"Shut up, Moocher."

Chapter
Five

"LIEUTENANT MONAHAN!"

Maggie and her dad were met at the door to Roma's by the host and owner, Mario Parisi. The Monahans had been visiting the restaurant since long before Maggie was born, and Mario always greeted them like they were family.

"And little Mary Margaret! Look at how you've grown!"

Maggie smiled and wondered if Mario realized that she'd stopped growing when she was fifteen. *Oh, well, what's nine years between friends?*

"Mario, is our usual table available?" Connor Monahan surveyed the restaurant as if ready to evict anyone who might be sitting at the table between the window and the open fireplace.

"Of course, Lieutenant. Right this way."

Maggie followed, wondering not for the first time why Mario acted like he owed her dad. She knew her dad was so clean he squeaked, but it seemed that some debt existed between the two. Then again, maybe Mario was just the overly obsequious type.

"Will it be the usual?" Mario asked as he pushed Maggie's chair a little too hard against the back of her knees.

"Of course," Connor replied, "prime rib with all the fixin's."

"Actually," Maggie said before Mario waltzed away. "I think I'll have the snapper."

"Snapper?" Connor looked as if Maggie had ordered a peanut butter and jelly sandwich. With a side of jellybeans.

"I'm just not, um..." Maggie stopped herself. Did she really want to get into an argument about eating red meat? "I'm trying to cut down. Have to keep my figure, you know."

"Well, I suppose I can understand that. Though I think girls nowadays are too skinny."

Maggie shrugged and smiled at Mario, who nodded and winked. Maggie knew it was a friendly gesture, but it seemed slightly seedy. She quickly turned back to her father.

"So tell me what's been keeping you so busy these days," Connor asked.

Making love to Anne had been a turning point for Maggie. All of her fears were washed away in a tide of passion and tenderness. She actually found it hard to remember why she'd been so frightened to enter into the relationship—to even speak to Anne. Now, she felt like a superhero: fighting crime by day, having hot monkey sex by night. Anything was possible. And then she found herself sitting next to her father.

"I, um, you know...not much."

Maggie gazed into her father's eyes and tried to determine whether he knew more than he was letting on. Had Moocher blabbed to someone who blabbed to someone else? Had someone seen her on one of her few dates with Anne?

"I understand you went on a training class with a couple of young officers a few months back," Connor probed. "David Ellison is the son of Detective Peter Ellison down in San Jose. We worked together on that kidnapping case in '82."

"Dave's a nice guy, but he has a girlfriend."

Connor frowned, his plan obviously thwarted. "So you're not seeing anyone special?"

Maggie thought about saying yes. She imagined her mouth forming the word, pictured her dad's face as the information penetrated his brain and his green eyes lost their sparkle and grew dark

"No." Maggie felt sick to her stomach. "No one special."

"You say that like it's a death sentence." Connor flashed a smile. "Don't worry about it; you're still young. Besides, it sounds like you've decided to concentrate on your career. That's probably a good idea for the time being."

Why don't you fill me in on my life plan, Dad. Should I pencil in a boyfriend for a year from March?

Maggie played with her bread and wondered if she could speed up time. Just a snap of her fingers and she'd be wiping spumoni off her mouth and reaching for the bill.

"Speaking of your career, have you thought any more about my suggestion?" Connor asked.

"What suggestion?" Maggie played dumb, hoping that by some divine intervention her dad would say something like, "My suggestion to buy that new bike you were eyeing in the store yesterday."

"My suggestion to put in for a transfer." No such luck.

"Dad, I love the bike patrol. And my arrest record is just as good as it would be on some of the other watches."

"Bike patrol was a good entry-level unit. But it's not

somewhere you want to stay for much longer, not if you want to be taken seriously."

"It's not like I'm working parking control."

God, I sound like a teenager. Please, Dad, can I have the car keys. I promise to be home by midnight.

"The point is, Mary Margaret, that until you settle down and start a family, you need to be serious about your career. So with that in mind, I had a little word with Bob Lockhart and—"

"You told my boss to give me a transfer? Dad, that's not right."

"I'm only doing what's best for you. What's wrong with that?"

Maggie knew it was a rhetorical question and kept her mouth tightly closed, her protests screaming through her head.

"Bob said he'd speak with you about it," Connor continued. "In fact, he said there might be an opening coming up soon. There might even be a position in the bomb squad."

"You need special training for that," Maggie protested weakly.

"So you get it." Connor shrugged. "You're more than capable of dealing with that and it will look good on your resume. Patrick is thinking of transferring to bomb squad down in LA. It'll be another step toward getting a job with the FBI if he plays his cards right."

Maggie's stomach tightened at the mention of her brother. "Well, I can't see myself in the FBI."

"I agree with that. It's perfect for your brother, though. Speaking of which, I think you should go down there. Maybe take the kids out—just you and them. You could go to Disneyland. They'd love that."

"Whoa." Maggie held up her hand. "What are you talking about?"

"You don't spend enough time with your brother and his family. I wish Patrick hadn't moved down there." Connor winced and Maggie remembered the bitter argument they'd had when his oldest had announced his new position with the LAPD. "But maybe it was the right decision. Anyway, you need to make the effort to keep in contact."

"Why me? He has three other brothers, you know."

"It's not the same."

Connor's expression told Maggie that he would provide no further explanation and accept no argument. Maggie felt the words on her tongue, just waiting to roll out. She took a sip of water, swallowing the words like bitter medicine.

"I know you don't get on that well with Patrick, but you're

adults now. Surely you can forget all that kid's stuff."

"Dad, you don't understand." Maggie's words were soft, with just a glimmer of hope. Hope that he would ask her to explain. He never had, and she knew, deep down, that he never would.

"I understand, all right. I understand that it would break your mother's heart to know that you kids didn't see each other every opportunity you have."

"Dad..."

"Dad, what?"

Please don't use Mom like that, Maggie pleaded in her head, but said instead, "OK, I'll give Patrick a call and set something up."

"Great." Connor's smile and twinkling green eyes almost made Maggie forget about the knots tying up her stomach. Almost.

"HEY, SWEETHEART, I know you're out with your dad, but give me a call when you get in." Anne paused in the middle of the message she was leaving on Maggie's answering machine. Was she being too pushy? "Um, or whenever you get a chance. I miss you."

She hung up quickly, wishing she hadn't left the message. But Maggie had looked so apprehensive the night before, more like she was going to face a firing squad instead of contemplating a nice meal with her father. From the few clues Maggie had let slip, Anne knew Maggie's dad put a lot of pressure on his daughter—as well as the rest of the family. But Maggie was a tough-talking cop. A little neurotic, of course, but surely she wouldn't let someone push her around. Would she? Then again, Anne had enough experience in her law practice with women who were victims despite being tough, intelligent, and independent in every other way. It was just a matter of the abuser knowing just what weak spots to hit...

Abuse? Anne put the brakes on her mental rambling. *Where did I get the idea that Maggie was abused? Wouldn't she have said something? She was just raised in a really strict household and is still struggling to shake off the shackles.* She nodded her head, satisfied with her explanation.

Then she remembered a shadow passing over Maggie's eyes. She'd been talking about her brother, Patrick. Anne's protective streak suddenly sat up and saluted and she felt the fine hairs on the back of her neck rise up against her T-shirt.

I can't push her, Anne decided. *I need to let her tell me in her own time.*

Anne sighed and picked up the book she'd been trying to read, and tried some more. After failing for another fifteen minutes, she threw it on the table. She picked up her workout clothes and tucked her cell phone in her bag, grabbing her keys and wallet and then heading out the door.

MAGGIE WAS HAVING a very strange dream.

She and Anne were playing beach volleyball, pitted against two gorgeous long-legged blondes. All four women were totally nude. She and Anne were playing really well, setting and spiking with a vengeance. But every time they scored a point, they had to walk under a huge barrel and have creamed spinach dumped on their heads. Just as she was serving for match point, a shrill ring catapulted her back to reality.

"Hello?"

It took a moment for Maggie to remember that picking up the phone and turning it on had to precede the greeting.

"Hello?" she tried again. She was more successful the second time.

"Hey, baby, what are you doing?" Anne's voice reminded Maggie of a perfect cup of coffee—really creamy, really warm, and really yummy.

"Hi, sweetheart." Maggie tried to purr back, but she was struck with nap voice. "I was sleeping," she added with a croak.

"Oh, yeah? It sounds like it." Anne paused, as if trying to decide what to say next.

"Sorry I didn't call you back last night," Maggie said to fill the gap. She had a pretty good idea that Anne was calling to offer post-parental-encounter support and was being careful to say the right thing.

"That's OK."

Maggie thought about making an excuse about getting in too late or being called in to work. Then she realized she didn't have to lie to Anne. "I just crashed after dinner. It was such an emotional trip, you know?"

"Yeah, I can imagine." Anne's voice sounded relieved, now that the subject was out in the open and Maggie was obviously being honest about it. "Well, anyway, you know how we were going out tonight?"

"Are you canceling on me?" Maggie asked in a tragic voice.

"No, Mom actually cancelled on me. I was going to take her to an estate sale in Napa, but she has to go into the office to get something done for tomorrow morning. I'm free now if you want to go out, or we could just—"

"Where are you?" Maggie interrupted excitedly, her head filling with ideas of what they could just do. She had a sudden image of Anne playing volleyball and tried to ignore the spinach.

"I'm on Highway Twenty-Four, just leaving Lafayette. I had to come out here to drop something off for Mom."

"Come to my apartment!" Maggie demanded. She realized she sounded just a little bit desperate, so repeated in a calmer voice, "Come to my apartment and we can figure out what we want to do."

"I think I'm having cell phone problems. I thought you just asked me to come to your apartment."

"I did. Why is that so strange?"

"Because we've been seeing each other for about two weeks and I've never seen your apartment—not even the outside. In fact, I don't even know exactly where you live."

"Did you say 'about two weeks'?" Maggie asked.

"What?"

"You said 'we've been seeing each other for about two weeks.' You're not even sure how long we've been seeing each other?"

"It's been two weeks, one day, and nineteen hours since our first date for coffee," Anne answered precisely.

Maggie sighed happily. "Wow. I guess you're not going to be the type to forget our wedding anniversary."

Anne was quiet for a moment, and Maggie could hear her words echo in the silence.

"Hey," Anne said after a few agonizing seconds, "I'm stuck in traffic in the tunnel approach, but I'll be through soon. You'd better tell me how to get to your place."

"Oh, yeah, I guess that'd help." Maggie hoped the phone wouldn't pick up the strained tone in her chuckle. "OK, well, you want to take the Broadway exit and head down the hill toward Oakland. Turn left on Livingston. It's near Tech High School. My building is in the first block on the right. It's the only apartment building on the street. I'm in apartment 2C."

"OK, got it. I'll be there in about ten minutes. Love you."

"Love you, too," Maggie said cheerily.

She hung up the phone and then threw it down, watching it bounce off the sofa cushion and hit the floor.

"Arrrggh!" she shouted at the ceiling. "You are so stupid, Mary Margaret! Stupid, stupid, stupid! Why the hell did you mention weddings? You've only been dating for two weeks, one day, and nineteen hours, for fuck's sake."

Maggie got up from the sofa and began pacing through her apartment.

"Did she notice? Maybe she didn't notice. She paused, didn't she? Was that a shocked pause, as in 'I only wanted to hang out with you for a few months and have some really good sex' or was that a thoughtful pause, as in 'You know, I can really see us settling down together some day'? Maybe it was just a reception glitch. Maybe I'm hoping for a miracle. OK, I think this calls for some healthy denial. I did not say anything about wedding anniversaries. Even if she brings it up, I'll plead ignorance."

Her pacing brought her in front of the bathroom mirror, and she forced herself to nod emphatically, sealing her promise to herself. While doing that, she noticed water spots near the sink. As she grabbed a towel to wipe at the spots, the full realization of the state of her apartment hit her like a flash flood in the desert.

Maggie knew her apartment wasn't dirty. There were no half-eaten pieces of pizza under the sofa or dishes in the sink growing new life forms. It was just in disarray. Complete and utter disarray. The bed was unmade, clothes were on the floor, books, videotapes, and CDs were stacked everywhere except on shelves, and the TV remote had disappeared weeks before. It wasn't pretty, and when it came to impressing Anne, Maggie was all about pretty.

Maggie decided to start at the front door and clean inward. If she didn't make it to the farthest reaches, she'd make sure Anne didn't wander. She stacked, straightened, and put away like a madwoman. When the door buzzer went, she was panting worse than a chubby kid chasing down the ice cream truck. She buzzed Anne in and tried to catch her breath.

"Hi," Maggie gasped in the open door. "Come on in."

Anne got through the door, closed it, and gathered Maggie into her arms. After a nice big squeeze, she leaned down and gave her a nice big kiss.

"Wow," Maggie said, "what was that for?"

"I missed you. I haven't seen you since Saturday. That's three whole days. It seemed like an eternity."

"OK, quite possibly the sweetest thing anyone's ever said to me." Maggie smiled and then gave her lover another kiss.

"Tell me what was sweeter," Anne challenged after their lips had parted.

"When my four-year-old nephew told me he wanted to marry me. But you'll get extra points if you give me another hug."

Anne complied, and Maggie squeezed her tight.

"You're awfully cuddly today," Maggie mumbled from her pleasant place between Anne's breasts.

"I know." Anne sighed. "I got my period and I'm feeling extra clingy. Hope you don't mind."

"Of course not. I love it." Maggie gave Anne a bigger squeeze and then moved her hands down to rub Anne's lower back. This elicited a groan of pleasure that shot straight through Maggie.

"If you don't stop groaning like that, I'm going to have to change my underwear," Maggie warned.

"Why don't you just take them off? It'll save you some laundry." Anne waggled her ebony eyebrows.

"Down, girl. You've got monthly issues."

"I think I can work around them. Of course, it might be nice to move out of the doorway..."

"Oh, my God, where are my manners." Maggie stepped out of Anne's arms reluctantly. She took Anne by the hand and led her two steps. "This is the living room where I do most of my...well, living. Through that door is the kitchen, where I do food activity like pouring cereal into a bowl. And this is the way to my bedroom." She took Anne's hand and led her toward the last room on the list.

"You don't need to tell me what you do in there," Anne said, allowing herself to be led.

"It's where I entertain all of my female admirers." Maggie grinned. "Hang on while I make sure the coast is clear."

They entered the room and sat down on the bed, which Maggie had made in her cleaning frenzy. Anne shifted over a lump and moved a pillow out of the way. She caught a glimpse of something small, brown, and furry and jumped off the bed.

"Shit!" Anne cried. "What the hell is that?"

Maggie looked around in confusion and then spotted the troublemaker. "Hey, it's OK. It's just my, um, teddy bear."

Anne approached the bed cautiously as Maggie moved the pillow and revealed the cuddly toy. "I must be on edge. I thought it was a rat."

"Thanks a lot," Maggie said indignantly. "I may not be the neatest person in the world, but I don't have rats running around in my bedroom."

"I'm sorry." Anne leaned down and kissed Maggie on the cheek. "I didn't mean to imply you were a slob. I guess I just didn't expect my tough cop girlfriend to have a teddy bear."

"Well, I've had Ambassador Squiggles for a long time. I got him before I was tough, or a cop, or your girlfriend." Maggie picked up the bear and played with his ears, gazing into his brown plastic eyes.

"Where did he get such a distinguished name?" Anne managed to ask the question with a straight face, which amazed Maggie.

"My mom named him."

It was one of the few distinct memories that Maggie had of her mother. Most of the others came courtesy of her dad or brothers telling her about things that had happened. Those memories were constructs, made of old photos and stories. But the memory of that Christmas was real: her mother pulling the box from under the tree, the green paper with red stars and white snowflakes, the teddy bear that was so big and soft and cuddly. Her mother was already terribly ill. Maggie could picture her mom's thin body, the dark circles under her eyes, and her skin so pale it seemed translucent.

His name's Ambassador Squiggles. It was like a secret shared by just the two of them.

"Tell me more, baby," Anne said softly, pulling Maggie into her arms. "When did your mom name him?"

I should tell her, Maggie mused, even as she felt the walls going up.

"It's history."

"I don't care," Anne said, keeping a steady hold. "I'm a big fan of history. I watch the History Channel all the time."

Maggie laughed and relaxed a little. "I got him the Christmas before my mom died. She died in February. I've rarely slept without him since. It's just a connection to my mom, I guess."

"I can't imagine what it was like for you to lose your mom at the age of three."

Maggie just shrugged and pulled out of Anne's embrace.

"It was tough, but we got by." Maggie found it impossible to meet Anne's eyes. She knew that she would see so much understanding in those blue depths that she'd have to dive in, but afraid that, once she started, she wouldn't be able to stop. And then what? There was nothing that Anne could do about the past. It was time Maggie got on with her life. She needed to concentrate on Anne and their relationship, and let the past fade away.

"If you ever want to talk about it, I'm here. OK?"

Maggie smiled and nodded, glad that the subject was once again safely closed.

"By the way," Maggie said, "Moocher has been dying to meet you. I told her maybe we could set something up for next weekend."

"Sounds good."

"I've got to warn you about Moocher, though." Maggie reached out and twirled a lock of Anne's ebony hair around her finger. "She can be a real tease. I'm used to it, and she isn't being mean or anything."

"What does she tease you about?" Anne's eyes narrowed. Maggie felt suddenly frightened for her best friend's life.

"Um...about us, mostly," Maggie replied carefully.

"What about us?"

"Well, she's kind of obsessed with sex and she's always asking for details about...you know..." Maggie paused, then added quickly, "Don't worry, I would never talk about it. And anyway, if I did start sharing, I think Moocher's head would explode. She's all mouth, really. Don't take her too seriously."

"Considering the fact that she's more or less responsible for bringing us together, and she's your best friend, I'll cut her some slack," Anne said. She added in a cold, even tone, "But if she's mean to you in my presence, she'll have to face the consequences."

"Sweetheart, please don't kill my best friend." Maggie laughed, patting Anne on the cheek. She watched sparkles of blue fire flickering in Anne's eyes. "Although your protective streak is incredibly sexy."

"Oh, yeah?" Anne purred seductively.

"Y-yeah," Maggie stuttered softly. She felt a tingly warmth traveling up from her toes.

"Well, let me show you how protective I can be." Anne leaned over to kiss Maggie. Her fingers began to explore, turning Maggie's warm tingles into sizzling jolts.

Ambassador Squiggles fell to the floor, thumping softly against the very clean carpet.

Chapter
Six

"IT'S SEVEN THIRTY-FIVE. She's late," Anne observed, taking a sip of her Corona. They had arrived at the Blue Room, a popular lesbian bar in Berkeley, before Moocher and her date. Ever since settling into one of the spacious booths, they'd been suffering disdainful looks from larger parties of women. It was making Anne antsy.

"She said seven-ish," Maggie replied. "Seven thirty-five is seven-ish."

"No it's not; it's seven thirty-ish. The ish goes in thirty-minute increments. Everyone knows that."

"I don't know that." Maggie threw a peanut in the air and caught it in her mouth. Anne had been amazed with her skill, watching as she threw the nuts higher and higher and never missing. Anne had tried one and nearly put her eye out.

"Well, everyone but you and Moocher know that, then," Anne replied caustically.

Maggie stopped throwing nuts and looked at her lover.

"I sound like an anal-retentive freak, don't I?" Anne asked. "I'm sorry."

"That's OK." Maggie grinned. "For a minute there, I thought we were going to break up over ish."

The phrase "break up" seemed to grow an appendage and grab Anne's heart, squeezing with staggering force. "I'm sorry," she gasped, trying to get her heart to start beating again.

"It's really OK. You go ahead and be as anal as you want, sweetheart. If it means we're always on time for appointments and my CDs are shelved in alphabetical order, then it's all good."

Anne smiled and felt her heart returning to a normal rhythm. It stopped again when Maggie let out a strangled "Oh, my God!"

"What?" Anne yelped.

"Moocher's here with Charlotte—AKA Charlie."

"Is that bad?" Anne tried to spot the new arrivals through

the crowded bar.

"It's the third date," Maggie explained, leaning across the table toward Anne. "Moocher hasn't gone on a third date with the same woman since 1997."

Anne opened her mouth to ask for additional information, but she got no more of the story before the couple arrived at their booth.

"Sorry we're late, guys," Moocher said. She waited as Maggie moved to Anne's side of the booth, then motioned for Charlie to sit before sliding in next to her.

"You're not late," Maggie said. "You said seven-ish."

"Well, I should have said seven-thirty-ish."

Anne flashed an "I am Queen of the Universe" smile at Maggie. Maggie engaged in an act of treason and stuck out her tongue.

"So, allow me to introduce my lovely friend Charlie," Moocher said. "Charlie, I think you met my partner Maggie a few months ago?"

"Yeah. Hiya." Charlie moved a wad of gum from one side of her mouth to the other.

"Hi, Charlie." Maggie grinned politely "Good to see you again. This is Anne, my girlfriend."

Oh, my God, Anne marveled, *Did she say "girlfriend"? She did, she called me her girlfriend.* She smiled broadly and Maggie grinned back, looking pleased with her daring.

"It's great to see you again, Anne." Moocher smiled. "You've made my little Mag-a-Muffin so happy these past few weeks."

"Mag-a-Muffin?" Anne nearly snorted beer out of her nose.

"Moocher, you are so dead," Maggie snarled.

"How about some drinks?" Moocher ignored Maggie's ire. "What are we having?"

"Something extremely expensive," Maggie replied caustically. "Twenty-year-old scotch."

"You don't drink scotch. You'll get another Corona. I'll spoil you and get you a Corona Extra. Anne?"

"I'll have another beer as well, thanks." Anne smiled at Moocher. "Need some help?"

"No, you two sweethearts continue to cuddle. My Charlie-Girl will help. Come on, babe." Moocher took Charlie's hand as she stood from the booth, then put her other hand on the small of Charlie's back and gently guided her across the bar.

"OK, what the hell is the story with Charlie?" Anne whispered urgently when the couple was out of earshot.

"She's a blonde bimbo with fake boobs," Maggie whispered back. And then added unnecessarily, "Very large fake boobs."

"I think her boobs weigh more than the rest of her body."

"Oh, definitely. I keep waiting for her to fall on her face."

"She'd bounce before her face made contact." Anne snickered. "By the way, why are we whispering? We're in a crowded bar and Moocher and Charlie are on the other side of it."

"You started it."

"I did not," Anne protested.

"They're coming. Stop whispering."

"Here we are, ladies." Moocher passed out the drinks. "Beers all 'round except for my girl, who's sticking with mineral water with a slice of lemon. She's my little designated driver."

"Moocher, why don't you just sit in your La-Z-Boy recliner and practice belching the National Anthem?" Maggie asked.

"What are you implying?"

"That your treatment of women is a bit Fred Flintstone."

"Wilma Flintstone, surely," Moocher corrected.

Anne laughed at the friendly banter, but Charlie looked like she was watching a foreign film with no subtitles.

"I need to go to the little girl's room," Charlie announced after taking a sip of her water.

"Allow me to accompany you," Moocher offered.

"No, thanks, I'm fine." Charlie got up quickly and moved toward the restroom, dodging past the two pool tables in the back and nearly getting a pool cue shoved into her cleavage.

"I think she needs to go throw up." Maggie winced as the pool cue whizzed past Charlie's chest. The players apologized and then leered at the well-endowed blonde. "Must have been at least a quarter of a calorie in that lemon twist."

"Be nice," Anne warned, but couldn't suppress a smile.

"You two are just jealous." Moocher sniffed. Then she flashed a lecherous smile. "But seriously, aren't her breasts amazing?"

"They're amazing, all right." Maggie snorted. "Amazingly artificial."

"You should be careful, Moocher," Anne added. "You could get lost between those things. Be sure to leave a trail of bread crumbs when you go in."

"Oh, my God!" Moocher cried. "You guys are ganging up on me already? Anne, I brought you two together, for Christ's sake. If it wasn't for me, Maggie would still be sneaking into the back of the courtroom and making goo-goo eyes as you argued your cases."

Anne smiled tenderly at Maggie, who was blushing a vibrant red.

"Moocher, I told you not to say anything about that," Maggie hissed.

"I think it's incredibly sweet." Anne reached out and stroked Maggie's cheek. She could feel the heat of the blush. "I saw you once."

"You did?" Maggie smiled shyly at Anne.

"Oh, for fuck's sake, you guys are making me sick. I might have to go join Charlie at the porcelain altar."

"Too late," Maggie announced, "here's your love bunny now."

"Hey, babe," Moocher said, standing up and kissing Charlie when she returned to the booth. "I missed you."

"So, what do you do for a living, Charlie?" Anne asked politely. She managed to meet the woman's eyes and not let her gaze wander downward.

"I'm a manicurist," Charlie replied. "But I'm thinking about going back to school."

"Really?" Maggie said. Anne could hear the forced enthusiasm in her voice. "What do you want to study?"

"I want to be a nurse. Except I don't like blood very much." Charlie looked worried. "But I think they get orderlies to deal with blood and bed pans and icky stuff like that."

"I'm not too sure about that," Anne said. Then she added helpfully, "Next time you go to the doctor's office you may want to ask the nurse if you could have a chat with her about it for a few minutes."

"Hey, that's a great idea." Charlie smiled warmly at Anne, who felt a little pang of guilt.

Anne decided to take her own advice and try to be nice. Maggie followed her lead, and after a few more beers, the conversation soon settled into a nice, warm place. Moocher regaled them with tales of her college days in Chicago. Maggie once again shared her story of her one drunken night of lesbian passion, but was reluctant to go into the details.

"Because I can't remember any more," Maggie protested when Anne and Moocher begged for more information.

"OK, start at the beginning," Anne said. "Who was this woman?"

"She was in my English class—Romantic Poetry."

"Of course." Moocher grinned.

"I used to sit in class and just watch her," Maggie continued. "Every movement she made just seemed so graceful and beautiful."

"Anne, I hope she's looking at you like that nowadays." Moocher took a swallow of beer. "If not, don't say anything."

"Honey," Charlie protested. "Shush. It's so sweet."

"So you never said anything to her?" Anne prompted.

"No way. I never had the nerve. I kept hoping she'd ask to borrow a pen or something, but we never exchanged a single word. Then one night, about halfway through the semester, I went to a party. I walked into the kitchen and there she was."

"And you said, 'Hey, baby, let's go find a quiet corner and exchange some bodily fluids,'" Moocher guessed.

"No," Maggie corrected, rolling her eyes. "I still didn't have the guts to say anything to her. Well, not at first."

"Uh huh," Moocher and Anne said in unison.

"Well, they were having this drinking contest involving tequila shots, and I thought it might impress this girl. I was pretty sure I could hold my liquor..."

"This was based on your prior experience with alcohol, which consisted of a sip of Irish whisky every St. Patrick's Day?" Moocher asked.

"Yeah," Maggie replied with an embarrassed grin. "I think I might have actually won the contest; I'm not sure. Then I saw my obsession walking down the stairs. I met her halfway and I distinctly remember hearing myself say to her, 'I really think you're beautiful. Want to go somewhere quiet?'"

"Not the best pickup line ever," Moocher commented.

"But straightforward and to the point," Anne noted.

"And she just took me by the hand and led me to the bathroom. I remember kissing her, and it was wonderful, but everything gets blurry after that."

"You definitely did other stuff?" Moocher asked.

"Oh, yeah. I remember fingers and mouths and a feeling like I was going to explode. I definitely, well, you know..."

"The waves crested and crashed on your sandy beach?" Moocher supplied.

"I came, yeah." Maggie smiled. "And then there was a whole new crashing wave rolling through my body and I spent the next hour leaning over the toilet, heaving my guts out."

"What did she do?" Anne asked.

"The minute she saw me turn green, she shoved me over the toilet and high-tailed it out of there. I didn't see her again that night."

"What about in class?" Anne asked.

"She never spoke to me again and avoided eye contact. I did the same."

"The bitch didn't deserve you," Moocher said. "I'm sure Anne would at least hold your hair out of the way as you blew chunks."

"I definitely would, baby." Anne pulled Maggie in for a squeeze. "But watching other people throw up makes me throw up, so I'd be puking right beside you."

"Oh, that's the most romantic thing you've ever said to me," Maggie replied with a sarcastic smile.

"Speaking of underage drinking, who's ready for another?" Moocher asked.

"No, it's my round," Anne said. "Same again, everyone?"

Once Anne and Maggie had gotten another round, the friends settled in for more tongue wagging.

"So, Maggie," Charlie said, "Moocher told me about your bicycle stunt work to catch that purse snatcher the other day."

"What stunt work?" Anne asked, looking sharply between Maggie and Moocher.

"It wasn't stunt work. I just jumped off my bike to tackle the kid," Maggie explained with an embarrassed shrug.

"She flew off her bike," Moocher corrected. "Looked like a fucking superhero or something. Of course, when she landed, she got the wind knocked out of her, and she floundered on the ground while I made the arrest."

"I wasn't floundering," Maggie said indignantly.

"Were you hurt?" Anne eyed her lover with a worried expression.

"Just a few bruises, mainly on my butt." Maggie squeezed Anne's arm. Anne knew she was trying to be reassuring, but it wasn't working. "It's no biggie."

"That sounds so exciting," Charlie said.

"That's nothing," Moocher replied with a wave of her hand. "One time, we tried to make a simple arrest for public urination."

"Moocher, don't you dare tell this story," Maggie warned.

"Yes, tell the story," Charlie begged.

"Well, the guy was kind of crouching down in a dark corner against a building. So in my best macho voice I said, 'Sir, step into the light and let me see some ID.' He stands up and he's fucking seven feet tall and at least three hundred pounds."

"He wasn't that tall," Maggie interrupted.

"Let's put it this way, he towered over me and made Maggie look like a munchkin. So all of a sudden, this wall of humanity is stomping toward me. To stop him, Super Mag jumps on his back. She's pulling her nightstick across his neck to cut off his air supply, but that hardly slows him down. He starts thrashing around, trying to throw Maggie off, and she just hangs on. Looked like she was riding a bull in the rodeo."

"Did you get hurt?" Anne asked. She tried to sound casual, but Maggie looked up quickly, her eyes full of concern.

"No," Maggie said, smiling her assurance. She grabbed onto Anne's slightly clammy hand.

"Back-up arrived," Moocher continued, "and we started placing bets on how quickly she'd be thrown. Cries of 'ride 'em, cowgirl' were heard."

"You all stood around laughing. I could have used a little help," Maggie said indignantly.

"Anyway, his brain finally realized it wasn't getting any oxygen, and he fell over like an elephant shot with a tranquilizer gun," Moocher concluded

"Speaking of guns," Charlie asked, "have either of you ever shot anyone or been shot at?"

Anne gripped Maggie's hand tighter.

"It's not like TV or the movies, you know," Maggie explained.

"One time we were riding north of campus," Moocher said. "It was a warm, peaceful Sunday afternoon. Nothing had been happening all day. With absolutely no warning, a shot rang out. I could literally feel it going right past my ear. Funny thing is, we never could figure out where the shot came from."

"Moocher," Maggie hissed at her partner.

Anne could feel the blood drain from her face. It was an odd sensation.

"Of course, if your dad continues to conspire with the lieutenant and gets you transferred, you may get to deal with gun-fire every night."

There was an awkward silence as Anne's eyes turned slowly to stare at Maggie. "What does she mean?" The flush of anger was sending the blood shooting back into her head, leaving her feely dizzy and sick.

"There's nothing to worry about, it's just..." Maggie's words trailed off as Anne rose from the wooden bench.

"Excuse me, I need..." Anne didn't finish the sentence as she stormed toward the restrooms.

ANNE PULLED A paper towel from the dispenser and patted her face dry. She turned as the door opened, expecting to see Maggie. Instead, Moocher entered the small restroom.

"Hey," Moocher said softly.

"Hi." Anne flashed an embarrassed grin.

"You OK?"

"Yeah, yeah, I just needed... I mean, I was just..."

"I'm sorry I stuck my foot into it," Moocher said.

"Why didn't she tell me?"

Moocher sighed and leaned against the sink. "Maggie learned a coping mechanism at an early age: that if you don't talk about your problems, they go away."

"That's stupid." Anne sneered. She threw the paper towel in the trash, her hands still shaking with the sudden emotions.

"I know it's stupid. They don't go away, just get buried deeper where they do the most damage. But it's the way her family reacted to the death of her mom. It's a learned behavior that you can't change overnight."

"Is she going to be transferred?"

"No. She doesn't want to, and I don't think the lieutenant will put the transfer through just because her dad wants it." Moocher paused until Anne met her eyes. "But you know it doesn't make her job any safer."

Anne felt her stomach tighten. The anger she felt because Maggie had kept something so important from her had distracted her from her initial reaction to hearing about the danger of her lover's job.

"I guess I thought if I didn't think about it, it wouldn't be true." Anne shook her head ruefully. "Now who's the one being stupid?"

Moocher shrugged. "You just came face to face with the reality that the love of your life works in a very dangerous profession, and the thought of her getting hurt is enough to—well, send you running for the toilet."

"Yeah." Anne rubbed at the sudden ache in her forehead.

"Look, Anne, it's really not as bad as we make it sound. Maggie is perfectly safe."

"How can you say that?" Anne frowned. "You work in one of the most dangerous professions on the planet."

"You're right. And, yes, Maggie could get hurt on the job, or even get killed. It does happen. But you could get hurt or killed walking down the street."

"My odds are a little better." Anne smirked.

"I'm not so sure about that."

"I just can't stand the thought of her getting hurt."

"I know." Moocher reached out for Anne's arm and gave it a squeeze. "But we've been partners for two years and the worst thing she's suffered is a broken finger. I swear to you that I'll always watch out for her."

Moocher looked directly into Anne's eyes and added, "And with that in mind, what are your intentions?"

"Huh?"

"I don't want to see Maggie hurt any more than you do." Moocher crossed her arms over her chest. "So if you're planning on playing with her for a while and then moving on, please leave now."

"I don't... I mean, I wouldn't..." Anne felt like an amoeba under a microscope. "I love Maggie. I would do anything for her. Things are a little intense right now."

"Maybe too intense?" Moocher prompted.

"I'm not saying that. Not exactly." Anne was floundering again.

"Look, I think I understand where you're coming from. Maggie's already talking long term, isn't she?"

"She's let a few things slip." Anne shrugged.

"And you're scared of commitment. Like I said, I understand. I'm the queen of commitment phobia. My therapist used my case for a paper. It was published in a fucking psychiatric journal. So I know what I'm talking about. What you have to do is take the fear and use it. Be the ball. Do you understand?"

"Um, no," Anne admitted.

Moocher laughed. "OK, forget the ball thing. I don't really get it either. All I'm saying is that fear is normal in a relationship. It keeps you on your toes. But don't let it rule your life. If you love her, then love her. Ride that wave for as long as it lasts. If you fight it, it's going to dump you to the bottom of the ocean. But if you don't even get on the board, I'll hunt you down and permanently disfigure you. Any questions?"

"Still a bit heavy on the sports symbolism," Anne replied with a broad smile, "but I think I got it."

"Good." Moocher grinned back. "I think I'm getting pretty good at this pep-talk stuff."

Anne squinted dubiously. "Be the ball," she murmured as she headed out of the restroom.

"I WISH YOU'D told me," Anne said, running her fingers through red-gold hair.

They'd called an end to the evening by mutual agreement. When Anne had returned from the restroom, she'd flashed Maggie a smile and watched gratefully as the tense set of Maggie's shoulders eased. Anne had mumbled reassurances all the way home. Once they entered the cottage, she lit a few candles and put on some soothing music, then led her lover to the couch.

"I'm sorry," Maggie said. "I was just hoping that my dad was blowing hot air."

"But he upset you. I've known that all week. I just couldn't help you without knowing what he said."

"I feel so stupid."

Anne smiled, remembering her own words to Moocher in the restroom. "Promise me you'll talk to me when you're upset."

"I will." Maggie leaned against Anne's shoulder. "You promise me, too."

"I promise." Anne said the words, but was glad that Maggie was focusing on the anger instead of the fear of Anne's mini-meltdown. Anne wasn't ready to talk about her panicked feelings, not until she came to terms with them herself.

Anne rubbed Maggie's shoulders. The muscles under her fingertips were stiff with tension. "I know what you need."

"To win the lottery?" Maggie said in a dreamy voice.

"Not at this very minute, no."

"OK, I'll do that later. What do I need at this very minute?"

"First, you need this." Anne gently turned Maggie around and leaned down to give her a long, slow kiss.

Maggie smiled, then frowned as her eyes looked out the window. "Can your mom see us?"

"Relax. She's not home. Even if she was, what difference does it make?"

"It's just weird."

Anne knew that public displays of affection were still difficult for Maggie. Adding a parent into the mix made things even more complicated. An accepting parent was a completely alien concept for Maggie.

"Look, Mom's out of town for another week, but when she gets back, we'll get together and talk. You'll like her, and she'll love you." *And maybe she'll have some things to say that'll make you feel a whole lot better.*

"Sure," Maggie said, not sounding at all sure. "But let's get back to what I need."

"Well, you might have noticed on previous visits that I have an extra-large Jacuzzi tub. I remodeled this place myself and I made the bathroom my highest priority. The tub is big enough for two and—"

"Yes," Maggie interrupted.

"You didn't let me finish."

"I knew what you were going to say. Yes, I would love to share a bath with you. Let's get wet." Maggie stood and hurried off toward the bathroom.

Anne followed, laughing at her friend's enthusiasm. Maggie's shoes and socks were trailed through the hall, and when Anne finally caught up to her lover, Maggie was reaching for her shirt's buttons, her feet patting against the cold tiles of the bathroom floor.

"Hold on," Anne said. "I think you might need a little help with that."

"With taking my clothes off? I don't think so; I've been doing it by myself since I was two."

"I've found that you're never too old to learn a new way of unbuttoning," Anne said, walking up to Maggie.

Maggie looked down and watched her shirt being slowly unbuttoned. A line of concentration formed in her forehead, as if she really was learning something new.

"And taking off a bra takes years to master." Anne reached behind Maggie and unfastened her lover's bra with one hand.

"I have to admit, you are adept at that particular skill," Maggie said softly. She smiled at Anne, maintaining eye contact even as Anne used her thumb to softly stroke an awakening nipple.

Anne reluctantly left Maggie's breasts and continued with the task of undressing her lover. She began to unbutton Maggie's jeans. "More tricky unbuttoning. Pay attention."

Maggie looked down, watching intently as Anne unbuttoned the jeans and pulled them slowly down. The air in the cottage was cool, and goose bumps rose on Maggie's chilled thighs. Anne noticed and ran a hand across the soft, pebbled flesh. A shiver traveled through Maggie and she quickly stepped out of the pants. Anne simply grinned and folded the jeans, carefully placing them in a neat pile with the other clothes.

"I think you forgot something." Maggie looked down at the pink panties she still wore.

"I didn't forget," Anne replied in a low rumble. She wrapped her arms around Maggie and kissed her deeply, then dipped her fingers under the elastic of Maggie's panties, teasing around the edges. She reached under the material to cup the soft skin of Maggie's butt cheeks, then withdrew her hands and completed the torture by running a fingernail along the crotch of the panties. Maggie closed her eyes tightly and hissed her pleasure.

"Let's get wet." Anne echoed Maggie's earlier request, but in a much more sultry tone.

"Already am," Maggie replied dreamily.

Anne chuckled, then quickly undressed as Maggie kicked off her briefs, tossing them in the corner of the bathroom. Anne leaned over and turned on the taps, dumping a packet of lavender bath salts into the stream of hot water. The small room soon filled with steam and Anne cracked open the window. She knew it would soon be a lot hotter. Once the water level was high enough, she turned on the Jacuzzi jets and stepped into the tub. She sat down and scooted back, spreading her long legs to the edges of the tub.

"Get in between my legs," she requested.

"With pleasure." Maggie stepped carefully into the tub and plopped down gently. The warm bubbly jets instantly worked on Maggie's tense muscles, and she let out a loud moan of pleasure.

"Tilt your head back a little."

Maggie did as she was told, and Anne filled a small bowl with water, tipping it over Maggie's hair. Anne smiled at Maggie's blissful purr. She squeezed shampoo into her hand and massaged it into Maggie's hair, then spent a little extra time massaging Maggie's scalp. The moans continued.

Anne rinsed the shampoo out of Maggie's hair, running her fingers through the strands. When it was wet, Maggie's hair was a darker red, with individual strands of gold that caught the light. The wet hair also made her ears stand out; Anne leaned over and took an earlobe between her lips, sucking the lobe and running her teeth over it softly. Maggie's answering moan came from a deeper place than the ones before.

Anne released the lobe and picked up a sponge. She squeezed some bath gel over the sponge and then rubbed it against Maggie's back, moving it in slow, soothing circles.

After a few moments of sensual washing, Anne turned off the Jacuzzi jets. She wanted to be able to hear and be heard. She leaned back again, pulling her lover with her.

"Lean back against me," Anne said.

Maggie complied, leaning against the soft cushion of Anne's breasts — soft except for the nipples, whose hard points poked into Maggie's shoulder blades.

Anne put aside the sponge and soaped her hands. She then reached over Maggie's shoulders and rubbed her hands over Maggie's breasts. She ran a soapy finger over the nipples, watching them pucker and harden like her own.

"I love your breasts," Anne whispered, leaning down to Maggie's ear, as if sharing a secret.

Maggie's only reply was a slow shudder.

"Your areolae are so beautiful," Anne added, continuing to softly run her finger over the pink skin.

"Areolae," Maggie repeated. "That's a mighty big word."

"I have a very large vocabulary."

"Oh, do you?" Maggie said. Then she added in a lower voice, "Teach me."

Anne heard the husky tone of passion in her lover's voice

and leaned over to place a soft kiss on the back of her neck. "These are your mammary glands." She softly rubbed and squeezed Maggie's breasts. The nipples were already hard and striving forward, as if trying to escape. Anne trailed her hands downward, running her fingers over Maggie's stomach and circling her belly button.

"This is your navel," Anne said. "You have an innie."

"Mmm hmm." Maggie closed her eyes as Anne moved her hands down smooth thighs, moving slowly inward. Maggie's legs parted to allow better access, and Anne dipped her fingers into the short red curls.

"Your mons pubis," Anne said, cupping the mound softly. She moved her hand down and again softly cupped Maggie's sex. "Your vulva."

Maggie trembled in her arms and Anne felt as if she were holding a priceless artifact, a sacred treasure that had been bequeathed to her. She felt unworthy, but accepted the gift to honor the giver. She placed another soft kiss on the back of Maggie's neck.

Her fingers trailed over soft folds of flesh. "The labia majora," she whispered, continuing the lesson. Her stroking fingers circled and came closer and closer to the crease in the center. Finally, they dipped in and parted the softer folds of flesh. "The labia minora," she said softly into Maggie's ear.

Maggie's own moisture was thicker than the bath water around it, and Anne felt it between her fingers, spreading it up and down softly. She reached down farther with her fingers and circled Maggie's opening, nearing and then darting away in a teasing motion. Maggie's hips twitched slightly, trying to force the connection. Anne finally complied and dipped in her forefinger. She sighed to control her breath and whispered, "The vaginal opening."

Maggie's moans were louder now and Anne continued to tease her. She reached down a little farther. "Your anus," she said, the tip of her finger dipping into the tight orifice. Maggie shuddered and let out a squeak of pleasure. Anne filed away the response for another time, when her access would be better. She moved her hand up again and approached the last point of interest on her journey.

"Your clitoris," she said and smiled at the deep growl of pleasure as she gently ran a finger over the nub. She brought the flesh between her first and middle fingers and rubbed it with a soft but rapid touch. With her other hand, she took a nipple between thumb and forefinger, pinching it.

Anne felt Maggie trembling beneath her, teetering on the

edge. "Let go, love. I'll catch you," Anne said. She closed her eyes as Maggie cried out loudly, the sound echoing against the tiles. Anne held her tightly, once again cupping her sex as the orgasm sent powerful waves through the smaller woman.

When Maggie's body finally relaxed, Anne pulled her back, wrapping her in her arms. "Just rest awhile now," she said, trailing soft kisses down Maggie's shoulder.

"We'll turn into prunes," Maggie complained in a sleepy voice.

"I love prunes." Anne smiled, softly nipping the soft skin below her.

"I love you," Maggie said, and settled back into the soft warmth.

Chapter
Seven

"YOU LOOK NICE." Anne examined her lover's cream-colored linen pants and turquoise silk blouse. The color of the blouse matched Maggie's eyes exactly.

Maggie rose from the seat of her car and opened her arms to give Anne a better view. "Are you sure I look all right?"

"My mom wouldn't care if you wore shorts and a T-shirt and were barefoot." Anne smiled. Maggie obviously had some misconceptions about her mom. She hoped to quickly rectify that situation. Her first step had been to arrange a dinner as soon as her mom returned from her business trip.

Anne took Maggie's hand and led her up the path toward the back door of the main house. She was surprised to find her lover's hand clammy with sweat. She put her arm around Maggie's shoulders and felt a tremble roll through the smaller woman's body.

"Maggie, it's just my mom." Anne looked down at her lover in concern. "She's not going to eat you or anything. She's a vegetarian."

Maggie smiled apologetically but didn't reply. That worried Anne even more.

"If you don't want to do this tonight, I could..."

"No," Maggie blurted out. "I just don't handle parents very well. I'll be OK."

Anne tried to smile again. She didn't know what to do or say, but she was saved by the sound of the back door opening. The bright light spilling from the open door illuminated them as they stood on the path.

"Come on in here, you two," Jill called out, beckoning the two women inside. "Stop sneaking a kiss in my backyard."

Anne glanced down at Maggie, who put on a brave smile and walked toward the house. They climbed the steps side by side and entered the kitchen.

"Mom, this is Maggie."

"Pleased to meet you, Mrs. Doyle." Maggie smiled shyly and stuck out her hand in greeting.

Anne's mom ignored the offered hand and enveloped Maggie in a hug. "None of that Mrs. Doyle crap. I'm Jill."

" 'Hey you' works, as well." Anne's comment earned her a swat with the kitchen towel that Jill was conveniently holding. "Ow, that hurt." She pouted, rubbing her hip where the towel had snapped.

"Good." Jill turned back to Maggie. "Pay attention tonight and you'll learn some of the more effective punishment techniques for Anne. She's like a puppy. I find a firm voice and well-enunciated commands work wonders. If all else fails, hitting her on the nose with a rolled-up newspaper gets your point across."

Anne scowled at her mom but was happy to hear a little giggle from Maggie.

"I've made some Ethiopian dishes for tonight." Jill moved to the stove and lifted the lid off a pot. She tasted the reddish-brown stew and added some salt, stirred the stew a few times, and then put the lid back on. "Why don't you show Maggie the house and then set the table? I started but got side-tracked."

Anne took her lover by the hand and escorted her through the door into the dining room. Maggie stopped just inside the room and gazed at the twinkling glow of the crystal and china in cabinets built into the walls. The walls were inlaid with dark wood, a darker shade than the hardwood floors. She looked across the room through an archway that opened into a large living room.

"Come on," Anne said, "I'll show you around."

They entered the living room. Thick Persian carpets covered the floor and the furniture was perfectly arranged. Original oil paintings of Northern California landscapes adorned the walls. There was a large open fire, and on the mantel several porcelain figurines shared space with a picture of Anne. Maggie approached the photo and gazed at the young woman staring back at her. Anne walked up behind her lover and looked as well. It was her high school graduation photo, taken when she was sixteen. The face that looked back at them reflected a mixture of belligerence and vulnerability.

"You were beautiful," Maggie whispered.

"I was a gangly kid with two left feet and bad skin." Anne scowled at her younger self. "The school hired a professional photographer to take the graduation photos, thank God. I was liberally airbrushed."

"You liar." Maggie continued to gaze at the photo. She

reached out a finger and traced the face. Anne could almost feel ghost fingers touching her own cheek.

Maggie's attention was finally drawn from the photo to the rest of the room. She peered around the room, reminding Anne of a kid on a school trip, standing in a museum.

"This house is amazing," Maggie said reverently.

"It's been in my family since it was built." Anne smiled proudly. "My great-grandfather was an architect. He worked with Julia Morgan. He designed the house and made sure only the best workmanship went into it. Don't you wish they still made houses like this?"

"No one could afford them if they did."

"I guess." The mention of money made Anne uncomfortable. "Anyway, we need to set the table, or I'll get my nose swatted with a rolled-up newspaper."

They moved back to the dining room and quickly finished their task. Anne noticed Maggie looking intently at a heavy crystal wineglass.

"Mom's a real bargain hunter." Anne heard an unspoken apology in her words. "She gets a lot of this stuff at estate sales. She has a knack for seeing what goes with what. I always tell her if the law thing doesn't work out, she could become an interior decorator."

"Well, it sure beats my family's house. Dad still uses jelly glasses and a mug that says 'Keep on Streaking.' I think we got the silverware a piece at a time with each fill-up at the gas station."

"It doesn't bother you, does it?" Anne asked, suddenly realizing that being out wasn't the only thing that set her apart from her lover. Money wasn't important to her. She thought—hoped—that it wasn't important to Maggie either.

Maggie's eyes were clear, no shadow of doubt dancing in their depths. "Nope." She grinned, then looked serious. "I have to admit, I was a little taken aback when I first walked in. But then I realized this doesn't define you. You would be the same woman I fell in love with even if you grew up in a cardboard shack."

"I love you, too." Anne leaned down and kissed Maggie slowly and tenderly.

"Careful. Hot dish coming through, hot dish coming through!" Jill rushed into the room and set the casserole dish on a trivet in the middle of the table. Anne and Maggie regretfully let go of each other with an almost audible smack and moved to help.

It didn't take long before all of the food was laid out, and they sat down to eat. Jill noticed that Anne had set the table so that she sat between her mom and Maggie. It didn't exactly balance the table, but she figured Anne had a good reason.

"Now, Anne, give a demonstration of how to eat Ethiopian," Jill instructed. "By the way, I don't know why you bothered laying out utensils."

Maggie looked confused and watched Anne tear off a flat piece of moist bread and use it to scoop a dollop of stew out of the casserole dish. Anne brought it to her mouth and pushed it carefully past her lips.

"Well done." Jill clapped. "Maggie, you might have noticed that Anne didn't touch her lips with her fingers. That's considered terribly bad manners."

"Because those fingers might have been anywhere." Anne wiggled her eyebrows suggestively. Maggie blushed.

"Anne," Jill scolded, "stop teasing her."

"It's true."

"It probably has more to do with going to the bathroom," Maggie said, trying to get some back.

"Ewww, gross," Anne said. "I'm trying to eat here."

"When you kids are finished, please join me in a civilized meal." Jill sighed.

Anne and Maggie smiled at each other and then turned to Jill. "We're sorry," they said in unison. All three women laughed and began to eat.

They spent the next twenty minutes trying to eat like proper East Africans, and failing miserably. The food was simple and filling, and eventually Maggie's powers of consumption faltered.

"That was absolutely amazing." Maggie sat back and sighed. "I've never tried this type of food before."

"There are several good places around town," Anne said. "But I'm partial to Mom's recipes."

"I like to try different ethnic dishes." Jill shrugged. "What about you, Maggie? Do you like to cook?"

"Oh, no." Maggie shook her head. "But I'm not bad at opening boxes and pushing buttons on the microwave."

"I would have thought you'd be forced to cook, being the only girl in a house full of boys," Anne said.

"No, we survived on TV dinners and macaroni and cheese from a box. Everyone says that Mom was a great cook, but I was too little to learn anything from her."

Anne noted a familiar furrow in Maggie's forehead.

"It must have been so hard for you to lose your mother at such a young age," Jill said sympathetically. Anne had filled Jill in on the basics of Maggie's past. Now she took a deep breath and hoped her mom would find the right words to say.

"My own mother died when I was pregnant with Anne," Jill continued gently. "It was very sudden. I was devastated, of course. The worst thing of all was that she would never see her granddaughter."

"That's so much worse than what happened to me. I have nothing but happy memories of my mother, what memories I do have." She shook her head and then said dismissively, "It was a long time ago."

Anne had heard that phrase, or something like it, before. She remembered Moocher's explanation. *She's learned that if you don't talk about your problems, they go away.*

"Yes, it was a long time ago," Jill agreed. Anne smiled, knowing her mom wasn't big on problem avoidance. "But your mother's death helped to shape who you are. Tell me one characteristic you share with her."

"I don't remember," Maggie said quickly. She twisted the cloth napkin on her lap.

"Did your family ever tell you of something?" Jill was speaking softly, but persistently.

Anne watched the exchange silently, afraid to break the spell. Maggie shrugged, and Anne was sure she was ready to disengage from the conversation, but she looked up and began to speak.

"I was eating a whole bunch of pancakes one Saturday morning. Dad said, 'Maggie, you have some appetite. Just like your mother.' He used to tell me a lot about my mom, but never anything like that."

"What do you mean? What did he tell you?" Jill asked.

Maggie shrugged and Anne wondered whether any more words would come. Maggie had already shared more than she'd heard before.

It did take a few long seconds, but then Maggie continued. "Dad and Patrick used to tell us what Mom would think or say or do. You know, things like: 'Mom would want you to do your homework.' Dad used to tell us that Mom was taken to heaven because she was so good — like the saints. And if we were absolutely perfect, we could go up to heaven and be with her. Whenever I did anything wrong, Patrick would tell me I'd never see my mom again."

"That's such bullshit!" Anne squawked, breaking her silence.

"Anne, hush," Jill said.

"She's right." Maggie smiled at Anne's righteous anger. "I didn't realize it until I left home and went to college. Once I was away from home, I started to see how I'd been manipulated. I remember the first time I skipped Mass. It was the most terrifying and wonderful feeling I've ever had."

"Anne's father and I are both lapsed Catholics," Jill said with an encouraging smile. "We knew that we never wanted Anne exposed to any organized religion. I was horrified one summer when I found out she had been going to vacation bible school."

"I was in love with a pretty eight-year-old with big brown eyes," Anne explained. "I spent the whole time looking at her."

"You came home with a fish sticker for our car. I nearly had a heart attack."

Anne blushed as Maggie poked her in the ribs.

"So, when was the last time you stepped foot in a church?" Anne asked Maggie.

"A few weeks ago, right after we went out for breakfast." Maggie paused as Anne and Jill looked at her with interest. "When I was little, because I thought my mom was a saint, I used to talk to her in church. I know now that I can talk to her anywhere, but it seemed somehow fitting to go into church and tell her about Anne." She smiled shyly. "Tell her that her little girl was in love."

Anne smiled at Maggie, taking her hand and squeezing gently. She was overwhelmed with emotion, and bent down slowly, meeting Maggie's lips for a slow kiss. Maggie didn't hesitate to kiss Anne in front of Jill.

"You guys are making me cry." Jill dabbed at her eyes with her napkin.

Anne rolled her eyes. "Why are you crying, Mom?"

"Because you two are so beautiful and perfect. Like a miracle."

"You already knew I was beautiful, perfect and miraculous. I just happened to find someone equally beautiful, perfect and miraculous."

"Shut up, or I'll get my dish towel. What I mean is, you're like two sculptures, created by two different artists. On your own, you're very beautiful—yes, even you, smarty-pants." Jill poked Anne. "You're well-crafted and lovingly made by your respective sculptors. And then one day, someone came along and put the sculptures together, and they became one piece—a piece that is so much more: something absolutely breathtaking... Or is that just a mother talking?"

"That's just a mother talking," Anne answered, pulling Maggie into a hug and kissing the top of her head. She could tell that the smaller woman was approaching her emotional limits, and decided it was time to lighten the mood. "What's for dessert?"

Maggie's stomach growled at the mention of a tasty treat. Jill and Anne cracked up.

"That beast is out of control." Jill laughed. "Luckily, I have a berry galette and vanilla bean ice cream."

She got up and went into the kitchen.

"You OK?" Anne stroked Maggie's cheek.

"Yeah, I'm good." Maggie leaned into the touch and smiled broadly. "I'm great."

"AND JILL'S HOUSE is absolutely amazing. She has all of this crystal and china and porcelain figurines. But Anne says she gets most of her stuff from estate sales."

The day after her evening with Jill and Anne, Maggie couldn't wait to tell Moocher all about it. They were on their lunch break, but Maggie decided to check out a sale at the music store first. Despite her intentions, Maggie barely paid attention to the CDs around her as she related her story to Moocher.

"What type of CDs are you actually looking for?" Moocher asked. "You've been over every inch of this store and you haven't picked up anything."

Moocher flipped through a few selections and pulled out a CD, holding it out to Maggie. "How 'bout this one? Recordings of sled dogs?"

"Moocher, were you even listening to what I was saying?" Maggie put her hands on her hips and ignored the CD in her friend's hand.

"Yes, I was." Moocher rolled her eyes. She put the CD back and continued walking down the store aisle. "Jill this, Anne that...crystal, porcelain, blah, blah. You've been talking about your dinner with Anne and her mom all morning. I'm respectfully requesting a subject change."

"I wouldn't call that tone respectful," Maggie replied, only half-teasing. "But I will be happy to change the subject if I'm boring you."

"You're boring me," Moocher said bluntly. She turned back to Maggie and smiled apologetically. "Although I'm very glad that you had a good time. Now choose some music and let's go. I actually wanted to eat lunch on my lunch break."

"I want to get something really meaningful for Anne." Maggie eyed the new releases.

"What about the Barenaked Ladies? That's meaningful."

"How is that meaningful?"

"It means, 'Hey, lady, let's get bare naked together.'"

"Ha, ha, and again I say ha," Maggie replied sarcastically.

"Ooh, the new Dave Matthews." Moocher pointed out the CD. "Did you buy it yet?"

"No," Maggie replied dismissively. She spotted a promising display at the end of an aisle, and moved toward it.

"No?" Moocher followed her. "Wait a minute, is this the same person who waited in line all night for tickets to Dave Matthews? Is this the same person who said she would go straight if Dave Matthews married her and wrote songs about her?"

"I said I would *pretend* to be straight for the benefit of his public persona. I wouldn't *go* straight for anyone. And besides, that was a long time ago."

"Maggie, that was last February."

"I'm just getting tired of men whining on about how they love their girlfriends and how their girlfriends left them and how hard their lives are. I just find that I relate more to female singers."

"Hey, watch out with those sweeping generalizations. That one nearly hit me in the head." Moocher looked down at the display that Maggie was picking through and gasped in horror. "Magpie, you're in the opera section. Just carefully put the CD down and walk away slowly. I've got your back."

"I'm kind of getting into opera." Maggie carefully avoided eye contact.

"What?" Moocher squawked. "I, you...wha...?"

"What is wrong with you?"

"You've caused me to babble incoherently. The last time that happened was when my cousin told me about sex. I just felt that whole universe-shifting thing all over again."

"It's just that Anne is really into opera," Maggie said.

"Ooh, I get it."

"What does that mean?" Maggie scowled at Moocher's knowing smile.

"It means I get what's going on. You've been assimilated."

"What the hell are you talking about?"

"You've become one entity, my dear." Moocher shrugged. "You are the MaggieAnne. Anne doesn't like whiny male singers, so Maggie doesn't like whiny male singers. Anne likes opera, so Maggie likes opera."

"You are so full of shit." Maggie snorted.

"Do you need more examples? What about the whole vegetarian thing?"

"What 'whole vegetarian thing'?"

"When was the last time you ate meat?" Moocher continued before Maggie could attempt an answer, "Could it be since the day after you heard that Anne was a vegetarian? We went to Fat Burger yesterday and you ordered a garden burger. A garden burger! You've been ordering a bacon cheeseburger every Tuesday for the past three years."

"It's just easier to eat what Anne eats. When I started eating less meat, I just lost the taste for it."

"Whatever." Moocher shrugged and walked away.

"I don't see what the big deal is." Maggie followed Moocher, refusing to let the argument drop, especially when her friend sounded like a petulant teenager.

"You're right; it's not a big deal," Moocher agreed, her tone indicating just the opposite.

"Moocher, what the hell is your problem?" Maggie asked, catching up to her.

"I don't have a problem," Moocher snapped back, her feigned indifference crumbling like a sand castle before the onrushing tide.

Moocher's attacks of temper were like spring rainstorms: fierce but short-lived. Maggie waited until the anger in her friend's eyes flared and then died out. "Well?" she asked as Moocher took a deep breath.

"It's just that your life has been consumed by Anne." Moocher's tone was slightly more reasonable. "I know you're in love with her, and I'm happy for you. But you need your own existence. You are allowed to have your own interests and opinions and friends."

"I do have my own existence." Maggie kept her tone gentle, not wanting to re-ignite Moocher's anger.

"Well, it doesn't seem like it sometimes. You haven't gone on a bike ride for how long now? And what about Halloween? We have to get our costumes figured out."

"Oh, I forgot to tell you," Maggie said with a guilty grimace. "Anne and I are going up to her family's cabin Halloween weekend. I'll miss the party this year."

"And you were going to tell me this when?" Moocher replied testily. "It's only a few weeks away."

"I know. I'm sorry." Maggie bit her bottom lip.

Moocher obviously wasn't quite finished with being pissed off. "We used to do stuff every weekend. You always called me when you did your laundry because you were bored. Now it's like I don't even exist outside of work. I thought I was your best friend. Am I just your partner now?"

"No." Maggie grabbed Moocher's arm and gave it a gentle squeeze. "You are still my best friend. I know I've been ignoring you and I'm sorry. It's this love thing. It's just so overwhelming.

I..." She blew out a frustrated breath, fluttering her bangs. "I can't explain it."

"I know that." Moocher patted the hand that was still squeezing her arm. "I'm being a selfish bitch. Forget everything I just said."

"No, you're not a selfish bitch. Well, maybe a bitch, but not selfish."

"Nice." Moocher smirked.

"Look, I'm the one who was selfish. I ignored you completely, and I'm sorry. Sometimes I feel like I'm addicted to a drug. I don't just need to be near Anne, I need to inject her. I need to overdose on her. I've never felt anything like this. It's so intense. I'm sure it will settle down, but in a way, I don't want it to."

"Maybe it won't. You and Anne have something amazing. I envy you." Moocher reflected for a moment. "Maybe that's where this is coming from. I'm just jealous."

"I don't know about that."

"I do know something, though. I know that I want you to be happy. I'm sorry I started this whole tirade of crap. Can we rewind the conversation? Tell me more about your dinner with Anne and Jill last night."

At the mention of dinner, Maggie's stomach monster growled indignantly.

"On second thought," Moocher said, "buy your opera CD and let's go eat."

Chapter
Eight

"YUM. CHEEZITS." MAGGIE examined the choices on the shelf before her. "Let's see...traditional, extra cheesy, or the exotic white cheddar." Her hand drifted in the air between the brightly colored boxes. She made her choice and threw it in the cart. "Can't go wrong with the old reliable."

Buying food for a road trip was one of her favorite chores. She had already hit the candy aisle, and was now going for the salty snacks. Drinks were still to come.

The first few bars of "Love is in the Air" wafted around her like a spritz of air freshener. For a moment, Maggie wondered if the Muzak had gone haywire, then remembered that she'd recently changed her cell phone ring to something mushy and romantic.

"Hello?"

"Mary Margaret."

Gee, Dad, thanks for calling up to tell me my name. I knew I'd forgotten something.

"Hi, Dad," Maggie answered pleasantly. She hoped her teeth weren't grinding loudly enough to be heard.

"Just wanted to let you know that this weekend is a go for Disneyland."

Connor could have said something in Swahili for all the sense it made to Maggie. "Sorry, Dad. What was that again?"

"Disneyland," Connor replied unhelpfully. "This weekend will work."

"Disneyland. This weekend. Work?" Maggie thought repetition might help her understand.

"I called your brother and he said this weekend is great. The kids are off school on Friday, so you can get in a little early and have a nice meal out. The park is putting on some kind of Halloween costume contest Saturday night. The kids are really excited about it."

Halfway through her dad's reply, Maggie felt her stomach

drop. "Dad, I can't go down south this weekend," she said carefully. "I have plans."

"Plans?" Now it seemed to be Connor's turn to hear Swahili.

"I'm going away for the weekend. Up to the Sierras. Staying at a friend's cabin."

"Your niece and nephew are really looking forward to this. Especially Mark. He wants to wear his Halloween costume. He's going as Bugs Goodyear or something."

"Buzz Lightyear," Maggie corrected sullenly.

"Whatever. So change your plans. I'm calling to find out if you want to fly out of Oakland or San Francisco. I thought it would be a good idea if you left your car with Michael; he can give it a tune-up while you're gone. I'll drop you off at the airport."

"Dad, I'm not changing my plans." The words weren't quite as forceful as Maggie wanted, but she got them all out. She was pretty proud of that.

"Surely your friend will understand that family comes first. Who is this friend anyway? That partner of yours?"

Damn, I should have expected the delayed reaction.

Maggie decided to avoid the question and go on the offensive. "Dad, why is it every time I mention going somewhere with a friend, you assume it's my partner? What would be wrong with me going to a cabin with Moocher anyway?"

"Because people would get the wrong idea."

"The wrong idea that I actually like to hang around socially with my partner?" Maggie knew she was prodding her dad toward a response she really didn't want to hear. But she went there anyway. "You always hung out with your partners."

"This is different, Mary Margaret, and you know it."

Maggie felt like she was playing chicken with an oncoming freight train. She could ask why, but she'd just get an answer she already knew. *If I back down, am I admitting that I am wrong? That my love for Anne is wrong?*

"Well, it's not Moocher that I'm going with. And I can't change plans. We put down a deposit."

Maggie's stomach twisted at the lie. She tried not to look at the Cheezits and pretzels around her.

"I thought you said it was your friend's cabin," Connor said suspiciously.

"It's a pay-per-use time-share."

"Well, the kids will be really disappointed."

He just has to twist the knife, doesn't he?

"I'll make it up to them. Maybe I can take them somewhere nice when they come up at Thanksgiving."

"Well, I guess we can settle for that. I'll give Patrick a call. I'm sure he can explain it to the kids somehow."

"Thanks, Dad," Maggie took the opportunity to end the conversation. "I'll talk to ya later."

Maggie clipped the phone to her hip and then clutched her shopping cart. Guilt continued to twist and turn her stomach, and she wondered for a brief moment whether she would puke in the middle of the grocery store. Clean-up on aisle seven. No, that just would not happen.

"Love is in the Air" rang from her hip and she unclipped her phone warily. This time she remembered to check the caller ID. What she read settled her stomach like a spoonful of Pepto Bismol. She sighed with relief. "Hi."

"Hey, babe. What's up?"

Maggie pushed the phone call with her dad out of her mind. "I'm shopping for road food."

"Road food? Is that like road kill?" Anne chuckled.

"You're just going to have to wait and see on Friday morning. Are you coming over tonight?"

"Yep, I'll be there around eight."

"Okey-dokey. See you then."

"I love you, sweetheart."

Maggie let the words run through her, vanquishing the last of the unpleasant feelings in her stomach. "I love you too, Anne. So, so much."

FRIDAY MORNING WAS warm and clear, promising to be one of the last hot days of the year. Maggie took a deep breath of the October air, breathing in the distinctive dusty smell of autumn in the Bay Area.

"Maggie, we're only going away for a long weekend. What the hell do you have packed in here?" Anne hoisted Maggie's duffel bag into the back of her Subaru Outback and groaned loudly at the heavy load.

"Sweatshirts, long underwear, and a jacket." Maggie counted off the items on her fingers. She shoved her riding shoes into a corner and threw her pillow on top of the pile of luggage. "I get cold."

"Well, when we get to the cabin, you can carry all of your stuff up the hill. You won't be cold then."

"Yeah, whatever." Maggie turned to the collection of bags next to the car and pointed out a brown sack. "Could you put that bag right behind the driver's seat? Those have the road snacks in them."

"Maggie, this weighs a ton." Anne frowned as she lifted the grocery bag. "You know it's less than a four-hour trip. We are allowed to stop if we get hungry."

"It's just some soda, potato chips, Cheezits, Red Vines, and Oreos."

"Just?" Anne choked.

"Oh, and I threw in a bag of baby carrots for my little baby carrot." Maggie batted her eyelashes at Anne.

Anne just laughed and put the bag of food where Maggie had instructed. "Now, help me get the bikes on the roof rack," she said.

They carefully put Anne's brand new Kona mountain bike on the rack, and then put Maggie's old muddy Specialized Stumpjumper beside it.

"You're going to love the trails up there," Maggie said as she threw the front tires in the back.

"I'm still not so sure about that." Anne cast a worried eye at the bikes. "I haven't ridden a bicycle since I was a kid."

"You'll be fine. It's just like...well, riding a bicycle. You'll get the hang of it again."

"OK, but if I go flying off the side of a cliff, tell my mother I love her and give all of my money to a worthy cause."

"No way." Maggie shook her head firmly. "If you go over a cliff, I'm riding off right behind you."

Anne smiled and her eyes grew serious. "That's the sweetest thing anyone's ever said to me."

"Well, when we're lying in traction in the hospital, I definitely won't be saying sweet things to you. It all evens out in the long run."

Maggie eyed the back of the car and made sure there was nothing remaining to load, then opened the passenger door and got in. "Let's hit the road!" she ordered, buckling up.

Anne got in the driver's seat and started the car. She looked in the rearview mirror before backing out of the driveway, obviously having trouble peering through the pile of bags, pillows, and bicycle tires. "Maybe we should have hired a U-Haul."

"Do you want to re-pack?" Maggie asked.

"No, it's all right. Let the adventure begin."

"ANNE, IF WE'RE going this way, can we stop at the Coffee Mill?"

"We've gone three blocks. You already want to stop?"

"I was in a rush this morning and I didn't want to make a pot of coffee and then take the time to clean it up. Please." Maggie looked at Anne with puppy-dog eyes.

"You know those eyes will get you anything. You better save them for when you really want something and I'm being particularly stubborn."

"You're always particularly stubborn." Maggie rolled the eyes in question.

"I am not stubborn." Anne gasped. "I'm as pliable as Play-Doh, especially when it comes to you."

"Ha!" Maggie coughed.

"Ha? What do you mean, 'ha'?"

"I mean: ha! As in 'hardy-ha-ha, you are totally stubborn.' You never give up on an argument, no matter how wrong you are."

"That's not true," Anne protested. "If I'm wrong about something, I'm the first to admit it."

"OK, then admit you're wrong about not being stubborn."

"No."

"I rest my case." Maggie crossed her arms and smiled smugly.

"If you're not nice to me, I'm ditching you at a truck stop in the middle of the Valley."

"You are the most pliable, amenable, flexible person I know," Maggie quickly said, plastering on a fake smile.

"Thank you. You are the most observant person I know."

"Can we stop?" Maggie groaned. "Now I really need caffeine."

"YOU WANT AN Oreo?" Maggie asked as Anne merged onto Interstate Eighty.

"No, thanks," Anne murmured, looking at traffic in her side mirror.

"Soda? Baby carrot?"

"No, thanks," Anne replied in a distracted voice.

"Champagne? Caviar?" Maggie tested.

"No, thanks," Anne repeated in the same preoccupied tone.

"You aren't even listening to me." Maggie looked over at Anne, who was still focused on her mirror. "What are you looking at?"

As Maggie asked the question, a motorcycle passed on their left, driven by a woman in red leathers. Her blonde hair spilled from beneath her helmet and streamed behind her. Anne's eyes tracked the bike as it passed.

"You're girl-watching?" Maggie gasped.

"No," Anne said guiltily. "I was just waiting for her to pass so I could change lanes." She changed lanes to prove her point.

"You were checking out the babe on the Harley," Maggie accused indignantly. "I know that look."

"You're crazy."

"You got that same look when we went into the chocolate store with your twenty-dollar gift certificate."

"I was not looking at that woman on the Harley. I swear. I only have eyes for you, babe," Anne vowed.

"I caught you, and I'm seriously considering making your life a misery for the rest of the weekend." Maggie paused dramatically. "But, I have to admit, I don't really care."

"Yeah?" Anne asked hopefully.

"Yeah. You can look all you want, just don't touch. Ever."

"I swear." Anne's expression grew serious. "I would never cheat on you. No matter what happens. I hope you know that."

"I do," Maggie said, equally serious. "I can't even imagine it. Just know that it will never happen."

"Good. Now that we have that cleared up, I have a question for you."

"Shoot."

"Have you ever considered buying a Harley?"

"I HAVE TO pee," Maggie announced.

"We haven't even hit Davis yet."

"I had a large coffee."

"And your bladder's the size of a peanut."

"Isn't the phrase supposed to be 'the size of a pea'?" Maggie asked.

"But the bladder isn't round. It's more peanut-shaped, isn't it?"

"Don't be so pedantic."

"Do you want to pee beside a bush on the side of the road?"

"You're so mean today." Maggie huffed loudly and said in a singsong voice, "Dear, sweet Anne, please will you pull over so that I may urinate? I would greatly appreciate it if there is toilet paper and a lock on the door, but I will leave that up to your discretion."

"You are such a goof." Anne shook her head, chuckling.

"Oh, look, the world's largest fruit and vegetable stand. I bet they have a nice toilet, and we can buy some stuff for the weekend. I love barbecued corn on the cob."

"I don't believe it's the largest fruit and vegetable stand in the world," Anne said. "How can they claim that? Do you think they really went to every fruit and vegetable stand in the world and did a comparison?"

"I don't know. But it's the next exit."

"Is it the largest in square feet, or the largest in number of fruits and vegetables?" Anne changed lanes to exit.

"Again I say, 'I don't know.' Does it make a difference?"

"There are huge markets in the Middle East and North Africa, not to mention India and China. Surely this can't be bigger than every single market in the world."

"Anne?"

"Yes?"

"Cleansing breath and let it go."

"Right."

"ALL I'M SAYING," Anne griped as she opened the back of the car, "is that they could have signs warning that the largest fruit and vegetable stand in the world was ten fucking miles off the freeway."

"There wasn't enough space on their sign." Maggie carefully shoved the large bag of fruits, vegetables, honey and jam inside the car, then closed the hatch.

"They should have used the sign to say their stand was ten miles off the freeway instead of the obviously false claims of being the world's largest fruit and vegetable stand," Anne groused.

"It is a pretty damn big fruit and vegetable stand."

"Yeah, it's big," Anne replied. "But—"

"I know. It isn't the biggest in the world. Listen, I'm going to go check out how big the bathrooms are. You still good?"

"Yeah, I'll just stand around and breathe in the lovely smell of the Big Valley."

Maggie smiled and headed around the back of the open-air stand. Anne did as she promised and took a big sniff of air. It smelled like dust and growing things and bus fumes, the latter courtesy of the vehicle that was just pulling into the parking lot. Anne watched as dozens of seniors disembarked and headed into the fruit and vegetable stand.

"Well, it doesn't look that big to me," Anne heard one old guy say.

Anne chuckled, but then looked concerned as a teenaged boy came barreling out of the building, knocking into a woman's walker and nearly sending her flying. Anne rushed to help the woman get her balance, mumbling a sarcastic "nice" to the kid as he stormed past her.

"Fucking dyke," he snapped back.

Anne felt her blood boil, but she let it and the boy go. It wasn't worth the fight, even if he was brave enough to stick around for it.

"Are you OK?" she asked the woman, who was taking deep breaths.

"Yes, I'm fine. Those young kids. They always have to be somewhere right away. They need to take life at a slower pace while they can. Soon enough, they won't have a choice."

Anne nodded at the sound advice. In fact, she decided she'd take the long way to the cabin and show Maggie some of her favorite spots in the Sierras. She had a feeling Maggie would love the gold mine.

"Fucking asshole!"

Thoughts of sneaking a kiss in the dark of the old mine flew from Anne's mind as she heard the shouted curse. The fact that the teenager had been headed toward the back of the building, where Maggie was searching out the toilets, registered in her mind for the first time.

"Oh, dear, what was that?" The old woman looked around, as did a few of her friends who were waiting to make sure she was all right.

"It's OK," Anne said, knowing that it might not be. She spared a quick glance at the old woman to make sure she was all right, then ran toward the back of the building, her heart racing and her hands already bunching into fists.

She skidded to a halt next to her lover, who was breathing heavily over a body that lay on the ground. The boy's face was beet red and he clutched at his balls, dry-heaving into the dusty ground.

"Maggie." Anne's voice was strangled with fear.

"It's OK. Just a little disagreement, right?"

Maggie poked a toe into the boy's side, then kneeled down to look into his face. She pulled her wallet with her badge out of her back pocket and flashed them in the kid's face. "Unless you want to go to jail today, let's just both agree that this didn't happen, OK?"

The boy nodded wordlessly, still trying to get his breath back.

"Good boy." Maggie patted his face, then stood up. "It's OK," she repeated, flashing Anne a tight smile as she took her elbow. "Let's go."

Anne let herself be led away, the adrenaline still making her nerves tingle and leaving her slightly queasy. She swallowed. *OK, a lot queasy.*

"Are you OK to drive?" Maggie asked as they neared the car.

"Stupid asshole," Anne growled.

"Welcome to Redneckville, California. Where men are men and the farm animals are nervous."

Anne frowned at the joke.

"Sweetheart, I'm OK." Maggie rubbed Anne's back. "Are you OK to drive?"

Anne was terrified. She could feel the fear and anger and desperation rumbling through her body like a runaway freight train. But she realized that Maggie, despite her brave front, was probably feeling even worse.

"Yeah. Let's get the hell out of here." She pulled the keys out of her pocket and unlocked the car.

"As soon as we get to Davis, can you exit and hit the nearest gas station?" Maggie asked as Anne turned onto the road that led back to the freeway.

"Sure." Anne looked quizzically toward Maggie. She drew in a sharp breath as she noticed, for the first time, the raw scrape that extended along the outside of Maggie's left leg. "Jesus Christ!"

"He knocked me over." Maggie shook her head ruefully. "I didn't even see him coming. Bastard. Don't worry, it looks worse than it is. I just need to clean it out properly. But first let's put some space between this place and our next stop. If he's local, he may have friends."

"I'm sorry. I'm so sorry," Anne said. *Why wasn't I there when Maggie needed me? I should have followed the kid. I should have engaged him when I had the chance, and stopped him from going toward Maggie. It was my fault. It was all my fault.*

"Sweetheart, please, it's OK." Maggie seemed to read her mind. Or maybe the fear and guilt were filling her eyes. "He got a lesson that he won't soon forget, I'm sure."

"I should have been there, should have stopped him." Anne tried to pay attention to the road and continue to keep a firm grip on the steering wheel. She was beginning to regret having chosen to drive.

"Anne, can I just remind you that I am a police officer." Maggie reached out and squeezed Anne's knee, which helped settle its shaking. "I'm trained for this kind of thing. It was better that he tried his luck with me than with you."

Anne wasn't convinced of that. She could have at least warned Maggie, preventing the ugly scrape that was oozing blood.

"I should have been there," Anne repeated. She knew the truth of the statement, and didn't look at Maggie for denial or confirmation, just stared resolutely down the road.

MAGGIE KEPT HER eyes on Anne as they drove down the freeway. Anne's face was pale and pinched, her lips drawn in a tight, angry line. Maggie knew her lover was angry, but she wondered if Anne was angrier with the kid or with herself. Maggie had already told Anne that the incident wasn't her fault. Anne was obviously rejecting that, so Maggie decided to leave it until Anne cooled down and could consider it logically.

Besides, the adrenaline of the fight was working its way through her system, leaving her jittery. That, mixed with the ache from her wound, made her queasy. She leaned her head against the window, closing her eyes.

Maggie felt, rather than saw, the car leaving the freeway and she lifted her head and opened her eyes. Anne drove well into Davis before pulling into a gas station and convenience store.

"Wait here," Anne said as she got out of the car.

Maggie decided to do as instructed, wondering how long Anne's cooling off would take. From her attitude, she was still far from cool. More like blast-furnace hot.

Anne returned after only a few minutes carrying a bag of first aid supplies and a bottle of water.

"Thanks." Maggie tried to sound cheery and normal. "I'll just get this cleaned up and we can get back on the road. Won't take me long."

Anne didn't reply, just kept peering over her shoulder, looking apprehensively at every teenaged boy that drove by.

"Don't worry, he's already forgotten all about it." Maggie thought a moment and grinned. "Assuming that his family jewels are still in one piece."

Anne didn't smile back, but she did seem to relax slightly. Maggie took that as a good sign and set to work on her leg. She'd fallen into mud and gravel. Because she hadn't expected it, she'd gone down hard, and the gravel had been ground into the wound. She'd had far worse from bike accidents, but it was still an unpleasant task to clean out the little pieces of rock from the scrape.

"Don't worry, it's a lot worse than it looks." Maggie looked up at a still silent Anne, whose eyes were staring blankly, full of a horror far larger than the situation called for.

"Anne?" Maggie stopped cleaning her wound and waited for Anne's eyes to focus.

"I'm sorry. I just don't deal with blood very well. I should have told you."

"Oh, babe, it's OK." Maggie reached out and realized she was holding a bloody cloth. She hurriedly put it out of sight and reached out again. "Why don't you go back inside and get something to drink?"

"No." Anne gathered herself and seemed to shake the horror from her eyes, returning from wherever she'd been. "I can deal with it."

Maggie thought about forcing Anne to at least turn away, but she knew this wouldn't be the last time Anne would see her a little bloody and battered. Best to get her used to it. She returned to cleaning the wound, trying to remain silent so that Anne didn't get more upset. She could feel Anne trembling beside her. Each time Maggie jerked in pain, Anne jerked with her. Each hiss and muttered profanity was echoed. By the time the ordeal was over, both women were shaking and sweating.

"Now I need a drink." Maggie smiled as she placed the last bandage on the scrape.

"Yeah." Anne took a deep breath. "But I have to warn you: next time we see a sign for the world's largest whatever, I'm not stopping."

ANNE RETURNED TO the freeway and decided to make a beeline to the cabin. She wanted to wrap her arms around Maggie and not let go again until the weekend was over...or maybe just hold on for the rest of eternity. Guilt still gripped her heart. She couldn't believe she'd failed Maggie.

As she drove, she kept going over what had happened, replaying different scenarios. Why hadn't she stopped the kid when she had the chance? Why didn't she fight him? Why hadn't she noticed him earlier? It didn't matter what Maggie had said; it was Anne's responsibility to keep her lover safe.

And speaking of her lover, she realized that Maggie was awfully quiet. She turned her focus from the recent past to the woman sitting next to her and smiled when she saw Maggie, her head lolling against the headrest, sound asleep.

"I wont let you down again," Anne whispered. "I promise you."

"ARE WE THERE yet?" Maggie looked blearily out the window and saw the rolling foothills of the Sierras.

"Nope, not for another hour or so."

Maggie glanced at her lover. Anne looked much more relaxed. Her shoulders weren't hunched around her ears and her knuckles were no longer white from trying to throttle the steering wheel.

"Sorry I fell asleep." Maggie yawned. "Long car rides do that to me. I should have warned you."

"That's OK, you missed the suburban nightmare and a semi that nearly ran me off the road."

"And you didn't scream obscenities?"

"Of course I did," Anne replied. "You slept right through them."

"Damn, sorry I missed that." Maggie watched the rolling hills roll past for a while, waiting for her brain to wake up. When it did, she decided that it was time to leave homophobic farm boys behind in the dust of the valley. "Hey, I forgot to tell you that I spoke to Sean yesterday. He got the transfer to Yosemite. He starts in three weeks."

"That's great news. You told me how much he wanted that."

"Yeah." Maggie grinned, her eyes flashing with excitement for her brother. "He's really happy about it. I told him I'd take him out somewhere to celebrate."

"That's a great idea."

"And so, I was thinking..." Maggie's thinking had really not been much more than a brief flash that occurred when she'd spoken to her brother. She'd quickly stifled it, but it kept shining through. Up to this point, it had been a fantasy. Now, sitting next to Anne as they rose into the Sierras, and having easily vanquished an asshole, fantasies were becoming reality. "I'm going to tell him about me. About us."

Anne was silent for a moment. "Are you sure?"

"Yes. Don't worry; I know he'll be totally cool about it." Maggie wasn't so sure, but she knew if anyone in her family would accept her orientation, it would be Sean. "And I was thinking that if it goes well, I might tell the rest of the family at our next big get-together at Thanksgiving."

"Maggie, this is a big step," Anne said slowly. "You need to be careful."

"Are you saying that I shouldn't come out to my family?" Maggie's brow wrinkled in confusion.

"No." Anne glanced over quickly before turning her eyes back to the road that was beginning to twist and turn as they rose above the foothills. "I'm not saying that."

"What was it like when you came out in high school?"

"Well, you know the basic circumstances. I was in love with Rachel, and I thought the feeling was mutual. No, I know it was, but things got mixed up. She was weak and confused. She fell in love with the captain of the lacrosse team. Or maybe she just wanted to convince herself that she was in love with him. In love with a boy. That would make her normal." Anne's voice was bitter with sarcasm.

"When Rachel accused me of being some kind of predatory lesbian, I had a choice." Anne put her hand on top of Maggie's. "I could have denied everything. I might have pulled that off, at least long enough to survive until graduation. But I couldn't do that. Part of what Rachel said was true, I was a lesbian, and I wasn't ashamed of that. So I denied the parts that weren't true and admitted the parts that were."

"You never told me what happened when you outed yourself."

"Teenagers are sub-human. Our little incident earlier today proves that. I lost most of my friends. I concentrated on getting through the year, and things were a lot better when I went to college."

"What did your parents say?" Maggie asked.

"Oh, they already knew I was gay. I told my mom when I was thirteen. One day she sat me down to tell me about the birds and the bees and I said — in a surly voice, I'm sure — 'don't bother telling me about a boy's penis, because I'm not letting one of those nasty things anywhere near me.' Then I paused for maximum effect before saying, 'I'm gay.'"

Maggie could easily picture a thirteen-year-old Anne, and the story made her laugh so hard she made a piggy noise.

"Mom hugged me and said she was proud of me," Anne continued. "Not the effect I was going for. I wanted to piss her off."

"Why?" Maggie wiped the tears of laughter from her face.

"I was thirteen. My entire existence was directed at pissing off my mom. I was the demon seed."

"Yeah, I remember being like that, too."

"Oh, right. I so don't buy that." Anne shook her head. "You were going to Mass every Sunday, saying a Hail Mary because you called your brother a poo-poo head."

Maggie snorted indignantly. "Actually, when I was about thirteen I called Sean a fucking bastard."

"Really?" Anne obviously wasn't able to associate her image of sweet little teenaged Maggie with such a grownup potty mouth.

"Yeah." Maggie grimaced. "My dad overheard me and ordered me into the car. He didn't say one word, just drove me to the church in silence. When we got there, he dragged me by the ear to the priest and I had to say a confession immediately. He sure wasn't happy with four Hail Mary's and four Our

Father's, and he let the priest know it. Then I had to go home, apologize to my brother, clean his room, and wait on him for a whole week."

"Serves you right. That's a horrible thing to call your own brother."

"I know. I still feel kind of guilty about it. I'll apologize again next time I see him."

"Which brings us back to the subject of you coming out to him," Anne said, growing serious again. "The point is, my parents were very accepting of my sexual orientation. You don't have the same situation."

"But your high school friends weren't accepting."

"Maggie, it's not the same thing. In high school I risked being ostracized, but it was a temporary thing. A year later I was going to a liberal university in a liberal town where my sexual orientation was no big deal."

"So you're saying I should stay in the closet?" Maggie was now completely confused.

"No. I mean, maybe." Anne stumbled over the words. "I mean... I don't know." Anne blew out a frustrated breath and changed lanes, taking an exit and driving into a mountain town.

"Where are we going?" Maggie asked, looking at the little town that boasted a gas station, a small grocery store, and not much else.

Anne pulled into a parking spot in front of the store and turned off the engine, then she turned toward Maggie.

"I used to think I knew how I felt about this," Anne explained, looking into Maggie's eyes. "When you first told me that you weren't out, I thought you were...well, wrong, in a way. Now, things don't seem so black and white."

"Why?" Maggie took Anne's hand. She felt slightly stung at being called wrong, but was willing to hear Anne out.

"Because above everything else, I don't want you to get hurt. I couldn't stand to see that happen."

"I'm not a masochist." Maggie continued to hold Anne's hand and flashed a crooked smile. "I don't want to get hurt, and I certainly couldn't stand to lose the love of my family. They're so important to me."

Anne nodded.

"But," Maggie continued, "I just feel I need to be honest about who I am. I'm gay. Before I met you, it was almost like an abstract concept. Now, when I talk to my dad or one of my brothers, the fact that I'm keeping a secret from them haunts our conversations. I can't continue to have this happen. It's scary as hell, but I have to tell them. If they love me, they should love me no matter what. If they can't accept who I am, then they don't really love me at all."

"I hear what you're saying." Anne chewed her lower lip. "It's a common refrain. And I agree with the sentiment."

"But...?" Maggie raised her eyebrows.

"But be careful," Anne completed the thought. "That's all I'm asking. Be sure about this. Really sure. Pick your moment and your delivery, and remember that there's no going back."

"I will." Maggie squeezed Anne's hand. "I promise."

Anne leaned down and gave Maggie a soft, lingering kiss.

"You know, this is the last chance to get supplies before we get to the cabin." Anne pulled away from the kiss.

"Oh, really?" Maggie grinned. "Well, I think our Cheezit supply is running dangerously low."

"I think you're right."

Anne flashed a dazzling smile and Maggie felt her heart begin to pound. Then she thought about coming out to her family, and her heart pounded even more. She wondered which would kill her first, joy or terror.

MAGGIE'S FULL BLADDER prodded her out of a lovely dream. As she surfaced into consciousness, she looked around blearily. She wallowed in confusion for a moment before remembering that she wasn't in her bedroom. She was in Anne's cabin, and *oh, isn't this nice?* She had Anne's arm wrapped around her middle.

Having Anne's arm wrapped around her middle, while soft and warm and cuddly, also caused more pressure on her bladder. She winced and struggled out from under the arm, managing to limbo her way free.

Now came the adventure of finding the bathroom in the dark. She girded her loins—which were, quite frankly, still sore from earlier activity with Anne—and made her way out of the room. She took baby steps and held her arms out like a zombie. After a few tentative steps, she jammed her hand against the doorframe and stifled a curse. At least she'd found the door.

Thankfully, the bathroom was right next to the bedroom, and she just needed to trail her hand against the wall to find it. Once successfully in, she closed the door and turned on the light. The sudden stunning brilliance made her curse again and close her eyes tightly.

She stretched out her leg as she sat on the toilet and winced as the long scrape burned. Once she could open her eyes in the bright light, she was pleased to see that the wound still looked

clean and wasn't seeping blood any longer. Once they'd arrived
at the cabin and unpacked, they'd enjoyed a long soak in the hot
tub. Its warm water had been good for the scrape.

After relieving her bladder, Maggie took a big drink of
water, starting the whole cycle again. After a second glass, she
felt much better. "Major fluid depletion," she mumbled to
herself, smiling at the memory of the reason for her condition.
Their lovemaking had started pretty much the moment they'd
entered the cabin until, around midnight, they'd both finally
crashed.

Maggie turned off the light and then stood still, letting her
eyes adjust again to the darkness. She shivered in the cold night
air and wished she'd put on her pajamas before falling asleep.
Quickly but carefully, she retraced her steps back into the
bedroom, and then took little steps again toward the bed.
Thankfully, on her return journey across the room the moon
came out from behind clouds, and its soft light helped to guide
her.

Maggie crawled back into bed and snuggled under the
covers. While she had been in the bathroom, Anne had rolled
over to face away from her, but had not woken. The moonlight
highlighted Anne's black hair with silver. Maggie reached out
and carefully took a strand of it, letting the soft silkiness run
through her fingers.

She began to drift back to sleep, but was nudged awake by a
low moan from her lover. A moment later, Anne moaned again
and turned onto her back, throwing out an arm as if to ward off
something. Maggie stroked Anne's arm.

"Shh, it's all right sweetheart," she whispered softly. But
Anne became more frantic, flinging out her arm again. Her
elbow connected with Maggie's upper arm as she came awake
with a final gasping cry. Maggie winced in pain and reached out
to grab Anne.

"It's all right, I've got you. You're all right." Maggie spoke
softly but steadily, holding on to Anne while the tendrils of the
nightmare withdrew.

"Oh, man," Anne finally whispered, taking in deep,
steadying breaths, "that was a bad one."

"What was it about, sweetheart?" Maggie stroked her lover's
hair. Anne was holding onto her, both arms wrapped around
Maggie's waist.

"A giant teddy bear." Anne's voice was filled with horror
despite the absurdity.

"A giant teddy bear?" Maggie tried to keep a straight face.
She was glad it was dark.

Anne took another deep breath and seemed to wake up more fully. "I know it sounds bizarre, but it was after me. It sounds stupid now, but in the dream I was scared shitless."

They were quiet for a while, just holding each other until their breathing evened out. Maggie smiled when she realized their lungs were perfectly in sync. "You doing better now, baby?" she whispered gently.

"Yeah." Anne yawned, but sounded wide awake. "I haven't had a dream that bad since I was a kid."

"Did you have a lot of bad dreams when you were little?"

"Nothing really unusual." Anne pulled back a little from the death-grip she still had on Maggie. "I had a pretty active imagination. I'd have bad dreams, and then think there were monsters in my closet. That kind of thing."

"I had one monster under my bed. Whenever I needed to go to the bathroom in the night, I had to launch myself off the bed and halfway across the room. He had very long arms."

"I used to just lie there, frozen with fear," Anne recalled. "Until I got up enough nerve to call out for help."

"I bet your mom didn't mind as much as my brother Patrick did."

"Did your dad work graveyard?"

"No, usually swing shift. He got home around midnight. After work, an earthquake wouldn't wake up my dad. In fact, I can think of two occasions when it didn't. So Patrick was on bad-dream duty. He'd come in and tell us to stop being stupid."

"Well, my mom wasn't on dream duty when I was little. It was always my grandfather — he lived with us when I was a kid."

Maggie could just make out Anne's eyes as they glittered in the moonlight.

"Poppy never made me feel stupid when I thought there were monsters in my closet," Anne continued. "He'd always open the door and look way inside. Then he'd look in every dark corner of the room. After that, he'd sit on my bed and tell me a story."

"That's so nice."

"Yeah." Anne sighed at the memory. "When I was eight, I decided I was too old to be scared of monsters. The first time I had a bad dream, I just threw the covers over my head and closed my eyes tight."

"Did it work?" Maggie asked.

"No. I spent the rest of the night jumping at every sound, dozing off only to be jerked awake when the house creaked. But I was stubborn. I never called for Poppy in the night again."

They both sighed, lost in their memories of childhood.

"I suppose we should try to get back to sleep," Anne said softly.

"Yeah, I suppose you're right."

Maggie rolled over and Anne wrapped an arm around her waist.

"Maggie, can I ask you a question?" Anne said, her voice hesitant.

"Sure."

"How much do you pay for rent?"

"Talk about coming completely out of left field." Maggie chuckled.

"I'm serious."

"I'm Maggie, how do you do?"

"Ha ha."

Maggie stifled her laughter. "Sorry. Anyway, my rent's nine fifty."

"Shit, that's outrageous!"

"I thought it was a pretty good deal. But what can you do? It's the Bay Area."

"Well, I'm paying five hundred a month to my mom for my place..."

"You spoiled brat!" Maggie gasped. She knew Anne's mom could easily get three times that much rent for the cottage.

"I know, but she won't take any more than that. Anyway, I was thinking..." Anne's words trailed away and Maggie patiently waited to hear her lover's thoughts.

"I mean, I was going to say..." Anne started again, but the words stopped just as suddenly as before.

"What, sweetheart?" Maggie didn't have a clue as to what Anne was trying to convey.

"I, um, what..." Now the words were coming out, but tripping over each other.

"Breathe, sweetheart." Maggie gave Anne's arm a little pat. She felt a tendril of fear begin to whisper in her head. What could be so bad that Anne, her quiet but articulate girlfriend, couldn't bear to voice it?

Anne took a deep breath and then said in a steady but rapid stream. "OK, let me start this all over again from the top. Forget everything I just asked you about rent. What I want to say is this: I don't want to wake up alone any more. I want you to make the monsters go away. I want to fight *your* monsters. I want to make you hot cocoa when you can't sleep. I want you to be there in bed next to me, every night. Do you want to move in with me?"

Maggie could tell that Anne was holding her breath, and she

really wanted to put her out of her misery, but it was her turn to experience complete vocal shutdown.

"If you don't want to now, or ever," Anne said frantically, "then that's cool. I mean, I can understand—"

"You know. You have an amazing ability to render me totally speechless. It's something that many have tried and few have achieved." Maggie turned her head back and smiled broadly at Anne, whose eyes were still wide with panic.

"Yes," Maggie said, just to make herself clear. "I would love to move in with you. And not to save on rent."

"I love you," Anne whispered.

"I hope so. Few people would want to move in with someone they hate."

Maggie felt Anne squeeze her middle. No longer a post-nightmare death grip, this hug spoke of devotion.

"Mine," Anne murmured as they both drifted back to sleep.

"Yours," Maggie mumbled, letting herself sink into happy oblivion. "Forever."

Chapter
Nine

"YOU KNOW, WE could have gone to somewhere a little nicer than an ice cream parlor, Sean." Maggie grabbed two menus and followed her brother to a booth.

The restaurant was crowded. A group of rowdy kids, apparently celebrating a birthday party, had pushed together tables in the middle of the large room. Sean and Maggie had waited ten minutes for a free booth, and quickly made their way to it before it had even been cleared of dishes.

"This isn't just an ice cream parlor, this is Fenton's," Sean pointed out as he settled into the red vinyl seat. "Besides, this is probably the last time I'll get decent ice cream for months."

"I guess you'll have to make do with whatever they sell in the grocery store up there."

"It's one of the downsides of being stationed at Yosemite."

"But look at the upsides," Maggie said enthusiastically. She still couldn't believe that her brother had finally received his dream assignment.

"Oh, yeah," Sean said with a faraway look. "I am so stoked about this."

"I'm really happy for you, Bro." Maggie graced him with a broad smile.

"So let's celebrate by eating so much ice cream we make ourselves sick."

"Um, I think I'll pass on that, thanks." Maggie shook her head and held her stomach.

"Remember when we were kids and you agreed to eat that huge banana split? The ice cream parlor gave anyone who could finish it a free T-shirt."

"Oh, don't remind me." Maggie groaned. If she closed her eyes, she could still see the piles of vanilla, chocolate, and strawberry ice cream, topped with pineapple, chocolate, and strawberry sauce and mounds of whipped cream. The bananas had been the size of her forearm. She had to tip her head back just to spot the cherries that towered above her head. "Why the hell did we want a T-shirt anyway?"

"I think it was more for bragging rights at school. We could say you ate it, and we'd have the shirt to prove it."

"So you guys all pitched in your allowance, and then sat there and watched me stuff my face."

"I still can't believe you managed it. You were just a little thing. How old were you?"

"Eight," Maggie replied. "I think the banana split weighed more than I did."

"And you held it together all the way home on the bus."

"Barely." As she'd sat on the bus, the tastes had returned in random patterns. The diesel fumes from the bus made the whole experience just that much more special.

"I've gotta admit, I've never seen such colorful—"

"Sean, if you keep up this story, I'm gonna lose my appetite," Maggie interrupted. "I'm already considering forgoing ice cream."

"OK, OK, I'll drop it." Sean chuckled, his blue-green eyes twinkling.

The waiter finally approached to take their order.

"I'll have the grilled ham and cheese and a coke," Sean ordered.

"And I'll have egg salad with extra pickles on the side and water. We'll order our ice cream later."

"So, I've been going on about Yosemite since I picked you up," Sean said when the waiter left. "It's time for you to share. What's been happening in the world of Mary Margaret Monahan?"

"Nothing much." Maggie concentrated very hard on the ice cream menu.

"Oh, come on. You haven't caught any criminals lately?" Sean prompted. "Gone on any great bike rides? Eaten any huge banana splits?"

"Oh, well, I did forget to tell you that I'm moving." Maggie said it as if she'd just remembered. "I need to give you my new phone number."

"What? Did you find a cheaper place? I thought your rent was about as good as you were going to get for the size."

"I'm moving in with someone, so the rent is going to be a lot less."

"Wow. Again you surprise me. You said you'd never get a roommate. Are you sure she's gonna be OK to live with—won't screw you on the rent or anything?"

Well, she might screw me, but not on the rent.

"No, it's her place actually, so I'm kind of paying rent to her," Maggie explained vaguely. "She's really nice. You'll like her a lot."

Shit, how the hell do I say this?

They were interrupted with the arrival of the food, and Maggie took a big bite of her sandwich and a bigger gulp of water. Unfortunately, the breather didn't last long.

"Anyway, I guess it's worth moving in with someone if you end up with a bigger place," Sean said.

"Um, yeah, but it's not really that much bigger. It's a cottage, built behind a house in North Berkeley."

"I don't get it. Why move in with someone and not even get a bigger place?" Sean furrowed his brow. Then he smiled. "Oh, but you said your rent's a lot less. What are you saving up for, Sis?"

"Nothing special." Maggie speared a few pickles with her fork and shoved them into her mouth. She chewed, trying to gather her emotions so that she could remain nonchalant. It was tough, considering her heart was threatening to beat her to death from the inside. She swallowed, and continued in a voice she hoped didn't sound too strained, "I just thought it would be nice to have a little extra spending money, not have things be so tight."

Maggie felt out of control and tried to put on the brakes. *You are going to tell him. Don't go any further away from the truth.* "Anyway, I met Anne a few months ago and we really hit it off." Maggie tried to steer the conversation back in the right direction.

"It's always good to have a roommate you like. Maybe you guys can go out on double dates and stuff."

"I don't think so." Maggie tried not to blush and failed miserably.

"Oh, what's this I see?" Sean teased. "Are you telling me you already met someone?"

"No." Maggie realized that to her brother "someone" meant someone male. "I mean, yes...sort of."

"Woohoo! Tell me all about him."

"No." Maggie looked around to see how many of their fellow diners appeared to be listening in. She spotted one pair of shifting eyes, and lowered her voice. "There is no 'him,' " she hissed.

"I don't get it." Sean looked confused. "Then what does 'yes, sort of' mean?"

"I met Anne. My new roommate."

"Yeah, I know you met Anne. We already established that.

Is this conversation going backward?"

"Sideways, I think. Definitely sideways."

"So, are you dating someone or not?"

A direct question, requiring a direct answer. I can do this.

"Yes?" She hadn't meant for it to come out as a question, but it somehow had.

"Are you asking me or telling me?"

"Telling you," Maggie replied, more firmly this time. She took a deep breath. "I'm dating someone. I'm in love with someone."

"And again I say 'woohoo.' " Sean smiled, but his confusion was obvious. "What's his name, what does he do for a living, and what are his intentions toward my sister?"

"Slow down." Maggie took another drink of water, felt her throat tighten, and struggled to keep the fluid moving in a downward direction. She looked at her brother, as if by looking into his face she could predict his reaction. She gazed into the eyes that were twins of her own.

Maggie sucked air into her lungs and said with one large exhale, "Her name is Anne, she's a lawyer, I love her and she loves me. She wants me to move in with her, and I hope to spend the rest of my life with her."

She silently held her brother's gaze and watched his eyes slowly blink as the words registered one by one, and then were connected to make a coherent thought. Sean held her gaze, but said nothing. His face held no emotion that Maggie could decipher.

"Um," he finally mumbled. "Wow."

"Is that a good 'wow' or a bad 'wow'?" Maggie winced as she waited for his answer.

"It's a 'wow' wow. It's a...well, a surprised wow, I guess."

"Surprised like when you got that model of the space shuttle for Christmas or surprised like when Tiffany dumped you in tenth grade?"

Sean leaned toward Maggie and replied in a whisper, "Surprised like my little sister just told me she's gay."

"You don't have to whisper. I'm not ashamed. Are you?"

She still couldn't read her brother's reaction. She felt queasy as she waited for something to happen, whatever it might be.

"I'm not ashamed of you," Sean replied. "I'm just... I mean, are you sure?"

A burst of nervous laughter escaped from Maggie. "Um, yeah, I'm sure. Sure I'm gay, and most definitely sure I'm in love with Anne."

"How long have you —"

"Known I've been gay?" Maggie interrupted to complete her brother's sentence. She suddenly realized that she was handling the conversation better than Sean. Her declaration of love had energized her. She wanted to shout out that truth and make everyone understand it.

"I've always known, Sean, since I was little." Maggie smiled at her brother, who now looked puzzled. "You and the other guys knew it too, really. Didn't you?"

"No," Sean said quickly. "You were always a tomboy, but lots of girls are like that."

"You know it was more than that. The kids called me a dyke in junior high. Remember? I didn't even know what the word meant, but you told me to ignore them, that it didn't matter."

"I told you that because I thought they were wrong."

"Does it matter after all, now that you know they were right?" Maggie felt tears sting her eyes.

"No." Sean shook his head firmly. "It doesn't matter. I'm sorry. I just...it's a surprise, that's all."

"There's that word again."

"I'm sorry I'm freaking out about this. I am really not a homophobe. I just didn't think..."

"That your own sister was a lesbian?" Maggie smiled to take the sting out of her words. "I'm sorry about telling you like this. I just wanted to let you know. I mean, I'm so happy, Sean. I've never felt this way before."

"I'm happy for you, Mags. Really." Sean mimicked his sister's lopsided grin. "I'd like to meet her."

"Oh, you'll love her. She's funny and smart and drop-dead gorgeous."

"Is she like your partner?" Sean asked, finishing off his sandwich with a huge bite. Maggie was pleased to see he hadn't lost his appetite. That was a good sign.

"Like Moocher? No, not at all, why?" Maggie was confused at the question.

"I just thought that she'd be..."

"Oh." Maggie realized where her brother was going with his train of thought. "You mean you just assumed she was butch?"

"I don't know." Sean looked completely adrift. "You're so feminine, I thought she'd be...the opposite. Isn't that how it works?"

"No." Maggie tried not to feel angry at her brother's stereotyping. "There aren't rules. I don't think Anne and I are very butch or very femme. We're just us."

"Sorry, again." Sean winced. "I must sound like the biggest butthead in the world. I live in the fucking Bay Area; you'd think I'd be a little more enlightened."

"It's OK." Maggie smiled. "I know this is new for you. It's new for me to be out. But I have to come out, Sean. I can't hide any more. I don't want to. Being with Anne is so wonderful, there's no way I want to cover it up."

"How 'out' do you plan on being?" Sean asked, his eyes widening.

"We kissed in public the other day, walking down Fourth Street."

"I was thinking more in terms of coming out to other people. As in the rest of the family."

"Oh, that." Maggie picked through her potato chips, looking for the biggest one. "Well, I was thinking about bringing up the subject at Thanksgiving."

"Thanksgiving? As in this Thanksgiving? As in, three weeks from now?"

"Yeah." Maggie ate the chip she'd found.

"No," Sean said, shaking his head. "Mistake. Big, big mistake."

"Sean, are you listening to me at all?" Maggie growled softly in frustration. "I don't want to hide this any more. I need to be honest about who I am."

"I know how you feel, Mags. I really do. But you've got to think about this carefully. Michael will probably get used to it. And what does she do for a living again?"

"Lawyer."

"OK, then Liam won't care. She's got money, and that's at the top of Liam's priority list."

Maggie smiled, thinking about her stockbroker brother, who had always thought up moneymaking schemes when they were growing up.

"But, Sis, the rest of the family..."

"It'll be hard, I know. But I have to do it."

"Dad is going to freak. And what about Patrick?"

"What about Patrick?" Maggie asked, lifting her chin in defiance.

"Patrick will go ballistic. You know that. He'll never accept it."

"Then so be it," Maggie snapped. "Patrick doesn't run our lives. We're all adults now."

Despite her bravado, Maggie's hands shook, and she tried to hide them on her lap. Sean was too quick for her, and reached out to take hold of the nearest one. He gave it a comforting squeeze.

"Patrick doesn't control my life anymore," Maggie said. Her

voice shook, matching her hands. "It's time he realizes that. And if he doesn't accept who I am, then fuck him."

"Maggie, I'll support your coming out, but please—I'm begging you—do this slowly. Let's talk to Michael first, then Liam."

"Then what?" Maggie pulled her hand from her brother's grasp and waved her hands in the air, stressing her points. "Will we ever tell Dad and Patrick? You, Michael and Liam will know, but you'll have to constantly watch what you say around everyone else? I don't want to handle it that way."

Sean blew out a frustrated gust of air and rubbed his temples. "Can you just wait, then? Thanksgiving's always hectic, with kids running around and the football on the TV and shit. Wouldn't you rather do it at a quiet time, maybe one person at a time?"

"OK. I'll think about it. I'll try to come up with a good strategy. I know Anne's worried about it, too."

"Did you tell her about our family?"

"I've told her a bit," Maggie said evasively. "I've told her about some of my issues, probably too much. It's a wonder she hasn't run as far away from me as possible."

She thought about being held in Anne's arms and talking to her, feeling so many things that had weighed on her shoulders for so many years just float away.

"You really love her, don't you?"

"Haven't I said that about a hundred times already?" Maggie smiled, picturing her lover's face.

"At least a hundred." Sean laughed. "But I'm a slow learner."

"Are you two ready to order your ice cream?" the waiter asked, surprising them.

"Um, yeah," Sean said. "I'll have a medium hot fudge sundae with Swiss milk chocolate ice cream."

The waiter wrote down the order and turned to Maggie.

"I'll have a banana split," Maggie ordered. "But make it a small one, please."

Sean shook his head, rolling his eyes.

"Don't you say anything."

MOOCHER SLOWLY BACKED the U-Haul toward the open door of the large storage locker, watching Maggie's waving hand.

"OK... OK... OK..." Maggie kept waving Moocher back. "Whoa." She held her palm out.

Moocher kept backing up.

"Whoa," Maggie said louder, holding her palm out higher.

Moocher kept backing up.

"Whoa!" Maggie yelled, waving her arms.

Moocher finally stopped, the bumper of the U-Haul just inches from the wall.

Maggie stormed toward the driver's door and craned her neck to look up at Moocher's smiling face peering down at her. "What part of 'whoa' didn't you understand?"

"People are always overly cautious." Moocher shrugged, getting out and inspecting her parking job. "There, you see? Always wait for the third whoa."

"I'll remind you of that the next time I see a snake on the bike trail."

"Well, let's start unloading this crap."

"Um, Moocher," Maggie trilled. "How do you propose we get to the back of the truck?"

Moocher looked again at the back bumper of the U-Haul. It was right against the wall and overlapped the open door on both sides. "I'll just pull her up a little ways," she said, ignoring Maggie's self-righteous cackle.

On the second attempt, Moocher stopped at Maggie's first cry of "whoa."

"Tell me again your plan of action for today," Moocher said, descending again from the truck.

"Well, first trip I brought all of my stuff over here that I don't think I want to have at Anne's. She and her friend Roz will bring all of the stuff that she doesn't think she needs—because we need the room, or I have a better one, or whatever. In addition, Anne's mom is taking this opportunity to get rid of some of the stuff she doesn't want any more. We'll go through it and maybe pick out some of her stuff if we like it. Once we have all of that sorted out, we'll take what we want to keep from here to the cottage. Then, we'll take the stuff from my apartment that I know I need to the new place. Make sense?"

"Oh, it makes sense all right. Sounds like something General Patton would dream up. I'm just trying to figure out how the simple act of helping my best friend move turned into a military maneuver."

"Stop complaining and move your sorry ass, soldier!" Maggie ordered, lifting the back door of the truck. She pulled out the ramp and climbed up into the back, picked up a small box, and carried it back down and into the far reaches of the locker.

"Don't tire yourself out right away!" Moocher yelled, the

words echoing in the empty locker.

"Shut up or I'll put you on report!" Maggie snapped back.

"Ooh, I'm so scared."

"You should be."

"OK, General, help me get this horrible couch out." Moocher grabbed one end.

"What's wrong with this couch?" Maggie took the other end and carefully backed down the ramp.

"Didn't I throw up on this couch?" Moocher eyed one corner suspiciously.

"No, that was the chair."

"Oh, right, same baby-poo-brown fabric. Some things you just never forget."

They dumped the couch in the back of the locker and went for the mattress.

"What are you guys doing about a bed?" Moocher asked. "Does Anne have a queen-sized?"

"Moocher, are you implying that Anne and I will be sharing a bed?"

"Ha ha." Moocher rolled her eyes. "But seriously, sleeping together in anything smaller than a queen-sized bed is certainly fun for a while, but it becomes a royal pain."

"I like it—queen-sized...royal pain. How long did it take you to think that up?"

"OK, that's the last piece of advice I ever offer you." Moocher scowled, crossing her arms indignantly.

"I'm sorry." Maggie laughed. "Yes, we're going to be suffering a smaller bed until we can figure out how to get a bigger one into the cottage. Anne was thinking about doing some major renovations, because right now a queen-sized bed will take up most of the bedroom."

"That's why they call it a bedroom."

"Well, I like a place to put my alarm clock and my clothes," Maggie said. "Silly me."

"Hey, speaking of you and Anne sleeping together, you still haven't given me the full scoop on coming out to Sean. You told me it went well. What exactly happened?"

"Well, he said 'wow' quite a few times." Maggie smiled at the memory, still feeling a little giddy from the relief of finally coming out to her brother.

"I bet he said 'wow.' Not to mention, 'you're fucking shitting me.' "

Maggie and Moocher walked up the ramp and picked up her bed's box springs.

"Well, not in so many words. He was definitely shocked and

surprised, but he ended up being really cool about it. I can't wait for him to meet Anne. He's going to love her."

"Who wouldn't? She's beautiful, smart, funny...did I mention beautiful?"

"That's exactly what I told Sean." Maggie laughed. "I think he expected something a little different."

"What do you mean?"

"Think flannel shirt and work boots," Maggie explained, laughing when she realized Moocher was wearing exactly that. "Or maybe leather, tattoos, and lots of piercings."

"Oh, I get it." Moocher sighed. "He figured his baby sister got seduced by a big, bad-ass dyke on a bike."

"Oh, yeah, I think that's exactly the mental picture he had."

"Mind you, it's a nice image."

Maggie let her eyes go out of focus and pictured a leather-clad Anne, and then a nipple ring, and... She cleared her throat and tried to hide her blush. "Um, yeah."

"Or maybe the cowboy look," Moocher mused. "I can see cowboy boots, tight black jeans, a silk shirt, and a Stetson."

Maggie felt her face burning and struggled to push the image from her mind's eye. "Moocher, stop this now, please." She fanned herself with her hand. "You're giving me the vapors."

"You starting to feel the down-low tickle?"

"Oh, yeah," Maggie admitted. "Big time."

"Let's take a break. I think you need a drink of water."

Maggie sighed and nodded, going to the cab of the truck and taking two bottles of water from the cooler they'd left in the passenger seat. She cracked one open, handing it to her friend.

"So, I haven't told you my big news," Moocher said after taking a long swig. "I broke up with Charlie."

"What?" Maggie gasped. "When? Why?"

"Halloween." Moocher sighed and moved back to the rear of the truck, taking a seat on the bumper. Maggie sat on the ground, leaning back against the wall of the locker. "It just wasn't meant to be. She was just too...well, stupid."

"She was a bit of an airhead," Maggie carefully agreed.

"She was such an airhead a bee could fly in one ear and out the other and she'd ask if you heard something buzzing. The final straw came when we went to a costume party for Halloween last weekend. I had a great outfit. I wore gray pants and a gray T-shirt and I glued Barbie dolls all over me."

"And you were...?"

"A babe magnet."

"Oh, that's funny." Maggie chuckled.

"Yeah, I thought so. But Charlie spent the whole evening saying 'I don't get it.' It drove me fucking crazy. When I dropped her off that night, I told her it just wouldn't work out."

"Was she OK about it?"

"Yeah, she was fine. I think maybe it's one more thing she didn't get. She's probably still wondering why I haven't asked her out this weekend."

"Ooh, speaking of weekends," Maggie said, perking up, "You want to go on a bike ride next Saturday? I was thinking about doing Mount Diablo."

"Oh, my God! You're actually going to leave the house for an extended period of time without Anne?"

"Yes, she does let me off my leash occasionally." Maggie rolled her eyes.

"Keep your sordid secrets in the bedroom, thank you very much."

"Shut up, Moocher." As the three words left her lips, Maggie wondered how many times she'd uttered them. "Seriously, though, Anne and I had a talk about what you were saying a couple of weeks ago. About us doing too much together. We agreed that we needed some quality time apart, especially now that we're moving in together."

"Maggie accepts Moocher's advice: our exclusive story on page nine," Moocher joked.

"Shocking and extremely rare, I know. Anyway, Anne has to work on Saturday, so I thought it was a good time."

"Um, let me point something out to you, Magpie." Moocher held up a finger. "I think the idea was that you guys do things apart. If she's working anyway, how is this achieving your independence?"

"It's different because I won't be sitting around the house waiting for her to call. I'll be out doing something."

"And you won't be taking your cell phone?"

"Yes, of course," Maggie said. "I mean, come on..."

"Oh, God, I don't know who's more whipped, you or Anne." Moocher laughed and shook her head.

"I am not whipped!" Maggie cried indignantly.

"You are so, so whipped."

"Am not."

"Are so."

"Am not!" Maggie picked up her half-full bottle of water and threw it at her friend. Unfortunately, the cap wasn't completely on, and water sprayed out on impact. A dripping Moocher froze, and then glared menacingly at Maggie.

"Moocher." Maggie got up and held out her hands, "that was

an accident, I swear. I thought the cap was on." She began to slowly back away.

Moocher walked toward her just as slowly, drops of water plopping from her wet bangs. Maggie couldn't stop a giggle from escaping at the sight. The giggle was like a red cape to a bull, and Moocher stormed at Maggie, who ran as fast as she could, but was hampered by more giggles. Moocher caught her at the end of the row of storage lockers, and put her in a headlock. She reached out and rubbed her knuckle into the top of Maggie's head.

"Ow, ow, ow," Maggie cried between giggles. "I'm sorry, I'm sorry."

"Say 'uncle,'" Moocher said, grinding harder.

"No!" Maggie squawked.

"Say 'uncle.'" Moocher applied even more force.

"No!" Maggie gasped and giggled as she struggled to get out of the headlock.

"What are you doing to my girlfriend?"

The voice sounded right behind Moocher, and she immediately released Maggie. "Nothing. We were just goofing around. And it was all her fault anyway."

"No it wasn't." Maggie rubbed her head. "She was being mean to me."

"Do you kids need a time-out?" Anne folded her arms across her chest and tried to look parental.

"No," Maggie and Moocher said in unison, hanging their heads as they walked with Anne back to their truck.

"Have you guys done any work at all?" Anne asked, peering into the locker.

"Maggie unloaded that box while I carried out the furniture," Moocher said.

"You fucking liar!" Maggie cried.

"Girls, would you shut up one second? I want you to meet my friend Roz."

Roz peeked from around the back of the truck.

"Roz, the redhead belongs to me," Anne said, pointing to Maggie. "And the other one's some stray. We fed her one day and she followed us home. We call her Moocher."

"Hi, Maggie. Hi, Moocher." Roz flashed a bemused smile.

"Hey," Maggie waved.

"Michelle," Moocher croaked.

"What?" Roz asked.

"My name. Michelle. M-m-my real name."

Maggie leaned toward Anne and whispered, "Did you just hear her voice crack?"

"Yeah, I think I did," Anne whispered back.

"Pleased to meet you, Michelle." Roz extended her hand.

Moocher took it carefully, shook it, and then gave it back reluctantly. "It's great to meet you, too," she finally managed.

"Why don't you two start unloading? I need to take a look at Anne's stuff." Maggie dragged her lover by the arm and away from Moocher and Roz.

Once they were out of sight and out of hearing range, Anne and Maggie burst into helpless giggles.

"That was the funniest thing I've seen in a long time." Maggie wiped away tears of laughter.

"Oh, yeah."

They carefully peered around the side of the truck and saw Moocher and Roz speaking quietly.

"Is Moocher blushing?" Maggie gasped. "I think I can see little hearts floating in the air around them."

"Our little girl, she's all grown up. It seemed like only yesterday she was in diapers."

"Now she's asking for the keys to the station wagon."

"You know we have to torment her endlessly, right?"

"Oh, you know it."

They stood a few more minutes, watching love bloom in the mini-storage lot.

Chapter
Ten

ANNE STARED AT her notes and sucked on her pen, a habit that often resulted in some nasty ink accidents that she tried to forget. She reached to the bookshelf to check a reference, grunting as she pulled down the huge book.

Why can't they make law books smaller? she mused for the millionth time in her life. *Do they really think it impresses people? And who are 'they' anyway?* She pictured a room full of old, fat white men making up all the rules for society.

"Lawyers must have huge leather-bound tomes with new editions every year!" one crotchety old man shouted in Anne's fantasy boardroom.

"Women shall not be considered dressed up unless they're wearing uncomfortable hosiery and torturous shoes!" another man announced.

"Christmas decorations must be displayed the day after Halloween and not removed until Valentine's Day!"

"Christmas!" Anne cried, panic dissolving her fantasy. "What the hell am I going to get Maggie for Christmas?" It was almost Thanksgiving, certainly not too early to begin thinking about this most important of questions. She sucked more frantically on her pen as she thought and then rejected idea after idea.

"Hey, babe, am I interrupting a special moment between you and your pen?" Maggie smiled as she walked through the door, carrying a plastic bag out of which drifted some wonderful smells.

"Hi! What are you doing here?" Anne grinned. They'd only been living together for a few days, but Anne found that being around Maggie left her wanting even more. Seeing her lover's smiling face was a wonderful surprise.

"You've been working too hard and skipping lunch." Maggie held her hand up as Anne began to protest. "Oh, no, don't you dare try to deny it. I have my spies."

"Mom." Anne growled.

"Yes, and everyone else in this office that loves you. Anyway, I decided to take matters into my own hands. I'm a proactive kind of girl, you know."

"And that's why I love you." Anne cleared a space on her desk for the food.

"Of course it is." Maggie put the plastic bag down and pulled out the little white cardboard containers. "So I told Moocher to get her own lunch. I had to go on a mission of mercy."

"Thank you," Anne said as she ripped the paper off a pair of chopsticks and dug into a container of tofu and bok choy. "I guess you can be my girlfriend for a little while longer."

"Thank God! I was getting really worried about that." Maggie bit into a spring roll.

Anne and Maggie ate for a few minutes, making small talk, enjoying each other and their food. Their threesome was interrupted by a knock on the office doorframe.

"Anne? Sorry to interrupt." Julie, one of the two paralegals in the firm, looked into the office hesitantly. "There's a woman here who says she needs to talk to you. Said it's urgent."

"Tell her Anne's having her lunch." Maggie replied before Anne had a chance to swallow her bite of vegetable kung pao.

Anne smiled at Maggie's protective streak. Her lover had almost growled.

"I told her you were having lunch," Julie replied. "But she said she's on her lunch break too, and she can't come back during office hours."

"Ask Mona or Rachel if they're free," Anne suggested.

"She said she'd only speak to you," Julie said with a helpless shrug. "Said she's an old friend."

There was movement behind Julie and a then a woman's voice floated into the room. "Anne, please, you have to talk to me."

Anne stood when she heard the woman's voice, but Julie blocked the doorway, turning toward the visitor.

"Ma'am, I told you to wait a few minutes." Julie held her hands up toward the woman, who ignored her completely and barged into the room, her gaze fixed unwaveringly on Anne.

Out of the corner of her eye, Anne saw Maggie rise to her feet. True to her police training, Maggie seemed to be preparing herself for a confrontation. Anne prepared herself as well, though she knew much more about the kind of threat that had just waltzed into her office.

The woman had always been beautiful. Curly chestnut hair

tumbled to rest atop her shoulders. Her green eyes curved upward slightly, like a cat's, and were complimented by high, well-defined cheekbones. Her patrician nose and firm chin, together with smooth alabaster skin, had always reminded Anne of a classic statue.

But while the woman's face was a picture of perfection, her body told a quite different story. She was gaunt, with an unhealthy thinness rather than a natural one. Her clothes were neat but threadbare, and hung on her like a big sister's hand-me-downs. Her fingers were rough and stained with nicotine, and even though she didn't currently hold a cigarette, she held her hand away from her body as if she did. Anne could see scars and remnants of needle marks on her hands and neck, and though the woman wore long sleeves, Anne knew there would be more marks on her arms. The woman's eyes were clear, but from the looks of her ravaged body, she hadn't been clean for long.

"Simone." Anne's voice was guarded.

"Hey, Hot Shot." Simone smiled, a dimple creasing her left cheek.

Anne felt herself soften under Simone's smile. It always had that kind of magic over her. "It's all right, Julie," she said, not taking her eyes off Simone. "I'll see her."

Julie nodded and left, closing the door behind her. Anne heard Maggie clear her throat and remembered, guiltily, that her lover was standing next to her.

"I'll just, um..." Maggie stuttered.

Anne turned, frowning. "Oh, Maggie, I'm sorry. I need to, uh..."

Within seconds, a thousand emotions traveled across the features of the three women. Anne felt flustered and uncertain, and knew her face betrayed her. She glanced at Simone, and then to Maggie, then back to Simone. Simone looked curiously at Maggie, then her eyes reflected comprehension, and she openly appraised Maggie, taking an obvious interest in the police uniform. Maggie's brow wrinkled in confusion, her innocence betraying her. After a moment, though, realization glowed from her eyes, realization that the woman that stood before her had been Anne's lover. When Anne saw that dawning awareness, she turned away. She had to focus on Simone. She could explain things to Maggie later.

"It's OK, I need to get back to work." Maggie gathered the Chinese food, closing the white containers and putting them back into the plastic bag. Anne stared at the words "Thank You" written in English and Chinese in bright red letters on the white bag, transfixed by the reassuring phrase. The click of the door opening brought her out of her trance.

"Maggie, wait." Anne held her hand toward Maggie as if reaching for a lifeline.

Maggie paused, but didn't look up. "I'll talk to you later," she mumbled.

"I'll try to be home early tonight. I'll call you." Anne thought the words sounded pathetic once they passed her lips, but they seemed to make an impression on Maggie, whose shoulders eased slightly.

"OK." Maggie smiled tentatively. She spared one more uncertain glance at Simone, and then left, the bag of food rustling against her leg.

Simone closed the door with a soft click and sat in the chair that Maggie had vacated. "So. That was your current squeeze, huh?" She raised a challenging eyebrow, but Anne knew her well enough to recognize a glimmer of self-doubt in her eyes.

"Yes, that was my lover Maggie."

"Thanks for the introduction," Simone said sarcastically.

"I figured it would take too long to...explain." Anne slowly sat down.

"Our story is just too complicated?"

"That's a good word for it." Anne picked up her pen and started to doodle on the yellow legal pad. "If you've come about Katy, I can tell you that she's happy and healthy. I got a card from her parents recently and—"

"They aren't her parents," Simone interrupted sharply. "You may have forgotten that, but I haven't."

Anne froze and turned an arctic gaze on Simone. "I haven't forgotten." Her voice matched her eyes, and she was pleased when she saw Simone shiver.

"I want her back, Hot Shot."

Anne grimaced at the old nickname and the memories it stirred, memories filled with both joy and horror. "No," she said simply and forcefully.

Simone ignored Anne's response. "Help me get her back."

"I won't help you ruin that child's life. In fact, I'll do anything I can to stop it."

"I'm clean, Anne." Simone held up her hands to show they were steady and widened her eyes to show they were clear. "I've served my time, stayed out of trouble. I go to my Narcotics Anonymous meetings. Everyone is encouraging me to get back custody of my child."

"No!" Anne had tried to keep a tight grasp on her emotions, but they escaped, and she felt them rushing from her like water from a burst pipe. She slammed the flat of her palm against her desk. The sharp, ringing slap sounded unbelievably loud in the little office.

Simone jumped in her seat.

"She is in a stable, loving environment," Anne continued, anger making her voice crack. She cleared her throat and then continued in a steady growl, "She has a life that you could never give her. Why would you try to take that away from her?"

"She is my child!" Simone cried, her own anger overcoming her. She visibly gathered herself, taking a deep breath, and continued in a calmer voice. "She needs to be with me. I love her more than anything. I am her mother and I have a right to be with her."

"You gave up your rights when you chose your drugs over her." Anne closed her eyes in pain, unable to stop the replay in her mind of that afternoon: Katy screaming in her crib, dehydrated and feverish, and Simone unconscious in the bathroom, a needle still sticking out of her neck. Blood had backed up and leaked around the needle's entry point, dripping in a slow stream down Simone's neck, soaking into her white T-shirt and turning it crimson.

"I made a mistake." Simone leaned forward, her elbows on her knees and her hands clasped together. "I admit it. And now I want to make things better. You helped get Katy out of my life, and I agree that it was the right decision at the time. But now I want you to help me get her back. How can it be wrong for us to be together?"

Anne could feel her skin burning with anger and her pulse racing. A dull, throbbing pain settled in her forehead. "How long have you been clean?" she asked. "A year? Less?"

"I was in jail for nearly two years and I've been out for six months."

"That doesn't answer my question," Anne said impatiently.

"I had a few relapses. I needed to get away from some old relationships."

Anne rolled her eyes and snorted in disgust.

"Look, no one said you have to be perfect to be a mother," Simone argued. "But I have way more going for me than most. And I love Katy with all my heart."

"No, you don't."

Simone gasped, her eyes sparking with outrage. "How can you say that?"

"If you loved her, you'd let her be—let her grow up with the family who's fostering her. Let them adopt her and give her the life she deserves."

"The life you promised her?"

"What the hell is that supposed to mean?" Anne snarled.

"You failed her as much as I did." Simone paused, letting the words sink in. "You told me you loved Katy like she was your own. You said we'd be together forever, that if anything happened to me, you'd take care of Katy."

"I know I promised that." Despite her calm demeanor, the accusations were hitting their mark, boring under Anne's skin.

Anne remembered a quiet Sunday morning, waking up and looking at Simone, who slept in a beam of sunlight. Katy lay between them, and when Anne reached out to touch the little girl's downy hair, Katy looked up at her and smiled a toothless baby grin, her eyes full of devotion.

"Where were you the day I OD'd?" Simone's words replaced Anne's pleasant memory with one full of shock and revulsion. "I was convicted of child endangerment, but where were you?"

"It was already over between us." Anne could feel guilt as it roiled through her stomach.

"Yeah, you'd already given up on me." Simone sneered. "Walked out. And I accepted that. But you gave up on Katy, too."

"Don't you dare lay this on me!" Anne stood from her chair and leaned across the desk toward Simone. "I did everything I could to get that child away from you."

Simone stood, leaning forward until her face was inches from Anne's. "You left us, Anne. You promised you'd be there, and you left us. Now it's time to do the right thing."

The women's eyes locked, their breaths ragged from anger and frustration, guilt and recriminations.

"I am doing the right thing." Anne's eyes drilled into Simone's. "Now get out of my office."

Simone continued to hold Anne's gaze, sneering defiantly. "Fine," she finally said, turning away. "I'll do this on my own."

Anne waited until Simone had her hand on the door handle before speaking. "Then I'll see you in court. Because I'll do anything I can to see that Katy stays with the Perkins family."

Simone shrugged, but kept her back to Anne. She turned the doorknob and strode purposefully down the hall, her cheap pumps clicking on the hardwood floor as she left the offices of Doyle, Smith, and Goldstein.

ANNE DIDN'T HONOR her promise to come home early after Simone's surprise visit. Maggie stayed up watching old sitcoms, thinking about what she would say to Anne. Everything she thought of sounded accusatory. She didn't want to be accusatory. Anne didn't owe her an apology for having an ex-girlfriend. Even though the ex-girlfriend was a junkie. Even though Anne hadn't been able to take her eyes off the ex-girlfriend from the moment she walked into the office. Even though the ex-girlfriend was stunningly beautiful.

"Shit!" Maggie mumbled as the theme music to *Bewitched* started. The happy music mocked her as she fell slowly into sleep.

Maggie slept through Anne's arrival as well as her early departure a few hours later. When she woke up, she found a note on the coffee table.

Sorry I didn't get home early as promised.
I'll make it up to you tonight.

Anne

Maggie couldn't decide whether the fact that Simone wasn't mentioned was a good sign or a bad one. She got up and took a shower, then went to work, spending the day trying to ignore her stomach, which seemed intent on earning a Girl Scout badge in knot tying. She had never been so grateful that Moocher had pulled a different shift. She knew her friend would have demanded explanations—explanations that Maggie couldn't provide.

When she arrived home from work, Maggie was surprised and happy to see Anne's car in the driveway. She opened the door to the cottage and was assailed by the smell of good food.

"Wow, you made dinner!" Maggie stared at the meal spread out on the dining room table and then at her lover, who was placing the last dish of food on a hot pad.

"Well, I thought I should try to make up for yesterday." Anne grinned sheepishly. "Sorry about that."

"It looks great." Maggie felt at least some of her stomach's prize knots unwinding.

"Go ahead and change your clothes and we can eat right away."

Maggie scurried to the bedroom and changed quickly. She returned and sat down, digging without preamble into the curry and rice dish that Anne had prepared. As she ate, she watched Anne, who was eating slowly—almost absentmindedly. It was obvious that Anne was working things out in her mind. Anne's silent method of dealing with her problems was nothing new, but this time it was different. This time it wasn't a tough case that Anne was working on; it was an issue that affected them both. And Maggie had no idea how to break into Anne's internal cogitations.

Maggie's stomach went back to creating new knots as she and Anne exchanged small talk during the meal, unspoken words swirling around them like a dense fog.

Finally, as they were doing the dishes, Maggie decided to close her eyes and dive right in. "Is everything OK with...things?" She winced at her weak choice of words, deciding her dive was more of a belly-flop. She kept her face turned toward the cupboard and wiped at an imaginary smudge.

"Yes, everything's fine." Anne squeezed the dishrag so tight Maggie could almost hear the threads scream.

"It's just..." Maggie trailed off, unsure what it just was.

"I'm sorry. I know I owe you an explanation." Anne tried to smile. It was obviously forced and didn't hang around for long.

"You don't owe me anything." Maggie looked down at the towel in her hands. She couldn't meet Anne's eyes, unsure what she'd see in them, and terrified of that uncertainty.

"Well, I want to explain. I want you to know that I wasn't hiding Simone from you. It was just a painful episode from my past. I figured she'd kill herself long before she ever tried to walk back into my life."

"Kill herself?" Maggie turned confused eyes toward Anne. "Did she try to kill herself before?"

"No. She OD'd. It was an accident, I suppose." Anne shook her head and winced, as if telling even a small part of the story was agony. "It's hard to explain."

"It's OK, you don't need to tell me any more." Maggie couldn't stand to see the painful struggle in Anne's eyes.

"Let me start at the beginning." Anne leaned her back against the kitchen counter and took a deep breath. "I met Simone right after I finished law school. I passed the bar and was ready to save the world, you know?"

Maggie nodded, remembering her own idealism the day she started working as a cop.

"Simone was my first 'project,' " Anne continued. "I knew she was trouble from the first day I met her. But I was sure that I could help her. I figured love could conquer all."

"Including her drug addiction?" Maggie carefully asked.

Anne grimaced and shook her head, as if disgusted at her own idealism. "Yeah. And I know how stupid that was. It took me a little over a year to figure that out. I pretty much knew after a few months that it was never going to work, but I guess I stayed that long for Katy."

"Katy?" Maggie's brow wrinkled as she struggled to follow

the story.

"Her daughter. The result of an evening that she couldn't remember." Anne scowled, but then her eyes cleared and the ghost of a smile lifted the corner of her mouth. "Katy was a beautiful, sweet baby. And I loved her like she was my own. But I couldn't stay with Simone just because I loved Katy. So, eventually, we broke up."

Anne turned back to the sink with a shrug and draped the dishrag over the tap. Maggie wondered if that was as much of the story as Anne was willing to tell. There was still so much unspoken. She decided to push just a little more. "You mentioned that Simone overdosed?"

"That was later." Anne's words had a bitter edge. She sneered out the kitchen window.

"I'm sorry, I know it must be difficult for you to —"

"It's all right. You have a right to know the full story."

Maggie watched as Anne gripped the sink, her knuckles turning white with the effort. Maggie's stomach clenched. She didn't feel as if she had a right to anything. She wanted the conversation to be over, her lover's pain to stop, but she knew that Anne needed to continue — no matter how painful it was for both of them.

"I checked in with Simone periodically to make sure Katy was OK. I think I had convinced myself that Simone was clean, that Katy was safe with her. I was a fool." Anne's voice became flat and distant, all emotion pushed away. "One day I went over. I'd arranged to take Katy out for the day. When I got there, I could hear Katy screaming from the parking lot of the apartment complex. I ran up the stairs and found the front door ajar. I walked in and Simone was lying on the bathroom floor. She'd OD'd."

"What happened to Katy?" Maggie asked, her voice cracking.

"She was sick but OK. Simone got arrested for child endangerment and, because of previous convictions, got some heavy jail time. I made sure Katy ended up in a great foster home." Anne genuinely smiled for the first time that evening. "The only good thing about the story is that Katy is a happy, healthy, four-year-old."

Maggie could have left things there. It was the happy ending to the story that they both craved. But a question floated between them, like a feather caught in a draft. "What did Simone want yesterday?"

"She wants Katy back." Anne sneered, her words once again brittle with anger. "She thinks she deserves a second chance at motherhood."

Maggie's thoughts went to her own mother. And second chances. "Maybe if she could stay clean, work slowly with supervised visitations..."

"What?" Anne turned slowly, for the first time directing her anger toward Maggie. "She doesn't deserve to ever see or speak to that child again."

"I know what she did was a terrible thing," Maggie said carefully, "but if a child can be with her biological mother, as long as it's a safe, healthy environment..."

"Don't lecture me," Anne snapped, her blue eyes sparking. "You can't possibly understand the situation. So don't even try."

"All right, I just think — "

"This conversation is over." Anne pushed off from the sink and strode out of the room. Before Maggie could take a breath, she heard Anne call out a hasty farewell, and before she could turn to reply, the front door slammed closed.

"That went well," Maggie said to the empty kitchen, wiping at the angry tears that fell from her eyes. She thought about running after Anne, but there was no point. Instead, she turned back to the sink, cursing as she finished the dishes. "Damn, shit, damn, fuck, damn. I am so fucking stupid."

She continued to curse under her breath as she finished the dishes and left them to dry in the drainer. When she was finished, she sat on the sofa, but felt suddenly claustrophobic in the little cottage and went out to sit on the front steps.

She leaned her face into her hands, feeling hot, frustrated tears run into her fingers.

"Hey, Short Stuff, you OK?"

Maggie looked up to see Jill walking down the path between the main house and the cottage. She hastily wiped the tears from her face.

"Uh oh, what did my daughter do now?" Jill asked as she sat down next to Maggie on the steps.

"It was my fault," Maggie said forlornly.

"I somehow find that hard to believe." Jill handed Maggie a box of Kleenex and Maggie raised her eyebrows in question. "I saw Anne storm out of the cottage, and then a while later you came out. I figured you might need a box of tissues and a friendly ear. So, you had your first fight. You want to talk about it?"

Maggie felt a leftover tear seep from her eye and wiped at it with a tissue. "I met someone yesterday." Maggie looked up to watch Jill's reaction. "Simone."

"Ah." Jill nodded her understanding.

"Anne told me what happened — the overdose and Katy — and I tried to talk to her about it. But I just pushed her too far." Maggie wiped shakily at a tear that was tickling her cheek. "She's right, I can't possibly understand."

"That's not true," Jill said firmly. "Despite what my daughter might have said."

Maggie just shrugged, not sure who to believe. She'd done something wrong, that she was certain of. "I just wish she had stayed to talk about it. But she just told me the conversation was over and stormed out."

"Oh, Maggie." Jill grinned sadly. "Welcome to my nightmare."

Maggie looked up in confusion as Jill chuckled.

"My daughter can stand in a courtroom and speak so eloquently it takes my breath away. It's a skill that I'm not bad at myself — but Anne...Anne is brilliant. She knows just how much emotion to put into her speech, when to raise her voice and when to whisper, when to speak directly to the judge or jury and when to speak to the client as if no one else is in the room."

Maggie smiled, remembering a time when she'd crept into the back of a courtroom and felt her soul reach out to the ebony-haired, blue-eyed beauty that she'd first seen in an elevator.

"Unfortunately," Jill continued, "when it comes to talking about herself and her own feelings, my daughter is a bit challenged."

"She tells me she loves me all the time."

"And that's definitely an improvement." Jill smiled gently. "I actually think she spent her entire thirteenth year not saying one word. She communicated with grunts and lots of shoulder shrugs."

Maggie grinned at the image and blew her nose on a clean tissue.

"Her father and I both talk a lot — too much, sometimes. So we are firmly convinced that the hospital gave us someone else's child. Doesn't explain why she looks like a clone of her dad, but there you go."

"I shouldn't expect her to be something she's not — to do something that doesn't come naturally." Maggie sighed.

Jill echoed the sigh. "Anne needs to communicate. If she doesn't, she'll keep everything bottled up — and that hurts her and everyone around her. Just be patient with her. But don't stop poking and prodding."

"I don't want to upset her." Maggie rubbed her face where her sinuses ached from crying. "I drove her away. This is the first night she's gotten off early in ages. She should be resting now, not running."

"Maggie, you didn't drive her away. She left on her own. She's a big girl and she makes her own decisions." Maggie looked dubiously at Jill. "I know it's hard, Sweetie, but it's in her best interest and in yours to communicate. Come here." Maggie scooted over, and Jill put an arm around her and pulled her closer so that Maggie leaned back against her chest. Jill gave her a hug, rocking her slightly.

"Sometimes she treats me like I'm a child," Maggie said, trying not to sound like one. "I'm a cop. I understand all about the bad guys. I understand about the good guys, too."

"Is that what the argument was about? Not thinking that you understood the situation with Simone?"

Maggie nodded. She felt her body relax in Jill's comforting arms, responding to the gentle rocking.

"Oh, sweetheart, you need to realize that Simone is one of my daughter's biggest failures. That's how she sees it, anyway. I have a feeling most of her anger was hiding her fear. Fear for you. Fear that you'll become another failure."

"I don't understand."

"It's up to Anne to tell you about her fears, sweetie. I suppose I know a few things that make my daughter tick, but not everything. And telling you won't help the situation, since the problem is about Anne—and you—communicating. Together."

Maggie sighed and nodded. That she did understand.

Jill paused a moment, and then seemed to come to a decision. "Let me tell you a story. When Anne was a little girl— about three—my dad came to live with us. He had diabetes and had a leg amputated, so he couldn't really take care of himself. My mom died right before Anne was born.

"Dad and Anne absolutely worshipped each other. Anne could do nothing wrong in Dad's eyes, and Anne's world revolved around her grandfather—her Poppy. I was just starting my law practice, so I suppose I didn't think about the situation: that Anne spent most of her days with Dad, taking care of him, playing with him, watching TV with him. When she started school, I didn't notice that she didn't play at other kids' houses. She rushed home to be with her Poppy. I'm sorry to admit that I took advantage of the situation. When Anne got old enough, they took care of each other. We didn't need a baby sitter or nurse."

Maggie sat listening, picturing a young Anne playing at her grandfather's feet. She remembered Anne talking about her grandfather the first night at the cabin. It was the only time Anne had ever mentioned him.

"Anne would do anything for Dad," Jill continued. "One day when she was seven he got it into his head that he wanted to go fishing off the Berkeley Pier. So they got their fishing rods and tackle box, and Anne pushed Dad in his wheelchair three miles down to the pier, and when they were finished, three miles back up the hill. That night at dinner she seemed to be holding her fork strangely, so I reached over and took her hand. Her hands were covered in open blisters."

"Oh, poor thing." Maggie winced.

"I scolded Dad. He was sorry, of course. He just didn't think. Anne became furious with me for giving him a hard time. She said, 'They're my hands. I can do what I want.' "

"Stubborn even then."

"And loyal. I swear, she would have walked to the end of the earth for him." Jill grew quiet and stared into the distance. She rocked Maggie again.

"When Anne was nine, Dad had a stroke," Jill finally said. "He had to go into the hospital. Anne begged every day to go see him, but he was really bad off and barely conscious. Anne's dad and I debated about taking her for a final good-bye, and we finally decided that we should.

"The minute she walked into the room, Dad woke up and was able to talk to her. He told her not to cry. And she never did—at least not in my presence. They said their good-byes, and he died a few hours after she left."

"I didn't realize how much we had in common," Maggie said softly.

"In some ways the same, and in others very different. Like everything that happens in life, the death of a loved one affected you both deeply and helped form who you are today. Anne learned, at a very young age, about the rewards of taking care of someone who relied on her."

"But she couldn't save his life," Maggie said sadly. "No matter how hard she tried." An image of a woman in a hospital bed flashed into Maggie's mind, but she quickly slammed a mental door on the memory.

"That's true. And I'm afraid that pattern has repeated in her relationships."

"What do you mean?"

"She thought she could save Simone. That attempt nearly destroyed them both, along with a sweet, innocent little girl. Unfortunately, sometimes when you're a giver you get into a habit of choosing people who are takers. Anne gave and gave and they took and took—in different ways—until she was all used up."

"I don't ever want to do that to her."

"You've already given her so much, sweetie." Jill placed a kiss on the top of Maggie's head. "Just keep trying to get through that thick skull of hers, OK? Just let her know that you two are in this together."

"I'll try." Maggie pulled out of Jill's embrace when she saw her lover running up the driveway.

"I know you'll succeed," Jill whispered, and got up from the steps, waving to her daughter and re-entering her house through the back door.

"Hi," Anne said, her eyes catching Maggie's and then shyly dropping to her feet.

"Hi," Maggie replied just as tentatively.

"I'm sorry," they both said in unison.

"No, I'm sorry," they both said, again in unison.

They smiled, and Maggie held out her hand to Anne. "Come on in and take a shower, sweetheart. You're covered in sweat."

"I know. Hope I'm not too stinky."

"Well, I wasn't going to say anything." Maggie flashed a teasing grin.

"Oh, that's nice." Anne grinned, then grew serious again. "I really am sorry. I had no right to say the things I said to you. I haven't come to grips with Simone waltzing back into my life and the little bomb she dropped."

"I know, babe. It's all right."

"No, it's not all right. Just because I haven't processed it, I shouldn't have shut you down."

"Well, I'm going to give you space to process it. I know that's how you work through things. I'm sorry I pushed you."

Anne nodded. "I'm gonna go grab that shower. When I'm finished, you want to have a cuddle on the couch with me?"

"Yeah." Maggie's grin turned into a wider smile. "That would be great."

"SO, WHAT WERE you and my mom talking about?" Anne had showered, wrapped a towel around her hair, and pulled on an old, ragged T-shirt. She was sitting on the sofa, her legs spread out on the coffee table in front of her.

Maggie flopped down on the sofa next to her, and put her legs beside Anne's. Her feet reached the middle of the table, while Anne's hung over the far edge. "We talked about you, of course."

"I'm sure she told you to run far away from me as fast as you can." Anne smiled, but Maggie saw a glimmer of unease in her lover's eyes.

"No, funnily enough, she didn't." Maggie took Anne's hand and interlocked their fingers. She met Anne's eyes and said cautiously, "We talked about your grandfather."

Maggie watched as Anne's eyes widened a fraction and then narrowed again.

"He sounded like a great guy," Maggie said softly.

"He was. He was my best friend."

They were both silent for a moment, Anne lost in her memories and Maggie hoping that her lover would let her in.

"I was just thinking about something he used to tell me," Anne finally said. She reached out and pulled Maggie against her, just like her mom had done earlier.

"What's that?" Maggie felt the warmth of Anne's skin through her T-shirt. She took a deep breath, smelling the hint of lavender from the soap Anne always used.

"He used to tell me that I had a fairy that looked after me. Sometimes she sat on my shoulder and sometimes she played in my pocket. But she was always there when I needed her." Anne grinned, remembering her grandfather's serious expression when he told her about the fairy.

"Like a guardian angel?"

"Sort of — I suppose it was a non-religious version. Anyway, he told me that if I believed, really believed, I would be able to see my fairy. Of course I totally believed, particularly when I was little. I used to concentrate on my shoulder until my eyes crossed. And I'd thrust my hand into my pocket at odd times, trying to catch her."

Maggie chuckled. "Your mom must have thought you were crazy."

"Oh, I bet she did." Anne joined in with her own laugh, which rocked Maggie up and down. "Anyway, I used to say, 'Poppy, I can't see her; I can't see my fairy.' And he'd say to me, 'You keep trying, Annie. You keep believing. She'll be there when you need her.'"

"That's sweet." Maggie looked up at Anne and saw two clear blue eyes looking down into her soul.

"And he was right," Anne said, not breaking her gaze. "Just when I needed her, my fairy showed up in an elevator in the county courthouse."

Maggie was speechless for a moment. "You didn't stop believing," she finally whispered.

"Never." Anne leaned down to capture Maggie's lips in a gentle kiss.

Chapter
Eleven

"I CAN'T BELIEVE we're shopping the night before Thanksgiving." Anne moaned as she and Maggie walked through the grocery store parking lot. It had rained earlier in the day, and the asphalt was slick and covered in puddles, which Anne was careful to step around. "What the hell were we thinking?"

"Well, we could have come last night." Maggie purposely put her foot into the middle of a puddle and watched the rain water splash around her boot. "But when I got home from work you started giving me a neck rub, which turned into a back rub, which turned into..."

"Oh, yeah, it's all coming back to me now." Anne's teeth gleamed in a wide grin.

"Look out," Maggie warned as she dragged Anne from the path of a reversing Volvo. "If it's this crazy in the parking lot, what's it going to be like inside?"

"Ah-hah, I have a plan." Anne snagged a cart from the cart return. "I organized the shopping list by aisle, so I'll just read out the items and you grab them and load them into the cart."

"I knew there was a reason I fell in love with an anal-retentive freak." Maggie laughed.

"I thought you fell in love with my stunning good looks."

"Oh, yeah." Maggie gazed into her lover's clear blue eyes. "Your stunning good looks and your obsessive organizational skills. Both things I lack in abundance."

"Well, you are the most disorganized person I know. But I'm going to have to disagree with you on the lack of good looks." She paused as the automatic doors opened slowly in front of them. She leaned down to whisper into Maggie's ear, "You're the sexiest and prettiest woman in the world." She smiled as she watched the nearby ear turn as red as the poinsettias that lined the front of the store.

Once inside, the dull roar of a store full of frantic shoppers assailed them. They took a hard left and entered the dairy and frozen food aisle.

"OK," Maggie said, "start shouting out items."

"I will as soon as you give me the shopping list." Anne swung her cart out of the way of an old woman distracted by the dried fruit display.

"Why would I have the shopping list?"

"Because I put it right next to your wallet." Anne tried not to look annoyed.

"Why didn't you put it right next to your wallet?"

"Because." Anne stopped and sighed. "Never mind. No shopping list."

"You spent a lot of time organizing the list. Can you remember what we need?"

"We'll have to do our best. I'm not going home, that's for sure. It took fifteen minutes just to park. So, let's try to get enough food for tonight, tomorrow's breakfast, and all of the stuff that Mom asked me to pick up for her feast."

"Sounds like a plan. Orange juice?" Maggie stopped next to the juices.

"Yes, with pulp."

"Can we get the kind with just some pulp?" Maggie made a face.

"What's wrong with pulp? All of the vitamins are in the pulp."

"It's just too...pulpy."

"That's why they call it pulp." Anne shook her head at Maggie's pout. "OK," she said with a long-suffering sigh.

Maggie picked up the juice and put it in the cart. Anne repositioned it against one corner.

"Are you excited about seeing your dad tomorrow?" Maggie asked.

"Yeah." Anne smiled at the thought. "I haven't seen him since early summer. He took me to Hawaii for my birthday."

"Ooh, nice."

"Grab some milk for us, and Mom needs some whipping cream. Do we have any yogurt?"

"Not sure. Grab two just in case. So it's just your parents and you?"

"Uh huh. How many people are going to be at your dad's place tomorrow?" Anne checked the dates on the yogurt tubs.

"Dad," Maggie said, counting off on her fingers, "Sean, Michael, Michael's wife Shelley, Liam, Liam's girlfriend Kate, Patrick, Patrick's wife Diane, and their kids Mark and Megan. Oh, and me. Eleven."

"Yikes, I forgot about the rug-rats. How old are they again?"

"Three and five. And they're not rug-rats. They're the cutest kids in the whole world. Not that I'm partial or anything. Patrick and Diane are trying for more. And Michael and Shelley have started trying, so by next Thanksgiving there'll probably be four kids."

"Remind me to avoid that place like the plague."

Maggie frowned and looked wistfully at Anne. "I wish you were going tomorrow."

"I don't think that's a good idea." Anne pushed the cart ahead and stood next to Maggie, reaching out to squeeze her shoulder. "Maybe next year, huh?"

"I guess." Maggie pouted.

"Maggie, we talked about this. I thought you'd decided."

"I know, I know." Maggie waved her hand. "I just want to tell everyone how much I love you."

"Well, I appreciate that." Anne leaned over and placed a quick kiss on Maggie's cheek. "Just relax tomorrow and do what feels right. Then come home and we can cuddle and eat leftovers. Maybe tomorrow night we can share our own special version of giving thanks."

"Sounds like a plan to me."

Anne took control of the cart again, and swung around the aisle into fruits and vegetables. "Do you want stir fry tonight?"

"Yum."

"OK, then go pick out a zucchini." Anne chose a Chinese eggplant and put it in the cart. She turned to find Maggie still poking at the zucchinis and went to join her. "What's the problem?"

"I'm trying to find a good one." Maggie picked one up and flexed it. "This one's too rubbery. They should be firm."

"You like them firm, huh?" Anne smiled.

"Yep." Maggie picked up another one. "This one's firm, but too narrow."

Anne sputtered. "Need a wider girth?"

"Yes." Maggie looked at Anne, obviously confused

"What about this one?" Anne picked up a zucchini that was at least five inches in diameter.

"Are you crazy? That's way too huge. Look for one that's about three fingers wide."

Anne tried to hold in her laughter, but it burst out along with a small amount of spit.

"Jeez, what is wrong with you?" Maggie finally selected a zucchini and put it in the cart.

"Nothing," Anne wheezed.

"No, seriously, what are you laughing at?"

"I guess I should have figured a good Catholic girl like you would be familiar with zucchinis." Anne snorted.

"I have been eating them all my life," Maggie said. This made Anne snort again. "Tell me what you're laughing at or I'm leaving you here to finish the shopping by yourself."

"It's the zucchini," Anne gasped.

Maggie looked at the zucchini and then at Anne, and then back at the zucchini. Realization finally hit her. Anne watched the transformation as Maggie's mouth opened and the blood ran its regular course from her ears, down her neck and up into her cheeks. Maggie wordlessly left the fruit and vegetable aisle. The blush didn't leave until halfway through the beers and sodas.

"Diet Dr. Pepper," Maggie said, recovering from her embarrassment.

"Ugh." Anne picked up a six-pack while Maggie grabbed water.

"Don't you start on my favorite drink."

"Anyone that drinks carbonated prune juice—correction, artificially sweetened carbonated prune juice—is just sick in the head."

"I can't hear you, la, la, la." Maggie stuck her fingers into her ears.

"Oh, look." Anne stopped in front of the ice cream area. "Pumpkin-flavored ice cream."

"Oh, yeah, grab us some of that."

"I thought you couldn't hear me." Anne smirked.

"I used my psychic powers."

They turned the corner of the aisle and ran into a traffic jam. A store employee was trying to unload a box of pumpkin pie filling. People were grabbing the cans out of the box before he could put them on the shelf.

"Oh, that's scary." Anne squeezed through and turned down cheeses and international foods to get away from the mêlée.

"You know if you hadn't made your pie already, you'd be in there, too, tossing people aside."

"Thank God, again, for my organizational skills," Anne said with a smug smile.

"Thank you, God." Maggie looked skyward. She turned back to the food. "What do we need down here?"

"Mom needs some sharp cheddar and we need some stir-fry sauce."

Maggie picked up both items. "You want bagels and cream cheese for breakfast?"

"Sure. Get strawberry cream cheese and we'll get those

blueberry bagels. Red, white and blue."

"It's Thanksgiving. We can't have red, white and blue at Thanksgiving," Maggie protested.

"We got pumpkin ice cream. We don't have to eat orange and brown food at every meal, do we?"

"I guess not." Maggie pouted. She picked up the strawberry cream cheese and threw it in the cart. Anne rearranged some things and made sure that delicate items weren't being squished. "Are we done yet?"

"No. I think we're going to need to split up. It's getting harder and harder to get through this madhouse."

"OK. I'll get bagels. What other bread product do we need?"

"Bread crumbs if they have them or a really hard baguette," Anne replied. "I'll get wine and then loop around and get coffee. What kind of beans do you want?"

"Anything that's Fair Trade. Sumatran if they have it."

"OK. Let's synchronize our watches."

"Very funny." Maggie rolled her eyes.

Anne took the cart to the wider wine aisle, as Maggie made the move toward breads. They re-united a few minutes later.

"Is that it?" Maggie asked.

"Yeah. Now we just have to wait in line for a hundred years." Anne moved the cart into a line behind four other shoppers, and leaned her arms on the handle, stretching out her back.

"If you put the groceries away, I'll give you a back rub." Maggie rubbed her hand on Anne's back to give her a taste of what she was offering.

"Deal." Anne smiled at Maggie.

"I love you," Maggie said, leaning to whisper in Anne's ear.

"I love you, too." Anne placed a soft kiss on Maggie's lips, then pulled back a little self-consciously when she caught a glare from the woman in line behind them.

Maggie looked to where Anne had glanced. "You can stop staring," she said with a self-satisfied grin. "She's mine. And I don't share."

IT WAS A perfect day.

Maggie exited the freeway and headed down the El Camino Real toward Millbrae. The sun shone brightly in the clear blue sky and she rolled down the window, taking a deep breath of the cold air. It smelled of autumn in the bay area: dusty and minty, the smell of fallen leaves and eucalyptus bark. This favorite odor was mixed with the smell of two freshly baked pies on the seat beside her. She always brought pies to her family's Thanksgiving Day celebration, but this was the first time she'd actually made them — getting assistance from a horrified Jill who couldn't believe that a local bakery was Maggie's usual source.

"Making pies is the easiest thing in the world," Jill had promised. She'd said that about baking bread too, and Maggie was seriously questioning her definition of "easy." But with Jill by her side, it hadn't been too bad.

A bouncing football pulled Maggie out of her baking memories and she slammed on the brakes. She had just pulled into her old neighborhood. She should have been alert for flying footballs.

"Sorry!" her brother Liam shouted, waving to her as he retrieved the ball and threw it back toward Sean.

"Remember 1988!" Maggie yelled as she pulled up to the curb and parked. That was the year the neighborhood's annual football game had been interrupted by Mr. Sweeney, who had pulled out of his driveway and flattened their best football.

In recent years, only the Monahans were keeping up the tradition. But there was still a crowd gathered in the suburban cul-de-sac. The teams were boys vs. girls: Maggie's brothers Patrick, Michael, Liam, and Sean were playing against Patrick's wife Diane, Michael's wife Shelley, Liam's girlfriend Kate and a woman that Maggie didn't recognize, but assumed was Sean's latest "she's just a friend-friend" companion. Patrick's kids, Mark and Megan, seemed to be floating from one team to the other, giggling and screeching as their uncles tossed them around instead of the ball.

Shelley greeted Maggie at the car and helped her carry the pies inside. "Oh, my God," Shelly said as she placed the still warm pies on the counter. "These look homemade."

Maggie beamed proudly. "Yep, made with my own two hands. And a little help from a friend."

"Wow, learning how to bake. You know what they say about food and a man's heart."

I don't need a man's heart. I have Anne's. Maggie smiled, but felt a pang of regret that Anne wasn't standing beside her, meeting her family, beaming with pride at the homemade pies.

"So, Mary Margaret, I suppose you're going to go outside and play while your old man slaves away in the kitchen."

"Hey, Dad." Maggie turned and hugged her dad when he walked up behind her, giving him a peck on the cheek. She looked around the kitchen. "The turkey's in the oven and you're watching the parade on TV. Don't try to fool me."

"Well go out there and remind your brothers that Notre
Dame is playing in a couple of hours and I am not planning on
missing one minute of the game. So they better get their butts in
here."

"OK, OK, I'll go gather the troops."

The pandemonium of the football game was transferred
inside, although things did calm down slightly when the kids
were steered into the living room to sit with Grandpa. Growing
up, the Monahan kids would spend their Thanksgiving playing
until all of the neighborhood kids were called in to eat. Because
Connor always worked Thanksgiving for the overtime pay, the
kids settled for turkey TV dinners and store-bought pumpkin
pie. But when wives and girlfriends entered the picture, things
changed. Thanksgiving dinner was now a team effort and the
introduction of secret family recipes and lots of kitchen helpers
made it a culinary extravaganza.

Of course, the Monahan kids weren't the best sous-chefs in
the world.

"Michael, I said 'diced.' " Diane pointed toward two-inch
chunks of celery and onion. "The word 'diced' should give you
an idea of the size."

"And not the fuzzy ones hanging from your rearview
mirror," Maggie said.

"Where are the marshmallows?" Liam was searching through
cupboards.

"You are not putting marshmallows on top of my yams."
Shelley pulled a pot toward her protectively.

"Hey, last night I dreamt I was eating a giant marshmallow,"
Sean began.

"And when you woke up, your pillow was missing." Maggie
finished. "You've told that joke since you were six."

"And are you not smiling?"

"It's a grimace of pain."

The banter continued, the food was baked and boiled and
basted, everyone laughed. The happiness was buzzing through
Maggie like an electric current. She even teased Patrick and was
so shocked to see him smile she almost dropped the potato
masher.

They all helped bring the food to the table, Patrick carrying
the huge turkey. The grownups squeezed around the table and
the kids were seated at a card table to the side. A quick blessing
was said by Patrick, and then the family began to eat, Maggie
and the boys setting about the task in their usual efficient
manner.

Sean's friend, who Maggie had learned was named Dakota,

tried not to stare as food was shoveled into five mouths.

"Hey," Shelley said when she caught Dakota's terrified look. "You guys are scaring people. The food's not going anywhere."

"Notre Dame is playing in an hour," Patrick announced, as if that explained everything.

"Welcome to our nightmare," Diane said to Dakota, winking.

"I've only seen Sean eat like this on his own," Dakota said. "I had no idea what it would be like when the whole family ate like that. But I'm sure I'll get used to it after a few years."

Sean smiled and Maggie grinned. *So, the friend-friend is something more after all.* The ladies all seemed to pick up on the comment, and smiled and winked at one another. One more Monahan had been sorted out.

"So, Maggie." Diane—the head match-maker—turned her attention down the table. "When are you going to settle down?"

Anne's face seemed to float in front of Maggie. Her head was thrown back, her lips parted, her eyes hooded. It was a picture of ecstasy, a picture that had seared itself into Maggie's memory when they'd made love that morning. Maggie could feel the heat of her blush as it traveled across her face.

"Ooh, look at that blush," Kate crowed.

Maggie refused to look at Sean.

"Does this mean what I think it means?" Shelley asked excitedly. "Has our little Maggie finally met that special someone?"

Maggie was happy. Everyone was happy. Everyone loved each other. This was something she could share.

Sean coughed, but still Maggie didn't meet his gaze.

"Well..." This was something that she *should* share.

"Yes!" Diane clapped her hands.

"I have met someone and we've actually moved in together."

Maggie saw her father flinch. Connor had already lived to see three of his sons live together before marriage. But this was his daughter. *Oh, Dad, pre-marital sex is the least of your worries.* She grinned, feeling giddy.

"Who is he?" Kate asked. "How did you meet him?"

Everyone was looking expectantly at Maggie, all but Sean had a smile on their faces, happy and excited at her news.

"She's not a 'he,'" Maggie said proudly. "She's a 'she.' Her name is Anne and I met her at the county courthouse. I've never felt this happy in my life."

It had been a perfect day.

"SO HOW'S YOUR freshman Shakespeare class this year?"

Anne asked her father as she passed him the potatoes. "As brain-
dead as they are every year?"

"They're a bit challenged," her dad replied with a rumbling
chuckle. "I continue to be amazed at the lack of basic writing
skills some of these young people have. They were accepted by
Stanford University. They should be the cream of the crop."

"I blame it on television. How can you possibly string a
sentence together when all of your language skills came from
Barney?" Jill asked.

Anne listened as her parents launched into an amiable
discussion about the evils of television, and was once again
grateful that her divorced parents had always remained civil to
each other. In fact, they were so friendly when they were
together that Anne often wondered why they had split up in the
first place.

Anne was about to dive into the discussion and defend at
least some television programming when she glanced out the
dining room window and saw a car she didn't recognize pull into
the driveway. She squinted and tried to make out who was in
the car. The driver was definitely a stranger, but the passenger
was all too familiar.

"Shit," she said, interrupting her parent's conversation.
They turned and looked at her, then followed her gaze out the
window. They all watched as a very pale Maggie got slowly out
of the car.

"I need to..." Anne began.

"Go ahead, honey," Jill said, "I'll put some food away for you
guys for later."

Anne's dad nodded his agreement. Anne quickly smiled at
her understanding parents, and then rushed out of the house.

Maggie was halfway up the steps to the cottage when Anne
caught up to her. "Maggie, sweetheart." Anne tried to reach past
the man to get to her lover.

"Did you encourage her to do that?" he asked, placing
himself between Anne and Maggie. Familiar blue-green eyes
sparked with anger and Anne realized he must be one of
Maggie's brothers.

"What happened?" Anne asked, more to Maggie than her
brother. But the smaller woman didn't say a word. She stood in
the doorway, her eyes downcast, hugging herself tightly. Her
body vibrated with violent tremors.

"She told the family she was gay," the man explained. "Right
in the middle of Thanksgiving dinner."

"What did you people do to her?" Anne's voice was low and
full of venom.

"Don't!" Maggie cried suddenly, "Don't. Don't. Sean, it's not Anne's fault. I'm sorry. I'm sorry."

Anne's stomach clenched and she pushed forward past Sean, enveloping Maggie in her arms. For a moment, Maggie didn't move, standing frozen in the same position. Then she slowly unfolded her arms from around her body and attached herself to Anne. Sobs tore from her. Anne carefully led her into the cottage. She smiled apologetically at Sean and indicated with her head that he should come in.

Anne sat down on the sofa with Maggie in her arms. Sean sat down awkwardly in the chair across from them. Maggie's sobs were gut-wrenching, and Anne just held onto her, stroking her and telling her it would be OK. The emotional turmoil was sending waves of heat off of Maggie.

After about ten minutes, Anne turned to Sean and mimed drinking, then pointed to the kitchen. He nodded and left the room, returning with a cold bottle of water from the fridge. It took a few more minutes before Anne could get Maggie's attention.

"Sweetheart," Anne said gently, "calm down now and take a drink of water."

Maggie buried her head deeper into Anne's shoulder. Anne squeezed her tighter and held her for a few more minutes until Maggie's sobs subsided into hiccups.

"Come on, sweetheart, you'll make yourself sick. Take a breath and a drink. Please."

Maggie looked up with red, tear-filled eyes. She tried to take a deep breath, but she hiccupped again. Anne uncapped the water and watched as Maggie took a small sip.

"That's it, baby. It's going to be OK. You're home now. Everything's going to be OK."

Maggie's tears began again, running down her pale face. She said nothing, and her silence tore at Anne's heart. Maggie leaned her head back down against Anne's shoulder, and nuzzled into her neck. Anne wrapped her arms tighter around Maggie and just held her, rocking her slightly. After several more minutes, Anne could hear Maggie's breaths become even and deep.

"She's fallen asleep," Anne whispered to Sean. "I'm going to put her to bed. Then we're going to talk."

She stood up carefully and carried Maggie into the bedroom, placing her gently onto the bed and covering her with their quilt. She left the door open a crack so that she could hear if Maggie woke up, and then returned to the living room.

"OK, what the hell happened?" Anne asked gruffly. Her

hands were shaking, and she folded them into fists.

"It was a mess." Sean ran a hand through his short red hair. "It was a total fucking mess."

Anne looked at him sympathetically, and then handed him Maggie's bottle of water, which was still mostly full. He took a long swallow. "Everything was fine at first. We all helped get dinner. We were joking around, having a great time. When we sat down to eat, the ladies of the family started in on her. You know: 'When are you going to get a boyfriend, Maggie?' 'When are you going to settle down?' She started blushing. You know how she gets."

Anne smiled for a moment at the thought of her blushing lover. She was so innocent sometimes. She could picture Maggie at the dinner table, and the image tore at Anne's heart.

"So she just blurted it out, really," Sean continued. He smiled grimly. "Needless to say, the room went totally silent at the news."

"Why didn't you say something?"

"I didn't know what to say. It all happened so fast." Sean's chin quivered as he fought back tears. "I'm so sorry, Anne."

"It's OK." Anne rubbed at her face. "I'm just pissed off. I don't mean to take it out on you. What happened after that?"

"Dad got up and told Maggie to go into the kitchen. Patrick went in with them. We all just sat there. At first, Patrick yelled. Maggie yelled right back. She was great..." Sean trailed off.

"Who hit her?" Anne asked.

Sean jerked in reaction to the question.

"I saw the handprint on her face." Anne clenched her jaw.

"Maggie told Patrick he didn't control her life," Sean said with a tired sigh. "She said he was being a homophobic asshole who was poisoning his kids' minds with his hatred. I guess that's when he finally lost it and slapped her."

"And you all sat around doing nothing?" Anne asked in an outraged whisper.

"No! Liam, Michael and I were all halfway to the kitchen door when we heard Dad tell Patrick to take a walk and cool off. Patrick came out into the dining room, grabbed his kids and wife, and took them into the backyard." He added with a disgusted sneer, "As if they could catch something by simply being in the same room with Maggie."

"And then what happened?" Anne could feel a burning in her stomach, and folded her arms under her breasts.

"It got quiet. I could hear Dad's voice, but not what he was saying. Maggie didn't say a word. That lasted for just a few minutes, and then Maggie came out. She was pale and her eyes...it was like she wasn't there any more." Sean's own eyes had tears in them, and he wiped at them angrily. "She grabbed her bag and just walked out of the house. I followed her. There was no way I was going to let her drive like that."

"Thank you."

Sean nodded and wiped at his eyes again. "She never said a word the whole drive back here. Once we got to Berkeley, I asked her for directions. She pointed and nodded, but she still wouldn't speak to me. She didn't say anything until you came out of the house."

Anne nodded and realized she had been crying. She had no recollection of when the tears had started. "This is so fucked-up!" she cried in a strangled whisper. "How can her family treat her like that in her own home? This is just so completely fucked-up." Anne wanted to shout, but didn't want to wake up Maggie. She wanted to hit something. She jumped to her feet and started pacing the few steps possible in the small living room.

"No." Sean leaned back in the chair and looked up at Anne.

"What do you mean, 'no'?" Anne stopped in front of him.

"I mean no, it's not completely fucked-up. What Dad and Patrick did was horrible and evil and wrong. But she has you, Anne. You're her family. This is her home. You can fix this." He paused and looked at her with an intense stare. "Just love her."

Anne crumpled back onto the sofa at his words. "You're her family too, Sean."

"Yeah, and I won't give up on her. And Michael and Liam will be cool, too. I'm sure of it. I'll talk to them tonight. We'll bring her car back tomorrow, and if she's up to it, we'll take her out for pizza or something."

Anne smiled and was about to reply when she heard a low moan from the bedroom.

"I'll call tomorrow," Sean said, getting up and moving toward the door. "You go take care of her."

"Thanks." Anne moved toward the bedroom. She heard the front door click shut as Sean left.

"Anne! Anne!" Maggie cried out. Anne ran to the bedroom, slipping slightly on the hardwood floor.

"It's OK, baby. I'm here." She sat down and pulled the crying woman into her arms.

"Anne, he said...he said..." Maggie tried to speak through her sobs.

"Shh, it's OK."

Maggie took a deep breath and tried again. "He said my mother would be ashamed of me," Maggie said in a strangled whisper. "Do you think he's right?"

Anne had never hated — truly hated — anyone before, but at this moment she hated Maggie's father. The burning acid in her stomach erupted into the back of her throat, and she swallowed it down, taking a deep breath. She had to be strong now, for Maggie.

"He was wrong, Maggie. You know he was." Anne pulled away and took Maggie's face in her hands, looking into her eyes. "You are a wonderful, beautiful person. Your mother would be proud of you. She *is* proud of you, watching you from wherever she is. You know that. Try to feel her, Maggie. Listen to her."

She watched as Maggie's eyes focused inward. The smaller woman paused, and then took a deep breath.

"I feel her," she whispered. "She said she loves me."

Anne took the woman in her arms again, and rocked her softly. Tears fell from Anne's eyes, falling in soft drops into the red-gold hair beneath her cheek.

MAGGIE SPENT MOST of the night in Anne's arms, crying and then drifting off to sleep, only to be woken again by nightmares. She was listless the next morning, moving slowly through the house, her eyes empty of emotion, as if she had used it all up the day before. Anne's heart broke every time she looked at her lover.

But the arrival around noon of her three boisterous brothers brought the hint of a smile to Maggie's face. She was unsure about going out to eat, but they quickly persuaded her. Anne knew it would be a good thing for her lover, if only to get some fresh air.

Maggie had still been abnormally quiet on the walk to the restaurant, and never moved far from Anne's side. She would occasionally zone out, her gaze turning inward. Whenever this happened, Anne or one of her brothers would prod her out of it by a word or gesture.

"I think we should get two large pizzas," Sean proposed as they all sat down around a large table. "One stuffed spinach and mushroom and one thin pepperoni."

"Do you think that's enough?" Michael asked. Anne nearly laughed out loud, but then remembered she was sharing lunch with Maggie and three of her brothers.

"Let's get two orders of garlic bread, too," Liam suggested.

"Great. And salads for everyone?" Sean glanced around the table. Three red heads and one black one nodded back at him. He signaled the waitress.

Anne looked around the table. Liam, Michael, Sean and Maggie all had identical blue-green eyes—Liam's somewhat hidden behind wire-framed glasses. Each of the siblings had red hair, although all different shades. And each had a scattering of freckles over their fair faces, although Maggie's face was drawn and pale and dark circles shadowed her eyes.

"I'm just going to go to the ladies' room," Maggie said after the order was placed. Her voice was still gruff from crying.

"Do you want...?" Anne started to get up.

"No." Maggie smiled reassuringly at her lover. "I can manage. I'm all right."

Anne smiled back, and carefully watched until Maggie was out of sight down a side hallway.

"She looks like shit," Michael said when Anne turned back to the group.

"Better than when we first got here today," Liam pointed out.

"Is she OK, Anne?" Sean asked. "I mean, is she going to be OK?"

"Yeah, she's going to be OK." Anne looked into the three worried faces. "You guys showing up today and treating her normally has already made a huge difference. No matter what you might think about her sexual orientation, I'm glad you could put that aside and do this for her."

"I don't have a problem with it," Liam said. "I knew she was gay anyway."

"You did not, you dweeb," Michael said.

"I did too, moron."

Anne smiled at the two brothers. She expected them to stick their tongues out at each other. They probably would have, if the waitress hadn't arrived at that moment with their drinks.

"What about you, Michael?" Anne asked. "What do you think about it?"

"She's in love." Michael shrugged. "There's nothing wrong with love. It's all good."

Anne watched as the brothers exchanged looks and she realized that Sean had probably talked to Michael and Liam the night before and done a lot to get them over their initial reactions.

"You guys seem pretty open-minded. So, what's the deal with Patrick?"

She had obviously hit a nerve, as three sets of eyes suddenly found other things to look at.

Sean broke the silence. "It was hard for Patrick growing up. When Mom died, Dad couldn't stop working to take care of us, so Patrick had to become the man of the house. He didn't handle it very well."

"To say the least." Liam smirked.

"He just developed this superiority complex or something," Sean continued. "Like he was our master and teacher and priest all rolled into one. It was just the way he dealt with everything."

"He became obsessed with our morality," Michael added. "Especially Sean and Maggie, since Liam and I were older."

"And already a lost cause," Liam noted.

"Did Patrick hit you guys when you were growing up?" Anne's voice quavered as she remembered the handprint on her lover's face, and before that—the look in Maggie's eyes whenever she spoke of Patrick. She thought about questions that had never been answered; questions she had never asked.

"Patrick hit Maggie a few times," Liam replied, looking pained at the memory. Sean and Michael looked down at their plates. "Maggie drove him crazy. She just refused to be cowed by him. But Dad found out one day that Patrick had hit her and went off on him."

"Maggie once told me your dad strongly opposed physical violence," Anne said.

"That's right," Liam replied. "Patrick was too scared to hit her again after Dad found out. But Patrick still had control over us; he had other ways to get what he wanted."

"He sounds like a psychopath." Anne was happy to hear that the abuse had been stopped. At least Connor did something right. Not that it made up for what he'd done to his daughter the day before.

"No, Patrick's not crazy," Liam corrected. "He's just full of a lot of rage."

"That's complete shit." Michael's pale complexion turned ruddy with anger. "He's a fucked-up control freak and Maggie will be lucky if she never sees him again."

Anne noticed Maggie returning from the bathroom and titled her head slightly to get the brothers' attention. They all dutifully stopped the conversation.

"Were you guys talking about me?" Maggie looked at the guilty faces.

"Sort of," Sean admitted. "Mostly about Patrick."

"Oh." The little bit of color that had returned to Maggie's cheeks was suddenly gone.

"Subject change," Michael announced as the waitress arrived with their salads and garlic bread. "I want to know about you guys. How did you meet? I'm not into mushy stuff, but the wife is going to want to know all the details."

"We met in an elevator. Sort of." Anne smiled, happy to move the conversation in a new direction. She reached out and took Maggie's hand, giving it a comforting squeeze. "There I was, minding my own business, and there was the most beautiful woman in the elevator with me."

Maggie laughed, her expression relaxing just a little. "There were two people in that elevator. One was absolutely gorgeous and the other was a scrawny, redheaded cop. You figure out who was who."

"Hey, I'm the one who told you to eat your potatoes," Michael said.

"And I'm the one who told you coffee would stunt your growth," Liam added.

"Did she drink coffee even when she was a kid?" Anne laughed.

"Started when she was about twelve," Liam nodded. "Of course, it was more milk and sugar than actual coffee."

"She used to be so wired on the school bus in the morning that no one could get a word in edgewise." Sean laughed.

"She needed coffee to get like that?" Anne asked.

Maggie punched her in the arm. "I'm sitting right here. You don't have to talk about me like I was still in the restroom."

"So, going back to this elevator," Sean said, ignoring his sister. "You just started talking and that was that?"

"Um, no," Maggie admitted with a sheepish look. "Neither of us said a word to each other."

"Chicken shits!" Michael cried, making chicken noises and flapping his arms like wings.

"Guilty as charged." Anne blushed. "And two weeks later, I was in the cafeteria in the county courthouse, innocently buying lunch, when I noticed the same beautiful woman in line behind me."

"I didn't think you saw me," Maggie said in surprise. "You never even looked my way."

"I saw you before you saw me," Anne said with a guilty smile. "After that, I was so scared I didn't dare turn around."

"What were you scared of?" Maggie asked.

"I don't know. In the elevator, I felt this attraction to you. It was more than just 'woohoo, she's a hotty.' It was like a pull."

"Like a magnet," Liam offered. Anne smiled at him and he smiled back knowingly.

"But I completely fucked up and let you walk away," Anne continued.

"Or I fucked up and let you walk away," Maggie countered.

"You both gotta take equal blame on that one, I'm afraid,"

Sean said.

"And when I saw you again and I felt that pull again," Anne explained, "I just kept thinking about how much more I could fuck up, and how I really didn't want to fuck up. My rational mind said, 'just talk to her and ask her out' but my irrational mind said, 'she'll think you're a complete freak and you'll probably drool on yourself.'"

"Drool?" Michael said.

"It was my irrational mind," Anne pointed out.

"I felt exactly the same way," Maggie marveled. "Except I don't think I could have articulated it quite as well."

"That was well articulated?" Anne laughed.

"No," Liam, Michael and Sean said in unison.

"Shut up," the girls responded.

"I can't believe how silly we were." Maggie shook her head in amazement. "Thank God for Moocher."

"What role did she play in all of this?" Liam asked.

"When I couldn't bring myself to do it, she went up to talk to Anne in the cafeteria," Maggie explained. "She broke the ice, so to speak."

"Wow, you guys really were complete freaks," Sean said.

"Need I remind you of a certain love letter that you made me write for you when you were thirteen?" Liam said with an arched eyebrow.

"Ix-nay on the etter-lay," Sean said with a blush.

"Oh, no, no, no." Maggie looked curious. "I think I need to hear this story."

"If you've seen *Cyrano de Bergerac* or a certain episode of *The Brady Bunch*, you know the story," Sean replied curtly.

"To make a long story short, I wrote a great letter for his little girlfriend, and she agreed to go to the junior high graduation dance with him, but dumped him a week later," Liam explained.

"I ran into her a few years ago, though," Sean said, "and she told me she still had my letter."

"My letter," Liam corrected.

"Guys, stow it, pizza's coming," Michael announced, cutting off the impending argument.

The boys and Maggie all sat up straight and looked toward the approaching waitress. *My God,* Anne mused, *they look like soldiers getting ready to go into battle.* She continued to be amazed as the Monahans set upon the pizzas like efficiently programmed eating machines. No one spoke a word until the second slices were being parceled out.

"So," Sean said, "Anne showed obvious good taste by falling

in love with our sister..."

"Maggie showed her obvious gold-digger qualities by falling in love with a lawyer," Liam added, "despite her propensity for drooling..."

"And you both lived happily ever after," Michael concluded.

"Yeah." Maggie smiled broadly at her brothers, and then turned to Anne. "I'm not sure about the first two parts, but that last one is definitely true."

Anne felt relief flood her heart when she saw the sparkle return to Maggie's eyes. Forgetting their audience, the two women leaned together and exchanged a soft kiss.

"Oh, gross!" Sean yelled, covering his eyes in mock disgust.

"Get a room." Liam threw a wadded up napkin at the lovers.

"Hey, let them go for it," Michael said, "we'll eat all the pizza while they're distracted."

"Score!" The brothers cried in unison.

Anne and Maggie just kept kissing.

ANNE LAY HER head down on her pillow with a contented sigh. For some reason, the holidays were always the busiest time for her practice. So much for peace, love, and family togetherness, she thought. Families were far more inclined to fight when they were gathered around the turkey or the tree. Maggie's experience and Anne's current workload were proof of that.

Anne decided to put all of her unpleasant thoughts in the mental filing cabinet where they belonged. She focused her attention instead on the soft, warm, cuddly body next to hers.

"Are you tired, baby?" the soft, warm, cuddly body asked.

"Mmm hmm," Anne responded with a yawn.

"You're working too hard." Maggie frowned.

"And you're not? You're working double shifts, sweetheart."

"I have to; I took off Thanksgiving weekend, and now I'm asking for ten days at Christmas." She smiled wistfully "I can't believe we're going to Hawaii with Moocher and Roz."

"It'll be an adventure." Anne rolled her eyes.

"It's going to be fun." Maggie grinned. "Sun, sea, sand, alcohol — in no particular order."

"And you'll of course wear a thong for me?" Anne said with a teasing glint in her eye.

"Um, the answer to that question would be a huge, hairy *no*."

"Oh, come on Maggie. For me?"

"No. And, for special emphasis, I repeat — No. Not for you,

not for a million dollars, not if it meant saving the human race. I am not placing a strip of spandex into my butt crack."

"Not even to save the human race?"

Maggie paused. "Maybe to save the human race. If there was no one around except you, and you were wearing one, too." She considered that. "You know, you'd look much better in a thong than me. Your butt is way more beautiful than mine."

"Oh, please." Anne snorted.

"It is. Of course, we'd both have tan-line issues. Our butt cheeks are as pale as milk. People would think it was night and multiple moons had come out."

"You could start going to a tanning salon now," Anne suggested. "You have two weeks to get the perfect butt tan."

"You are absolutely insane. I am not tanning my ass and I am not wearing a thong. End of discussion."

"But, Maggie..."

"No."

"But."

"No."

"But."

"No, no, no. Zip it."

Anne stuck out her bottom lip.

"Zip it, and put away that face. I am not caving in on this one."

"OK," Anne agreed reluctantly. "It's probably a good idea if you don't wear a thong in public, anyway. Everyone on the beach would probably fall in love with you instantly, and I'd have to fight to keep you to myself."

"Shyeah, right." Maggie sneered.

"It's true." Anne leaned down and kissed Maggie softly. "It'll be hard enough as it is without the thong."

The corners of Maggie's mouth turned up in a small smile. "You're crazy. You know that?" she asked softly.

"Yeah, I'm crazy in love." Anne bent again to plant a firmer kiss on Maggie's lips. Her fingers reached under the edge of Maggie's T-shirt, searching for warm skin. As her tongue slipped between Maggie's lips, she felt the smaller body next to her stiffen, and she pulled away.

Two weeks had passed since Maggie had come out to her family during Thanksgiving dinner. She was almost back to normal. She laughed and joked and teased like she always did. Only sometimes would her gaze turn inward, usually at the mention of Christmas activities—which was why Anne was thrilled to be able to take her away from the Bay Area for the holidays.

But making love was still a problem for Maggie. They had done nothing beyond kissing and cuddling since Thanksgiving. Maggie would never initiate anything, and when Anne tried, Maggie would stiffen and pull away. Anne didn't know how to react. She certainly didn't want to push Maggie, but wondered if pushing was exactly what Maggie needed.

"I'm sorry," Maggie said.

It was the first time Maggie had said anything about how she felt, and Anne stroked her face, trailing her fingertips down Maggie's soft cheek. "There's nothing to be sorry about, baby." Anne hoped to encourage more words from her lover.

"I just..." Maggie's mouth remained open, but no words came out.

"What, sweetheart? Tell me what you're thinking."

"I just..." Maggie didn't get any further and her face scrunched up in frustration. Tears welled in her eyes.

"Oh, don't cry, sweetheart. Please don't cry." Anne felt tears sting her own eyes. She reached out and caught a tear as it fell from Maggie's blue-green eye. "Turn over; let me cuddle your back."

Maggie complied, and Anne spooned around her, her right arm wrapped around Maggie's waist, and Maggie's head tucked under her chin. This was their favorite sleeping position.

"I've got you, baby," Anne said, squeezing Maggie in a hug and kissing the top of her head. "You're going to be all right."

"I don't feel all right," Maggie whispered.

"How do you feel?" Anne whispered back, holding Maggie tightly.

"Dirty." Maggie's voice quavered. "Wrong."

Anne closed her eyes in anger, and was glad that Maggie couldn't see her. She needed to be strong, to say the right thing. She had no idea how to do that. Then she felt Maggie tremble in her arms, and she decided to wing it. "Is our love dirty and wrong?" she asked, trying not to sound hurt.

"No," Maggie replied emphatically, but she trembled harder. "No, I know it's not, but they made me feel so dirty and wrong and evil. Most of the time I can ignore it." Her words were flowing now. All of the frustration and pain was being expunged, and Anne held her tightly. "But when you touch me, there's something in my brain that brings the feelings back. It's like they put this switch inside my head that I have no control of. They control it. They control me."

She started to cry again, and Anne pulled her hip, encouraging her to turn back around. When she did, Anne wrapped both arms around her and hugged her close. She waited until Maggie's tears slowed down and her breath became a little easier.

"They do not control you, Maggie." Anne debated briefly about how to proceed, and quickly made a decision. *No second guessing*, she told herself firmly.

"Feel this hug," Anne continued. "Is this hug wrong?"

"N-no." Maggie squeezed tighter and snuggling her face into the soft skin above Anne's breast.

"Tell me what you feel when I hug you."

Maggie paused. "I feel warm and loved. I feel protected. It feels like home."

Anne smiled and kissed the top of the red-gold head. "I feel the same way." She let the hug continue for a moment, and then put a finger under Maggie's chin, lifting her head. She placed a soft kiss on Maggie's lips.

"Is that kiss wrong?" Anne asked softly.

"No." Maggie began to tremble again. "It's not wrong."

Anne waited, and Maggie tilted her head up again and kissed Anne more firmly.

"It's right," Maggie said when she drew back from the kiss. Her voice still shook, but a spark glimmered in her eyes.

Anne reached down and carefully caressed Maggie's breast, feeling the nipple harden through the thin cotton of the T-shirt. "This is not wrong," she said firmly, as her fingers danced and stroked. "This is right. This is good."

"Yes." Maggie closed her eyes. Her body moved instinctively into Anne. The trembling continued, but now love and desire, not fear, was the source.

Anne's hands moved down to the bottom of the T-shirt and once again sought out warm skin. She slowly pulled the T-shirt up and over Maggie's head, and then lowered soft lips to her breasts. She paid close attention to Maggie's responses, ready to slow down or move away at the slightest sound or feeling of discomfort. But Maggie's moans were only pleasurable ones.

"This is right," Anne said, after several moments of loving Maggie's breasts, and stroking her softly. "This is good."

"Yes," Maggie moaned. "This isn't wrong." She gasped, as Anne's hands moved below the waistband of her pajama bottoms.

Anne's fingers slowly teased, tickling her upper thighs and trailing through her golden curls. Maggie's need grew quickly, and she growled in frustration when Anne's fingers continued to tease.

"This is right," Anne repeated firmly. "This is clean. This is pure. This is divine."

"Yes," Maggie moaned, as Anne's fingers finally reached into her inner folds and stroked the warm, velvet flesh.

"Yes," she repeated, as fingers entered her and began a steady rhythm that thrummed through her soul.

"Yes!" she cried, as the orgasm ripped through her.

"Yes," she whispered breathlessly. Falling back into Anne's arms, she drifted off to sleep, wrapped in love.

Chapter
Twelve

"HEY, THIS PLACE is great. Look at that view!" Moocher was nearly bouncing off the walls as she ran through the condo. It was a beautiful timeshare owned by Roz's parents, built into a cliff above a private beach in Kauai. Thanks to a last-minute cancellation, the condo was open for the Christmas and New Year holiday, and the four friends had quickly arranged a dream vacation.

"This is a sofa bed," Moocher said, hopping on the couch to test its resiliency. "That'll come in handy if one of us gets kicked out of the bedroom."

Maggie and Anne had collapsed onto a loveseat that was positioned to provide a view over the ocean. They were both exhausted from working overtime prior to their holiday. Anne had even gone into the office that morning and only stopped working when she was in danger of missing the flight. Now, they snuggled and enjoyed the view, and marveled at Moocher's energy.

"Where's Roz?" Maggie realized she hadn't seen the woman since soon after they'd arrived.

"She's unpacking and making sure that the house is all set up," Moocher replied. She got off the couch, trotting across the room with an excited grin on her face. "I'm gonna check out the kitchen."

"She's making me tired just watching her," Anne mumbled, settling into the comfortable loveseat and shifting the warm body in her arms.

"Mmm," Maggie agreed wordlessly. "She slept the whole flight; no wonder she has energy."

"You could have slept, too, if you hadn't been so intent on joining the mile-high club."

Maggie grinned at the memory.

"Hey, there's food in the fridge!" Moocher yelled from the kitchen, "and some booze. It should get us through tonight until we can go grocery shopping first thing tomorrow."

Maggie and Anne were too tired to respond. It also would have been a little difficult, since their tongues were otherwise engaged in a little wrestling session.

"You think that sounds like a plan?" Moocher asked as she walked out of the kitchen, still grinning like a demented clown.

"Yeah," Anne replied.

Maggie was glad her lover answered.   She'd already forgotten the question.

"So we can either hit the beach or the pool right away." Moocher moved toward the windows and looked down at the pool directly below her and the beach farther down.

"Whatever," Maggie replied tiredly. Anne just grunted.

Moocher turned to them and placed her hands on her hips. "Since we planned this four weeks ago, I have been salivating in anticipation of seeing Anne in a bikini," she said indignantly. "If I have to wait another minute, I'm probably going to explode."

Maggie snickered. She couldn't blame Moocher one bit for her desire.

"What about seeing Maggie in a bikini?" Anne asked.

"Old news," Moocher said dismissively. "Shit, I've seen her covered in nothing but whipped cream. And I'll share that story with you if you get your bikini on and your ass outside. I'll grab the beers."

"What about Roz?" Maggie asked. "Is she ready to go out?"

"I'll go ask her." Moocher moved toward the stairs. Her face softened and she called out in a voice that could only be described as sweet. "Honey?"   She climbed the stairs to the bedroom in search of her lover.

Maggie and Anne exchanged glances.

"What is the deal with her?" Anne asked.

"I think it's alternate-universe Moocher. Did you notice her hair is parted on the other side?"

"I think I'm going to lapse into a coma from the sugar overdose." Anne smirked.

"Speaking of sugar, give me some," Maggie demanded, reaching up and tangling her fingers in Anne's hair. She pulled down with a gentle tug.

"Are you guys just going to sit there and suck face the entire time we're in Hawaii?" Moocher asked as she clumped down the stairs a few minutes later. Roz followed, wearing a swimsuit. Her skin glistened from recently applied suntan lotion.

"Moocher, be nice," Roz softly scolded.

Moocher instantly looked contrite. "Sorry," she said to Roz, and then turned to Anne and Maggie, "Sorry, guys."

Maggie had never seen a contrite Moocher. It left her feeling a little disoriented, like the time she'd seen her first grade teacher walking into the Hotsy Totsy Cocktail Lounge. It just wasn't right.

"OK, that's it." She stood up so she could gesticulate freely. "Roz, something horrible has happened. I'm afraid Moocher has been replaced by a pod person. I'm not sure when it happened, but this imposter is not Moocher. She's an alien look-alike. The real Moocher is just not this sweet, loving, or downright nice. Now, just be very careful and step away from her slowly."

"It's three against one," Anne said, playing along. "I'm sure we can overpower it."

Moocher scowled at them, crossing her arms over her chest. "Ha ha. Very funny." She snarled. Roz giggled at her lover's predicament.

"You see," Maggie said, "aliens don't have any concept of what we earthlings call 'humor.' More proof that she's not who she pretends to be."

"I think there's only one way to prove that she's an alien." Anne got up and moved with Maggie toward Moocher.

"I agree," Maggie replied.

"You guys are the aliens." Moocher looked around for an escape route. "You're communicating telepathically."

"Submersion in H2O," Anne suggested. "If she's an alien, she'll melt."

"That's the fucking Wicked Witch," Moocher said, moving away.

"Oh." Maggie stalked her prey. "She's learned our cultural references. Very good."

Anne and Maggie continued to step forward slowly, and just as slowly, Moocher inched toward the stairs. Roz, still standing on the lowest step of the staircase, continued to giggle. Suddenly, Moocher bolted, and Anne and Maggie sprang after her a split second later. She would have gotten away if she hadn't met a tall, solid body in her path. Roz held onto her until Anne and Maggie arrived. The three took possession of a squirming Moocher.

"Don't you dare do this," Moocher squawked. "I'm a trained police officer. I could get out of your hold, but I don't want to hurt you."

Maggie took advantage of a bare spot of stomach and gave it a tickle.

Moocher squealed.

"That doesn't sound like the response of a trained police officer," Maggie said with an evil grin. "More like the prize pig at the state fair."

Anne, Maggie and Roz managed to get Moocher up off the floor; they carried her outside and down the concrete steps to the pool. Moocher continued to rant, rave, and shriek all the way down. When she saw the tile surrounding the edge of the pool, she squealed louder.

"Hey, I think you just hit a note that the greatest opera singers rarely achieve," Anne commented.

"This is not funny," Moocher said indignantly.

"Sorry, honey, but I'm afraid it is." Roz was still giggling.

"One," Maggie shouted, starting the swing.

"Two," Roz said.

"Three," Anne finished, and Moocher flew through the air in an ungraceful arc, arms and legs flailing. She landed with a huge splash that got everyone wet.

Moocher spluttered to the surface and silently swam toward the three laughing women. She said nothing as she approached the side of the pool. She reached out her hand and Maggie bent down to take it, only to be met with a prodigious spray of water in the face.

"Ewww, you spit on me." Maggie wiped her eyes. "I hope you've had your shots."

"You deserved it," Moocher said as she clambered out of the pool. "That was cruel, and I will have my revenge. When you least expect it, expect it."

"OK, we're well and truly terrified," Anne said in a bored voice. "Now can we all get wet?"

There were grunts of agreement all round.

"You guys go get changed," Roz said. "I'll see if I can find some chairs and pool stuff."

After a few minutes, three pairs of bare feet slapped against the concrete, and then three bodies hit the water simultaneously. Roz threw in a giant inflatable whale and dove in after it. The ladies played a highly competitive round of Marco Polo for a while, until Anne and Moocher decided that lying in the sun was preferable to swallowing more chlorine-flavored water.

"She looks so much better than she did a few weeks ago." Moocher nodded toward Maggie, who was wrestling with the whale.

"Yeah." Anne sighed. "She's doing a lot better."

"I don't know what she would have done if she didn't have you. Thank God you were there."

"If she didn't have me, she probably wouldn't have come out to her family at all." Anne frowned.

"You're not blaming yourself for this, are you?"

"I don't know. I felt so helpless. I just wish I could have been there with her... I don't know." Anne blew out a frustrated sigh.

"You were there for her when she came home," Moocher said firmly. "You were there for her every day since. You are the best thing that's ever happened to her."

"I need to take better care of her." Anne sighed again and looked at Maggie, playing in the pool.

"She's not an invalid and she's not a child," Moocher said, poking Anne in the ribs. "You don't need to take care of her. Just be supportive. Just love her."

"Yeah," Anne replied, not really agreeing.

"I have to say, though, when I heard what happened I wanted to drive to Millbrae and beat the shit out of her dad and brother," Moocher said with an angry scowl.

"You and me both. But it wouldn't have changed anything. They'd still be homophobes and we'd just have sore knuckles."

"Yeah, but it would have made me feel really, really good."

"I hear you." Anne smiled as she pictured her fist connecting with a nose.

"What are you guys talking about?" Maggie asked suspiciously, and swam toward Anne and Moocher.

"Whether we should leave cookies or pineapple for Santa Claus tomorrow night." Anne laughed when Maggie's eyes lit up like a kid.

Roz swam over, obviously intrigued by the Santa mention.

"We are in Hawaii," Moocher said. "It seems a shame not to share some of the local delights."

"What about coconut cookies?" Roz suggested.

"Does Santa like coconut?" Anne asked.

Moocher licked her lips.

"Yeah, I think Santa likes coconut." Maggie laughed.

"Speaking of Santa," Anne said, "did you open the present from your brothers?"

"Yeah," Maggie replied with a small frown. "It was really strange. It was a Star Trek T-shirt. I don't even like Star Trek that much."

"Did it have a picture or writing on it?" Anne asked.

"It had the Star Trek logo on the front, and on the back it said 'To boldly go where no man has gone before.'"

Maggie floated at the edge of the pool while three people guffawed in her general direction. Moocher nearly lost a lung.

"What's so funny?" Maggie looked as if she would have stomped her foot if it wasn't a few feet from the bottom of the pool.

"Maggie, sweetheart," Moocher said. "When we go to the store tomorrow, you might want to look into purchasing a clue."

"Don't worry," Anne added with a chuckle. "I got her one for Christmas."

"You guys are pissing me off," Maggie hissed.

"Maggie, they used the slogan at this year's Dyke March in San Francisco," Roz said, taking pity on the pun-challenged.

"Why?" Maggie asked, a furrow developing between her brows as she thought through the phrase. "Oh," she finally mumbled. She slowly sank, letting the cold water soothe the burning blush.

MAGGIE WRIGGLED HER butt, creating a little dip in the sand under her towel. She rested her chin on her knees and sighed contentedly as she gazed out to sea, where the sun was just beginning to turn the clouds a soft salmon color. She turned her head and gazed at the huge package sitting next to her, wrapped in Scooby-Doo Christmas paper. She sighed again, this time in frustration, and turned to look at Anne, who was fully reclined on the big beach towel. "Can I open it now?"

"No, not yet," Anne replied without opening her eyes.

Maggie looked at the box for a few more seconds. "How about now?" she asked hopefully.

"No."

"Now?"

"Maggie, if you're not good, Santa will take it back and give it to another little girl."

"Will you tell me what it is?"

"No." Anne opened her eyes and glared at her excited girlfriend. "You'll be able to open it in a few minutes, as soon as the sun hits the sea. We agreed, right?"

"Is it a toaster?"

"Maggie."

"Jumbo pack of toilet paper?"

"Maggie."

"Folding bicycle?"

"OK, I'm leaving a note for Santa with the coconut cookies tonight. It'll be gone by the time you wake up."

"Anne, has anyone told you you're no fun?" Maggie asked with a pout.

"Yes." Anne closed her eyes again. "Lots of people, lots of times."

"Oh," Maggie said, wondering if her teasing had gone a little too far. "Anne?"

"What?" Anne snapped.

"You are fun, really." Maggie reached over and rubbed Anne's bare stomach, from bikini top to bikini bottom. "You're more fun than the huge cardboard box the refrigerator came in when I was five. You're more fun than putting a salamander in Jenny Poletti's lunchbox. You're even more fun than diving off the balcony into the pool."

"Please tell me you didn't dive off the balcony into the pool." Anne's eyes opened in shock.

"OK. Anne, I didn't dive off the balcony into the pool this morning when Moocher dared me to, and I wasn't responsible for that huge splash that got your trashy paperback all wet."

"You did it when I was going to the toilet, didn't you?" Anne narrowed her eyes accusingly.

"It wasn't that big a deal," Maggie explained with a dismissive shrug. "There was this little sign on the balcony that said, 'Owners are not responsible for any injuries sustained by individuals diving from this balcony into the pool below.'"

"And that didn't clue you in to the fact that it might be dangerous?" Anne sat up to look directly into Maggie's eyes.

"I just figured that meant that it was possible. Otherwise, why'd they have to put the sign there?"

"They put the sign there because some fool probably tried it before and cracked her skull open."

"Hey, I figured if something happened, at least I had a good lawyer. We had a loophole. The sign said they weren't responsible for people diving into the pool. They didn't say they weren't responsible for people missing the pool and landing on the concrete."

"That is not funny." Anne scowled.

Maggie looked into Anne's eyes and saw a glint of fear. She placed her hand on Anne's upper arm. She could feel Anne tremble under her fingertips. "Hey." Maggie waited until Anne met her eyes. "I'm sorry. I didn't think about getting hurt. Moocher and I dare each other to do stupid things all the time, we just—"

"It's OK. I'm just over-reacting."

"No, you're not over-reacting." Maggie gave Anne's arm a comforting squeeze. "I shouldn't have done it." She smiled, trying to lighten the mood, "Besides, we could have ended up in the emergency room on Christmas Eve. That just can't be fun."

Anne's mouth creased in a small smile.

"And red is really not my color," Maggie added.

"I don't know. I think you'd look good in red...something silky and skimpy."

"Like an erotic Santa costume?" Maggie suggested.

"Yeah." Anne ran a finger softly down Maggie's arm, "a sexy Mrs. Claus outfit."

"Is that what you got me for Christmas?" Maggie asked excitedly, gazing once again at the box.

"Maggie, why don't you take your eyes off the present and watch the sunset with me?"

Maggie turned back to Anne just as the sun dipped below a cloud layer. A beautiful mixture of pink and golden light illuminated her lover, as if God was casting her in a spotlight. The sight took Maggie's breath away and she froze, gazing at the perfection of Anne's face.

"Beautiful," Maggie whispered. She took a shaky breath and then reached out tentative fingers, delicately stroking Anne's face. Her fingers danced lightly over arched eyebrows, across a high cheekbone, down the gentle slope of her nose, and across the soft lips. Just as Maggie began to pull her hand away, Anne reached up and captured it, drawing it to her mouth and softly kissing the fingertips. Maggie made a small sound, halfway between a whimper and a groan. The two lovers moved together and met in a slow, searching kiss. They each claimed the other's soul, as their breath mingled and their hearts beat to the same rhythm.

Maggie pulled away and lay down, tugging on Anne's arm.

"You're missing the sunset," Anne said softly.

"Don't care," Maggie replied just as softly.

"What about your present?" Anne nestled against Maggie.

"You're all I need." Maggie placed a soft kiss at the pulse point on Anne's throat. "You're the best present I could ever hope for." She gazed into Anne's clear blue eyes. "Thank you for giving yourself to me."

"I'm yours. Forever."

"I CAN'T BELIEVE we've been here over a week; I don't want to go home." Maggie scrunched up her face in frustration.

"Let's just stay here the rest of our lives." Anne pulled Maggie back against her chest and kissed the back of her head. They were seated on the condo's balcony, sprawled on a lounge chair, Maggie nestled between Anne's longer legs.

They both sighed simultaneously as they looked out over the sea. The moonlight danced on the waves, and billions of stars glimmered in the sky, winking down at them as if sharing a private joke. Anne held tightly to Maggie and tried to hold tightly to the moment, not wanting it to slip away.

"This has been the best Christmas I've ever had," Maggie murmured.

"For me too." Anne nuzzled a sunburned ear. Maggie hissed at the sensation of cool lips on sensitive skin.

"I can't believe you got me a teddy bear for Christmas," Maggie said, turning to smile at the toy, which was sitting proudly in a patio chair next to them. "I love him."

"What about the earrings?" Anne asked, pulling lightly on one with her teeth.

"Oh, yeah, I like those, too," Maggie replied, in mock flippancy. Anne blew a soft breath through her nose, which tickled Maggie's ear. "Hey, don't snort in my ear."

"Sorry." Anne moved her lips to the nape of Maggie's neck and nibbled teasingly on the soft skin. "I love my pen, too."

"Give it its proper name," Maggie ordered solemnly.

"Sorry. I love my 'I'm a very important lawyer pen.' "

"That's better." Maggie smiled, then leaned forward and purred slightly when Anne hit a particularly sensitive spot.

"OK, ladies," Moocher called out, carrying a bucket of ice through the sliding door onto the balcony. "Get your hands, teeth, tongues, and big toes off of each other. It's time to ring in the New Year."

"Oh, goodie," Maggie said. She and Anne jumped up to help Moocher and Roz bring out various bottles of alcohol and mixers, as well as glasses, chunks of fruit, and little umbrellas. They set up a makeshift cocktail bar on the white plastic table.

"So, what are we drinking?" Anne asked, reaching for a bottle of Vodka. "Who's up for Sex on the Beach?"

"Well, you and Maggie should be quite familiar with that," Moocher replied, never one to miss an opening.

"You pervert," Maggie said. "Have you been watching us?"

"Oh, like you didn't have your eyes glued to the window when Roz and I were playing in the pool," Moocher said with a snort.

"You burst the whale," Maggie protested. "I thought it was some kind of explosion."

"There was an explosion all right." Moocher leered toward Roz, who swatted her on the arm.

"Isn't it amazing that we've spent more than a week together and we've hardly seen each other?" Anne commented.

"Well, I've certainly heard her." Moocher pointed at Maggie. "I'm surprised we haven't experienced the second coming of Christ. She sure screamed his name enough times in the past week."

Maggie blushed and glared at her friend. "I hate you," she

said, sticking her tongue out for extra emphasis.

"Kids, stop fighting." Anne handed out the cocktails and sitting back down on the lounge chair. "Here, get your lips around these babies."

Maggie took her drink and then sat down again between Anne's legs. Moocher took up an identical position between Roz's legs on the other chair

Moocher took a sip of her drink and her eyes widened. A slow smile spread across her face. "Ooh, Anne, quit your day job and become a full-time bartender. You'll make more money on tips than you can as a lawyer."

Anne laughed and sipped her own drink. She heard a slurp next to her, and realized Maggie had already made it to the bottom of the glass.

"Whoa, partner, slow down there. The night's still young and you're only a little thing."

"I was thirsty," Maggie said with an impish smile. She held out her empty glass, and Anne poured her an orange juice. "Hey!"

"I'd rather you weren't comatose at midnight. I want to give you a special New Year's kiss."

"You've got her pegged," Moocher said. "I could tell you some stories of little Maggie and alcohol..."

"Don't you dare." Maggie's eyes narrowed with menacing intent.

"Hey, that's a good idea," Roz said. "How about playing a little Truth or Dare?"

"Great idea!" Moocher cried enthusiastically.

"Yeah!" Maggie agreed.

"No way." Anne held out her hands. "No dares. You two are insane, and it'll all end in tears."

"OK, how about Truth or Truth?" Moocher suggested.

Anne looked intrigued at that suggestion. "OK, I think I could get into that." She smiled at her lover and began to formulate questions.

"What are the rules?" Roz asked, sucking a pineapple off the end of her little umbrella.

"We play Rock-Paper-Scissors to see who goes first," Moocher explained. "That person becomes the questioner, and can ask a question of anyone. If their chosen victim refuses to answer, the victim has to drink a shot and the questioner gets to ask another question—of the same person, or someone else. If the victim answers, they become the questioner."

"I guess it's one of those things you'll pick up as you go along." Maggie leaned forward intently.

"Before we start, I want that bear removed." Moocher snarled, pointing at the offending animal. "It keeps friggin' staring at me."

"He's not an 'it', he's a 'he,' " Maggie said indignantly.

"I thought it was a 'she,' " Anne said. "I bought her—I mean him—to be a companion to Ambassador Squiggles. Mr. S was getting a little lonesome since he has to sleep on the shelf now."

"Oh, I think he and Ambassador Squiggles will form a very intense relationship," Maggie said. "But don't let your prejudice show.   There's nothing wrong with same-sex couples, you know."

"My mistake. So, have you decided what to name him?"

"His tag says his name is Truffle," Roz said, picking up the bear and looking at his butt.

"That's not his real name," Maggie replied.   "That's like when they named slaves Toby or Chicken George."

"You are the queen of freaks." Moocher shook her head. "So what's his real name? Kunta Kinte?"

"No." Maggie sniffed. "It's Field Marshall Fluffy, actually."

"And that's better than Truffle?" Moocher asked.

"I think it's a lovely name," Roz said, straightening the bear's little knit scarf.

"You're all freaks!" Moocher cried. "I'm going to sell you to the next circus that comes to town."

"I don't think Ringling Brothers does that kind of thing any more," Anne said with a chuckle. "Let's play Truth or Truth. I want to see what dangerous little secrets we can reveal."

Moocher grabbed the bear from Roz's hands and threw him through the open sliding glass door into the living room, ignoring Maggie's squeal. "OK, Maggie and Anne go first. Fists out, you two," she ordered.

After three rounds of Rock-Paper-Scissors, Anne found herself in the driver's seat. She flashed an evil smile at Maggie. "My question is for Maggie," she said, leaning her head down and around so she could look into her lover's face. "Maggie, how did you end up naked and covered in whipped cream?"

"So...it was a shot of our choice, right?" Maggie reached for the tequila bottle, trying to ignore Anne, who was grinning at her from very close range.

"Anne, I can't believe you went this long without getting that story out of her." Moocher laughed. "You should have tried giving her a noogie. Gets her every time."

"I'll have to remember that." Anne watched as Maggie shook salt on her hand, licked the salt, took the shot, and finished with a bite from a lime slice.

"Expertly done," Roz commented. "Let's see you do that after ten shots."

"Let's find out. Ask her more questions that she doesn't want to answer," Moocher suggested.

"I get another question, don't I?" Anne asked, batting her eyes innocently.

"Yep, you're still up, my friend. Fire away."

"OK, my question is for Moocher," Anne said calmly. "Moocher, how did Maggie end up naked and covered in whipped cream?"

"That's not fair!" Maggie shrieked.

Anne snorted and looked at her lover, who was trying to mortally wound Moocher with her eyes. She was suddenly glad that Maggie didn't have super powers.

"Well," Moocher said, ignoring Maggie's glare, "at the end of your rookie year, you have a special meeting with your training officer and the captain. You have to dress up and sit there while they go over your performance for the past year. The night before Maggie's big day, a few of us took her out for drinks to celebrate."

"How many shots did she have then?" Roz asked.

"We lost count." Moocher grinned. "My date was drinking strawberry daiquiris—don't ask—and as I stared at the little dollop of whipped cream, I was struck by divine inspiration."

"She gets mean when she's drunk," Maggie said. "Be warned, Roz."

"We waited until Maggie was pretty much toast," Moocher continued. "The details are still a little blurry, but I remember stopping at the 7-Eleven and buying all the squirt cans of whipped cream they had."

"I woke up in the men's locker room at the station," Maggie said. "Covered in nothing but whipped cream."

"All she had to do was run across the hall to the lady's locker room," Moocher said with an innocent shrug.

"Yeah, just run across a hall that was always full of people," Maggie said. "I did manage to find one dirty towel, which I wrapped around my waist."

"Did you just go for it?" Anne asked, running her fingers through Maggie's hair to make up for laughing at her.

"I took a quick peek, and thought the coast was clear." Maggie winced at the memory. "So I just ran."

"As fast as her short, stubby legs would go," Moocher added. "We were standing casually in the hallway, waiting for her body to come zooming across."

"Couple of things I didn't realize, though." Maggie looked

chagrined. "First, that whipped cream melts very quickly when it gets hot; and second, that madly dashing while dying of embarrassment tends to really elevate your body temperature."

"She also didn't realize her training officer was going to choose that moment to walk down that particular hallway," Moocher said, prompting guffaws from Anne and Roz.

"Oh, you poor thing." Anne feigned sympathy while she tried to stifle her giggles.

"Don't try to pretend this isn't the funniest thing you've ever heard." Maggie pulled her head away from Anne's fingers, and turning it to give her lover an angry glare.

Anne offered an apologetic kiss.

"So what happened?" Roz asked.

"She froze," Moocher related. "Like a little wide-eyed, spindly-legged, cute-as-a-button doe in the headlights of an eighteen-wheeler. Her training officer just nodded and said, 'Morning, Rookie,' and kept walking."

"I got cleaned up and dressed as fast as I could," Maggie said.

"After chasing me through the locker room like a banshee," Moocher added.

"I then went to my meeting and pretended that the whole incident had never happened."

"Did he say anything?" Anne asked.

"Not exactly," Maggie replied, "but when he was commenting on my performance, he'd say stuff like 'she's very cool under pressure' or 'she's got tremendous assets' and he'd get this twinkle in his eye. The captain must have wondered why I was literally glowing red. My blush was so bad I think I raised the room temperature ten degrees."

"And the moral of the story is: never drink so much that you can't stop yourself from being stripped and covered in whipped cream." Moocher looked at her friends, her eyes twinkling with mirth. "Who's ready for more Sex on the Beach?"

They mixed the drinks and sipped for a while, still laughing at the story. Anne resumed playing with Maggie's hair and made plans for properly introducing her lover to the positive side of whipped cream.

"I can't believe we're wearing shorts and bathing suits on New Year's Eve," Maggie said, leaning into the head massage.

"Yep, in just a few more days I'll be back in a business suit and nylons," Anne grumbled.

"Moocher and I will be back in uniforms."

"Yeah, I'll be back in, um, lycra shorts and sports bras." Roz scratched her chin. "OK, I guess I don't have it so bad in terms of work clothes."

"That's OK, baby," Moocher said, patting a bare leg, "you have to work out with gorgeous women all day, watching them sweat and talking to them about their muscles. Just think about me sometimes when you're touching some woman's glutes."

"No one has better glutes than you, sweetheart." Roz reached to squeeze the muscles in question. Moocher squirmed away from the groping fingers. "I think it's your turn, babe."

"OK." Moocher tapped a finger to her lips and thought for a moment. "Roz, who was the first person you fell in love with?"

"I suppose you want me to say that I never truly felt love until I met you," Roz said, grinning at Moocher. "But I refuse to say something so cloyingly sweet. Besides, I fell hopelessly in love with Jennifer Cochran when I was seventeen."

"I always hated the name Jennifer." Moocher scowled.

"We worked together at Penney's," Roz continued. "She was older than me, maybe nineteen. And I'm sure she was straight, though I never dared ask her. In fact, I barely said a word to her. I used to just live for the days when we were both assigned to the lingerie department. I would sit there and stare at her while she straightened the bras and panties. Sometimes she'd run her fingers over the lace of a bra, or the silk of a slip, and I'd nearly faint."

"You never said anything to her?" Maggie asked, remembering her own experience of being in lust from a distance.

"We'd chat about work sometimes. She mentioned a boyfriend once, I think, but she was vague about him. Then, at the end of the summer, I quit and went away to college. I never saw her again."

"I'm sure she was a total bitch who would have used you and then left you crying in a ditch somewhere," Moocher said forcefully.

"Jealous much?" Anne laughed.

"It's OK, honey," Roz said, placing a kiss on Moocher's cheek, "I'm sure you're absolutely right. Now it's my turn to ask a question. So, babe, did you ever have a crush on someone you worked with?"

Moocher considered for a minute, and then fixed herself another drink. "Yeah, I did." She leaned back against Roz and took a sip of her cocktail. "There was this girl who joined the force after I'd been there for a while. I was attracted to her the minute I laid eyes on her. She was absolutely beautiful, in this sort of uncomplicated, adorable way. She had a wonderful sense of humor. Shit, she laughed at my jokes, so obviously she did."

Moocher's eyes were unfocused as she looked into her memories. "She was a true dichotomy. She had street smarts about some things, but was utterly naïve about other stuff. She swore like a sailor, but she blushed when I talked about sex. I knew she was attracted to women, but she never talked about a girlfriend. She was always tough and professional at work, but I once caught her crying after arresting a twelve-year-old punk. She told me it broke her heart because she knew his life was already wasted. I think that was the day that I truly fell in love with her."

Anne looked at Moocher while she spoke and felt a tingle of suspicion. She looked at Maggie, who was listening intently to her friend's story.

"Did you tell her how you felt?" Roz asked, gently massaging Moocher's shoulders.

"No, not really. I guess I was too chicken shit at first. Then, after a while, I realized that I needed a best friend more than I needed a lover." Moocher shrugged and thought about it a minute. "I love her, there's no doubt about it. I would do anything for her. I would die for her."

Anne felt Maggie twitch slightly when Moocher changed tense.

"She is my best friend," Moocher said, looking directly at Maggie. "And no matter what happens, I know she always will be."

Maggie unfolded herself from the chair and moved toward Moocher, who stood up to give her a hug. Anne looked over at Roz, who smiled and leaned toward her.

"Who knew they'd get all soppy when they got drunk?" Roz whispered.

"Hey, less of the snarky comments," Moocher said as she squeezed Maggie. "We're having a mushy moment here."

A reply was on Anne's lips, but she was interrupted by the sound of fireworks exploding nearby.

"Shit, we're missing New Year's." Maggie wiped the tears from her eyes.

"Happy New Year!" Moocher bellowed. She grabbed a horn that she'd brought in with the drinks, and blew on it, forcing out an obnoxiously loud bleat. "OK, let's forget the stupid song and have a group hug."

Her friends needed no further prompting, as they greeted the New Year tangled in each other's arms.

Chapter
Thirteen

"A PACKAGE ARRIVED for Maggie," Jill said as she helped Anne and Maggie carry their luggage into the house. It was raining hard, and they dashed quickly between the car and the cottage.

"For me?"

Maggie's eyes lit up with excitement, but Anne felt a tightening in her stomach. She had no reason to have a bad feeling about the package, but her body obviously had its own logic.

Jill smiled at the young woman's eagerness and ran to the main house, bringing the package back as quickly as she could.

"There's no return address," Maggie said.

Anne looked suspiciously over Maggie's shoulder and saw that the package was addressed to "Mary Margaret Monahan." She felt a strange sensation on the back of her neck and knew, if she were a wolf, her hackles would be rising.

"Let me open it," Anne said quietly but firmly.

"It's not a bomb." Maggie grinned. "I can't hear it ticking."

Maggie looked up and met Anne's eyes and Anne knew her eyes betrayed the anxiety she felt. Jill looked from Maggie to her daughter.

"Let Anne open it, sweetie," Jill said softly.

Maggie nodded, agreeing with them both, and handed the box to Anne. Anne went to get a small knife to cut the tape and then carefully opened the package on the coffee table. She looked inside and didn't at first understand what she was seeing.

"Oh." It was a soft exhalation more than a word. Anne looked up to see Maggie staring into the box, her eyes full of pain. "It's the toys I sent to Mark and Megan."

Anne suddenly realized what the box contained: a dismembered Barbie, her clothes and accessories torn to shreds, and what appeared to be the smashed pieces of a radio-controlled car. "That fucking asshole."

Anne heard her mother take a sharp breath, but she wasn't reprimanded for the outburst.

"Is there a note?" Maggie asked.

Anne looked inside and saw a piece of white paper at the bottom of the box. She could make out a few words: bitch, dyke, pervert.

"No," she replied, holding the box out of Maggie's line of sight. It was the first time she had ever lied to Maggie, and she didn't regret if for a moment.

"I thought he would let the kids have their presents." Maggie's voice sounded so lost. "Couldn't he at least let them enjoy Christmas?"

Jill moved forward and took the box from her daughter's hand. "I'm just going to get rid of this mess."

Anne gave her a grateful smile, then looked helplessly at Maggie.

Jill leaned close as she passed on her way out the door. "Just love her," she whispered in Anne's ear.

Anne moved to Maggie and put her arm around trembling shoulders. She led her lover to the sofa. They sat and Anne waited for tears or words to come.

"He always knew how to push my buttons."

Anne nodded, happy that Maggie had chosen words. It was better to talk about things, get them out in the open. Of course, it was now her turn to respond. And she struggled to find her own words.

"Your brothers told me that you drove him crazy when you were growing up," Anne said. Maggie shrugged, and Anne knew she needed to say more. "They said he hit you."

Anne could feel Maggie's body stiffen. She continued to hold on.

I should have asked her about this months ago, the first time I saw that haunted look in her eyes when she spoke about her brother.

Anne swallowed the guilt. She could let it consume her later. She needed to focus on Maggie. "It was more than just a few swats and slaps, though, wasn't it?" she prodded, worried when Maggie remained silent. "Sweetheart, talk to me."

"I can't." It was an agonized whisper and it tore at Anne's heart.

"Yes, you can," Anne said, making sure Maggie could feel the safe arms around her. "He can't hurt you."

"Yes, he can hurt me. He always knew how. When he hit me, he knew how to do it so the bruises wouldn't show. And when Dad found out, he was even more careful. He learned how to hurt me in other ways, too. Like this. He knew this would be torture for me. He will never stop hurting me."

Maggie's voice was becoming more and more hysterical, and Anne rocked her, shushing her softly.

"I will not let him hurt you," Anne vowed softly but firmly. "I will never let him hurt you again. Nothing will ever hurt you. I swear on my life."

Anne continued her promises, repeating them like a litany until Maggie's relaxing body signaled an understanding and belief in her partner's words.

"I love you." Maggie whispered.

"I love you too."

The words were simple, and comforting, and all they needed.

TWO WEEKS LATER, after fighting off colds that they'd both picked up on their return to the Bay Area, Anne and Maggie's life settled into a comfortable routine. Despite continuing to work long hours, they managed to spend quality time together in the evenings, as well as an occasional shared lunch. Before meeting Anne, Maggie had usually worked graveyard or swing shift—three to eleven p.m.—but she and Moocher both realized that this didn't work well with their partners' schedules. They had requested a change to an earlier shift and the request had finally come through.

The first day that Maggie arrived home before Anne, she arranged a surprise. When she heard the sound of tires on the gravel driveway, she was actually well prepared. She lit the candles she'd set out on the coffee table and then ran to check the lasagna in the oven.

The lasagna was ready, but the oven mitts were nowhere to be found. Maggie frantically searched, finally remembering they were in the laundry just as the car alarm chirped outside. She dashed to get them, then hurried back, her footsteps echoed by the creak of the front steps. The front door opened just as Maggie pulled the big glass dish out of the oven and slid it onto the stove.

"Shit!" she cried as her palm brushed the hot pan.

"Nice greeting," Anne teased as she shoved her briefcase behind the sofa and threw her keys on the little table by the door.

"Sorry," Maggie cried out, running in from the kitchen. "I burned my hand."

"Well, put it under the tap." Anne walked up to Maggie and

pushed her firmly back into the kitchen.

"It's not that bad. I was rushing so I could greet you at the door like the dutiful wife in a sixties sitcom."

"Well, you can be dutiful in a minute. First, run your hand under cold water."

Anne moved to the sink and turned on the water and then held Maggie's hand under the flow, wincing as the little burn turned red.

"I need to fix you a dry martini or something," Maggie protested.

"I hate martinis. A nice glass of wine and some of that yummy-looking lasagna will be just fine."

Anne yawned, and Maggie noticed the signs of exhaustion in her face—lines of tension around the corners of her mouth, bloodshot eyes, and the tense set of her jaw. They were both mostly over their colds, but Maggie was afraid that Anne would have a relapse if she didn't stop working so hard.

"You look tired, sweetheart," Maggie said softly.

"I heard from Simone today," Anne replied.

Maggie tried to read Anne's emotions from her face, but her lover's expression was carefully neutral. She decided neutral was a good idea. "Oh?"

Anne didn't reply for a moment. Then let out a deep sigh. "Let me go change and I'll tell you all about it over dinner."

"OK. Then you'll let me be dutiful."

"Sure. I can get into dutiful." She lifted her chin and her blue eyes went cold. She raised an imperious eyebrow. "Bring me wine and food, slave," she ordered in a low, menacing growl.

Maggie felt the hair on her arms rise and a tingle creep up her spine. She was overwhelmed by an interesting mixture of fear and lust. "Um." Her voice actually cracked, and she cleared her throat. "You do slave-master really, really well."

Anne smiled, her face returning to its normal demeanor. She playfully swatted Maggie's butt as she walked out of the kitchen. "Then hurry up or I'll have to bring out the whips and branding iron."

"Ooh, would you?"

ANNE PUT HER plate on the coffee table and leaned back into the couch. She sighed and rubbed her full stomach. "That was delicious, baby."

"Well, I had a little help, actually," Maggie said with a sheepish grin.

"Oh? Did Mom give you lasagna-making lessons?"

"Not exactly." Maggie's eyes flitted around, and then finally met Anne's. "She actually made the lasagna and I just baked it."

Anne gasped in mock outrage.

"Well, I was the one who had to figure out when it was done," Maggie continued defensively. "And I burned my hand taking it out of the oven." She held up her wound for extra sympathy points.

"Well, I suppose you have to start somewhere. You did a fantastic job of putting it in the oven and taking it out again, aside from your little mishap. And your skill at turning on the oven and setting the temperature was amazing."

"Thank you." Maggie smiled proudly. "I must say, lining up the numbers with the little mark was tough."

"At the rate you're going, in a few years you may even be able to use the stove."

"Oh, now, don't go too crazy. The stove is dangerous."

"I'll be there with you the whole time," Anne said. "I'll make sure no spattering oil burns you or anything."

"I can see it now: you'll force me to wear one of those asbestos suits."

Anne laughed at the image.

Maggie smiled but then grew pensive. "So we've done a pretty good job of ignoring the subject of Simone." She turned to Anne, waiting for the reaction.

"Yeah."

Maggie sighed inwardly, and realized she was going to have to do most of the work. "What did she say?"

"Pretty much the same old thing. She wants Katy back, she's hired a lawyer, and she's contacted the Perkins family — Katy's foster parents. I'm going to have to get in touch with them soon and see if they want me to represent them, or at least get them the name of someone who can do the job."

Maggie remembered all of the things she'd said before about the situation and how horribly they'd gone over. But she felt strongly about the subject, even more so now that her niece and nephew had been ripped away from her through ignorance and hatred.

"Anne, I know you feel strongly about Simone not ever seeing Katy again," Maggie began carefully.

"And I know how you feel about this, sweetheart."

There was tension in Anne's words, and Maggie could see the struggle in Anne's eyes to remain reasonable, to not fly off the handle as she had before.

"It's just that—"

"Maggie, no." Anne's eyes flashed blue fire. "I don't want to argue about this again. I know that you compare your life to Simone and Katy, but it's not the same. This isn't the story of a little girl who's been separated from a mother that loves her."

Maggie wanted to ask what it was, then, but she didn't want to fight, couldn't bear to see the anger in Anne's eyes. "OK." She reached out to stroke Anne's hand, which trembled under her touch. "You do what you need to do."

"I HEARD YOU got a call from Simone yesterday." Jill gestured for her daughter to enter her office and Anne complied, sitting in the visitor's chair.

"She's a crazy bitch." Anne rolled her eyes. "I contacted Joanne Perkins, and they've already hired an attorney: Lucinda Gutierrez."

"She's good." Jill sucked on her pen, a habit that she shared with her daughter. "Anne, you know I never liked Simone. And I will never forgive her for what she did to Katy."

"Mom, you are not going to defend—"

"No," Jill interrupted, meeting her daughter's angry blue gaze. "There is no excuse at all for what she did. And if it were up to me, I would never give her custody of Katy again."

"But?" Anne's eyes softened only slightly.

"But," Jill continued, "neither I nor you is in the best position to decide whether Simone has turned her life around."

"I know her better than anyone," Anne snapped. "I know she should never be given custody of Katy. And I'll do anything I can to stop it."

"Well, I trust you to do what's right." Jill leaned back in her chair. "What does Maggie think about all of this?"

"She doesn't understand," Anne replied dismissively.

"Look, I know you had a fight about this back in November when Simone first reappeared in your life."

Anne blew out a frustrated breath. "I told Maggie the basic facts then. But she doesn't know Simone. She believes in some fantasy world where every mother should be with their baby so they can all live happily ever after. She can't possibly understand the situation."

"Sweetheart, she's a cop. I'm sure she understands the situation. She's probably seen it quite a few times in her career."

"She listened to the facts and jumped to a simple solution. She doesn't know what it was like to--"

"To feel what you felt?" Jill interrupted. "Doesn't understand what you went through emotionally when you walked into the apartment that day? Did you tell her?"

"Yes, I told her."

"You said you told her the facts," Jill prodded. "You mentioned telling her 'the facts' a couple of times. But did you tell her your feelings? What you went through emotionally?"

Anne opened her mouth to answer, but realization caught up to her before her excuses. Her mouth shut with a click and she grimaced.

"I didn't think so," Jill said with a knowing grin.

"I guess I'd better try again, huh?"

"I think so."

"It's just so hard."

"Why, honey? Tell me why it's hard."

Anne opened her mouth to reply and once again had no words She shrugged helplessly.

"Anne, you look at Simone and Katy as your failure. As something you were responsible for."

"They almost died." Anne remembered that afternoon and, as always, horror filled her mind. "I should have been there for them."

"Anne, I've told you before, you were not responsible for Simone's life. You can be loving and supportive to your partner, but only to a point. If they want to ruin their lives—even if they are set on killing themselves—there is nothing you can do about that."

"What about Katy? She was just a baby. It certainly wasn't her fault that her mom was a junkie."

"No, but you had no way then of protecting her," Jill replied. "She wasn't your child."

"I should have done something." The guilt ate at Anne, just as voracious as it had been two years before.

"You did do something. You got there and got Katy out in time. You helped find her a new home and kept in touch with her to make sure she was doing OK. Now, you're going to make sure that Katy stays in a safe, loving environment."

Anne nodded. Her mom was right. She was back in control of the situation.

"So what's the problem?" Jill continued.

"What do you mean?" Anne furrowed her brow.

"Why can't you talk about this with Maggie?"

The control that Anne had felt evaporated like water thrown on a hot griddle. "Maggie just doesn't..."

"Understand? Yes, you've said that before." Jill's gaze held Anne's, pinning her to the chair. "And I've already established that's bullshit. So try again."

Anne felt like she had when her mom had smelled alcohol

on her breath after a high school party. The cough medicine excuse had gone over just as badly. Anne was facing the same problem as she had at sixteen. She had nothing else to offer. "I don't know."

Jill sighed and smiled, and Anne realized admitting ignorance was way better than the surly shrug she'd come up with as a teen.

"Maybe it's because Simone reminds you of something you see as a failure, and you're afraid that the same failure will happen with Maggie?"

"Maggie is nothing like Simone," Anne said quickly.

"That's true, in most respects." Jill nodded. "But you feel responsible for her, just like you felt responsible for Simone and Katy. Right?"

"Yes," Anne replied readily. "I can't stand to see Maggie hurt. This stuff with her family has been horrible. I'm so glad I can help her through it. I swear I will never let her get hurt like this again."

"Oh, sweetheart." Jill shook her head. "Listen to yourself. You can't stop anyone from getting hurt. Life doesn't work that way."

Anne did as her mother told her and thought about what she'd said. She knew where her mom was coming from. She'd had similar conversations with Jill before. Anne knew she took too much onto her shoulders. But sometimes other people needed that, needed her help. If she could offer that help, she'd do it, no matter how hard it was. Her shoulders were broad and strong.

"I know what you're saying," Anne said slowly. "I know I couldn't stop Maggie's family from hurting her. I can't change the way people think. But I should have been there for her, or told her not to go in the first place. There are ways I can protect her, and I've sworn to her that I will."

"OK." Jill frowned. "So, if all of that is true, why not talk to Maggie about it?"

"I have," Anne said, remembering her vow to Maggie to keep her from harm. "I just have trouble talking about Simone."

"I think you should try. Try to explain how you feel, not just your action plan. And then try to listen to what Maggie has to say. You may be surprised."

"OK." Anne nodded. "I'll try."

"Good." Jill grinned, her eyes twinkling. "And remember, making up is always fun."

"Oh, yeah." Anne smiled back, already imagining making up with Maggie.

Anne left her mom's office and returned to her own, thinking about what had been said. She knew she should talk to Maggie about the situation. Then again, if it just ended up hurting them both—reminding Anne of that horrible afternoon and Maggie of losing her mother—maybe it was best that they leave it as a taboo subject. Once she'd helped the Perkins family keep Simone out of Katy's life forever, then she'd try to talk to Maggie about everything. Until then, they'd just work on the making up part.

MAGGIE GAZED ACROSS the hills and breathed in the clean, fresh air. It was scented with bay and pine, and reminded her of her dad's aftershave. The memory made her wince and she pushed it away quickly.

It had rained for two weeks straight, but today the sky was a sharp blue, only an occasional fluffy white cloud floating along lazily like a sheep trailing behind the larger flock. It was a perfect day for mountain biking. Just enough mud to make you feel like you were alive. Hanging out with your best friend. She really should be happy. Anne had apologized, right? Everything was OK, right?

"Are you going to take all day to change that tire?" Maggie asked, her voice a grumpy whine.

Moocher looked down at her flat tire. "I'm trying to figure out if there is actually a tire under all this mud." Moocher pulled up some weeds to wipe away the muck. "You want to explain to me why you're in such a pissy mood?"

"I'm not in a pissy mood," Maggie snapped.

"Oh, OK." Moocher rolled her eyes. "Then you want to explain to me why you're in such a great mood?"

Maggie didn't reply and Moocher stared at her. Maggie met her gaze, trying to look innocent, but it didn't take long before she broke. "Anne and I sort of had a fight," she mumbled, looking away from Moocher.

"I see," Moocher said, putting her hands on her hips. "It's time for another pep talk, isn't it?"

Maggie just shrugged. She wanted someone to make her feel OK. As much as she loved Moocher, she didn't think her friend was up to the Herculean task.

"What was the fight about?" Moocher asked.

"Simone."

"Oh, Jesus." Moocher sighed. Maggie had told her about Anne's ex soon after the encounter in Anne's office. "What does the bitch want now?"

"Nothing new, just wants her daughter back. It drives Anne crazy and she won't talk about it. I want to figure out what's going on inside her head, but it's painful for her and I don't want to push her to tell me all the gory details."

"Well, that's understandable, Magpie. But gory details are part of the relationship deal. They're mandatory—like foot rubs and cleaning up your partner's puke."

"Ewww." Maggie scrunched up her face.

"Ewww, indeed, my dear, but still part of the partner contract."

"I don't remember signing anything to do with puke."

"Oh, it's in there. Sub-paragraph 999. Listed under things that you don't always want to do, but have to."

"OK." Maggie grinned. "I'll take your word for it."

Moocher grunted and turned back to her flat tire. "OK, so the bitch wants her kid back and Anne is going all super-lawyer on her ass. What's the big deal?" Moocher looked up from the bike when Maggie didn't reply. "Oh, I get it. You think that Simone getting Katy back isn't such a bad idea?"

"Not necessarily," Maggie shrugged. *Oh, God, it is so much more than that, but how can I explain it?*

"And Anne and you 'sort of' had a fight about it?" Moocher prodded. She must have seen the pain that comment evoked, and she hurriedly added, "But you guys made up, right?"

"Yes, we made up." Maggie smiled at the memory. They still hadn't spoken in detail about Simone, but they had definitely made up.

"And did Anne convince you that everything was going to be OK?" Moocher narrowed her eyes. She looked ready to go after Anne if the apology didn't meet with Maggie's full approval.

"Yeah, she convinced me, all right. In fact, she used her powers of persuasion all night. It's a wonder I have enough energy to make it up these hills."

"OK, over-share." Moocher held up a dirty hand.

"But Moocher, you used to beg for details of our sex life," Maggie said with a teasing grin.

"That was before Hawaii." Moocher shuddered. "I heard noises coming from your bedroom that curled the hair on my toes."

"You did not." The rush of blood into Maggie's face stopped suddenly when Moocher failed to keep a straight face. "Bitch!" Maggie stuck her tongue out at her friend.

"Ha! I had you going there for a second." Moocher continued to work on the tire, trying to get the tread pulled from the rim, but it kept slipping from her fingers and she muttered a long and creative string of expletives.

"Do you need some help with that?" Maggie asked, not making any move to help her friend.

"No, no, I've got it." Moocher stubbornly shook her head.

Maggie watched Moocher extract the tube from the tire and throw it aside, then run her finger along the inside of the tread. She made two full circuits and then growled.

"I can't find anything," she grumbled.

"Oh, for fuck's sake, give it to me. You've got hands like a sailor." Maggie reached over and took the tire from Moocher. She ran her fingers carefully along the tread, quickly discovering the source of the flat. She extracted the small bit of metal and threw it into the bushes. "Got it," she announced, handing the tire back to Moocher.

Moocher inflated the new tube slightly and then fitted it between the tread and the rim. She got the tube fitted but had problems reseating the tread. "Maggie," she whined.

Maggie didn't say a word, just held out her hand for the tire. She quickly worked the tread back onto the rim. When she was finished, Moocher handed her the pump.

"You want me to pump it up as well?" Maggie asked indignantly. "What did your last slave die of?"

"Need I remind you that I have two year's seniority on you?"

"That's at work, not in the real world." Maggie crossed her arms but relented when Moocher began to pout. She sighed and took the pump. Maggie worked the pump for a minute, and then felt around the tire to make sure the tube was inflating evenly. Satisfied that it felt OK, she pumped some more until she began to struggle.

"Here, let me finish it off." Moocher pumped several more times and then replaced the tire on the frame.

"Speaking of work," Maggie said slowly, "I meant to tell you. I'm thinking of asking for a leave of absence." She waited for a moment, then continued, forcing an upbeat lilt to her voice. "I've been thinking of reevaluating my goals. Maybe I'm not in the right profession."

Moocher remained silent, bent over the bike. She finished reconnecting the brakes, then rose slowly and turned to Maggie, her expression completely blank.

"Can you please repeat everything you just said, because I think you were possessed for a second," Moocher said calmly. "Your head didn't spin all the way around, but there was definitely some nasty goo flying from your mouth."

"I'm just wondering whether I'm really cut out to be a cop."

Maggie still refused to meet Moocher's gaze. "Maybe if I take
some time off I'll decide to stick with the police. Or maybe I'll
decide I want to be, I don't know, a teacher...or something."
Maggie's voice trailed off and she became very interested in a
loose thread on her bike glove.

"Where the hell is this coming from?"

"I don't want to upset Anne. I love her so much. She's been
hurt so many times before by people who claimed they loved
her. She wants me to be happy and to be safe. I'm just thinking
I should do something to ensure that will happen."

"So she told you she wants you to quit?"

"No, she hasn't said anything like that," Maggie said
quickly. "I know Anne wants me to be happy. She wants me to
do what's right for me."

"As long as it's right for her as well?" Moocher asked
sarcastically.

"What's that supposed to mean?" Maggie frowned. "We're
partners. Remember that contract you were just talking about?
Of course we need to make decisions that are right for both of
us."

"Manipulating you into going against everything you
believe in is not the same as making a decision that's right for
both of you!" Moocher snapped, finally losing her temper
completely.

"She is not manipulating me!" Maggie shouted back.

"Maggie, you wanted to be a cop all your life. Why would
you want to quit now?"

"I wanted to be like my father all my life," Maggie corrected,
tears springing to her eyes. "I thought he was a superhero. I
thought if I could be like him, I could be a hero too. Now,
whenever I see myself in uniform, I think of Dad and Patrick,
and I realize what a load of shit it all is."

"Oh, Maggie, you are a hero. You're the best cop I've ever
known. I have learned so much from you—about compassion
and respect and treating people fairly. Think of the hundreds of
people you've helped." Moocher walked up to Maggie, who had
buried her face in her hands. Tears seeped between Maggie's
dirty fingers.

"Your father and brother can rot in hell," Moocher spat.
Maggie took a breath and began to protest, but Moocher
continued. "I don't care that they're family. I hope they contract
some painful, lingering illness and are left out in the desert so
the buzzards can eat their eyes out. I swear I have never wished
death on anyone before. But they are scum."

"Moocher—"

"No. I don't want to hear you defend them. What I want you to understand is that they are twisted and evil people. You are goodness and light. Maybe you were motivated to become a cop because of your dad. That doesn't matter now. What matters is that you became a cop and you are a good cop. Don't throw that away because of him. And don't throw it away because you think it's what Anne wants."

"I love her." Maggie wiped her eyes with the terrycloth sides of her biking gloves.

"I know you love her, you doofus," Moocher said with a fond smile. She waited until Maggie looked her in the eye. "And I know that your love can get you over this mess. You've got to get past her fears and your pain. I mean, listen to what you've been saying. You don't even seem to understand all of the motivations behind this decision. If you don't get this straightened out, it's going to tear you guys apart."

"That's why I thought about quitting the force. If I could find something that I like doing—"

"Maggie! You're missing the point," Moocher interrupted. "Changing your life because it's something that Anne wants— correction, something that you *think* Anne wants—is not the answer. It may solve some issues in the short term, but it's going to make your life hell in the long term. Trust me on this."

"I don't know," Maggie said softly. "I just love her so much."

"Yes, we established that already. Or is there an echo here? You love her and she loves you. But remember this: she fell in love with a cop—a beautiful, smart, funny, crazy cop. That is who you are, and if she really wants to change that, then you've got to wonder whether she really loves you at all."

Maggie gasped. "How can you say that?"

"I hope I'm wrong." Moocher held up her hand just as Maggie was ready to grow fangs and go for Moocher's throat. "I'm actually quite sure I'm wrong. What I'm also sure of is that she will love you so much more if you remain true to yourself and who you are. And I know she'll give you the strength to get beyond the pain caused by your dad and Patrick."

"I need to talk to her about this." Maggie drew in a deep breath.

"No shit," Moocher said with a grin. "I sense a hell of a lot of gory-detail sharing in the foreseeable future. What are you guys doing for Valentine's Day?"

"Um, I don't know." Maggie frowned in confusion at the subject change. "Anne asked me to keep next weekend clear. I think she's planning a surprise."

"Nice little romantic getaway, huh? You'll be relaxed,

connected.   Add a little wine, maybe some chocolate—perfect time for a sensitive chat."

"Yeah." Maggie sighed and smiled.   "I think you're on to something."

"And speaking of sensitive chats, I think that was the last pep talk I have in me. Race you to the bottom of the hill?"

"Race, huh?" Maggie brushed her hands against her shorts, then picked up her bike.

"Yeah," Moocher replied, taking a drink from her water bottle.

"You're on!" Maggie jumped on her bike before Moocher had replaced the bottle.

"Bitch!" Moocher jumped on her bike and clipped in. She pedaled fast to catch up to Maggie, skidding in the mud. "If I ever said I liked you, I lied!"

"THANKS FOR BUYING me lunch, honey." Jill smiled at her daughter as they walked out of the café, arm in arm.

"Well, I have to throw you a bone once in awhile. Makes it easier when I ask you for something."

"Ah-hah, I knew you had an ulterior motive."

"Actually, I do have a favor to ask. I have to run an errand, and I'd love your company.   I need your opinion about something."

"Sure, lead on." Jill released Anne's arm and motioned ahead of her.

Anne pointed left down College Avenue, and they headed along the busy sidewalk, looking into shop windows as they ambled. It was only a few days before Valentine's, and Anne had the upcoming weekend all planned. She'd told Maggie to keep the weekend free, and, without telling her, booked a room in a bed and breakfast in Mendocino. It would be a lazy, loved-filled weekend away.

She smiled as she breathed in the cool, fresh air.   The weather was finally beginning to turn and Anne noticed some buds just beginning on the trees that dotted the avenue. After the trauma of the holidays and the tough start of the year, Anne felt that her life was settling in.   She shared the love of a wonderful woman.   Despite their difficulties, she felt like anything was possible. The first signs of spring were a life-affirming omen.

"Are you going to ask me for this advice or just keep walking down College Avenue with a goofy smile on your face?" Jill grinned affectionately at her daughter.

"Patience is a virtue," Anne replied, saying nothing more until they reached a small shop. "We're here."

"Where?" Jill looked up at the shop's name, carved in a wooden sign above the front window. "David and Sons' Jewelers." Jill looked curiously at her daughter, who motioned her inside.

The jewelry store was small but filled with a stunning collection of handcrafted, one-of-a-kind pieces. Anne approached one of the glass display cases, smiling at the older man who stood behind the case.

"Ah, back again." The man greeted them with a friendly grin. "Brought someone for a second opinion?"

"Yes," Anne replied. "My mom."

"Perfect. Moms always have the best opinions — sometimes whether you like it or not."

"Oh, I hear that." Anne smiled at her mom, who looked curiously toward her daughter. Anne turned to the jeweler. "You know the one I'd like to see."

"Yep." The man unlocked the back of the glass display case and removed a ring. He handed it to Anne, who took it carefully and turned to her mom.

"Wow." Jill took the ring from Anne and looked at it closely. "It's absolutely beautiful."

The ring had two strands of yellow and white gold, intricately intertwined and knotted around a diamond. It was incredibly delicate and absolutely stunning.

"So?" Anne asked.

"So?" Jill turned the ring and watched the diamond reflect the light. "You want my opinion? Well, I think it will make a wonderful Mother's Day gift."

The jeweler chuckled as Anne gave her mom a long-suffering look.

"I'm getting it for Maggie," Anne explained. "I'm going to ask her to be mine, in a sort of 'till death do us part, sickness and health' kind of way."

"You're going to ask Maggie to marry you?" Jill blinked slowly.

"Well, if the people who made laws weren't a bunch of homophobic bastards and it was actually possible for two women to get married, then, yes. Call it what you want, but in my universe I'm asking the love of my life to marry me. I'm planning to propose on Valentine's Day. Can you believe your daughter is actually that much of a romantic mushball?"

Jill looked at her daughter and then stared blankly at the ring.

"Mom, opinion required here." Anne waved her hand in front of Jill's eyes. "Do you think she'll like the ring?"

"Um, well... I mean, of course she'll like it, but, I mean..."

"Was there a 'yes' in there somewhere?"

Jill finally found her voice. "Anne, I think we need to talk about this."

"May I suggest the window seat?" The jeweler pointed in the direction of the bench seat that was currently bathed in sunlight. "In my experience, it's perfect for the kind of conversation that I think you two are going to have."

Jill met his eyes and they exchanged a knowing look. She handed him the ring, then took her daughter by the elbow and walked toward the bench.

"OK, Mom, what are you thinking?" Anne frowned.

"Anne, before I say anything let me first say that I consider what you're ready to embark on to be as morally binding as a legal marriage. You're making a lifetime commitment that you'll be obligated to make work forever, through good times and bad. That's a lot different than living with someone, as far as I'm concerned."

"I agree with you." Anne nodded her head emphatically. "This is it, the whole marriage enchilada. And I intend to swear to it in front of friends and family, as soon as we can arrange something."

"Anne, slow down," Jill said, holding up her hand.

"What do you mean, slow down?" Anne snapped. "I thought you'd be pleased. Shit, I thought you'd be ecstatic. Is it because we're lesbians? It's OK for us to live together, but not get married?"

"No!" Jill said forcefully. She looked around the shop, but the only other occupant was the jeweler, and he had moved to a back room. "No, this is not about you being gay. You know me better than that."

"Then what is it?" Anne felt a mixture of hurt and confusion. "Mom, you're the one who told us we're like two sculptures that are meant to be together. Or don't you remember that?"

"Yes, Anne, I do remember." Jill reached up and moved a stray lock of black hair behind Anne's ear. "I believe that your destiny is to be together forever. And I am ecstatic for you. I'm just having trouble getting my point across."

"And what is your point?"

"OK, let me try this another way." Jill took a steadying breath. "I want to tell you a story, a true story about two other souls that were meant to be together. At least, I thought so. I won't pretend that it's the story about two strangers, because it's not. It's the story of your father and me."

"Mom, just because your marriage failed, doesn't mean that ours will, too," Anne interrupted with a scowl.

"I know that, sweetheart, just hear me out. OK?"

Anne nodded and tried to calm down and listen.

"When we met, your father had just gotten his PhD and was an assistant professor. I was a freshman — his student. From the start, it was a relationship that was frowned upon, although I certainly wasn't screwing him for a passing grade. It was definitely his blue eyes and sexy smile."

That prompted a tiny grin from Anne.

"Our families were against the relationship because of the situation, and because we came from different backgrounds. My family had money. His didn't. He was a strict Catholic. My family went to church on Christmas and Easter, and maybe for a confirmation or christening. But we ignored what our families and society said. That's important, Anne. You and Maggie are also very different, but those differences mean nothing if you love each other."

"If you and Dad loved each other so much, what happened?" It was a question that Anne had never directly asked her mom.

"One of the most important things in a relationship is communication," Jill explained. "Sometimes, it's so hard to see when communication isn't working. When you live with someone and talk to him or her every day, you think you're communicating."

Jill waited a moment and Anne let the concept sink in. She nodded her understanding and Jill continued. "At some point, your father and I stopped talking. Oh, not about everyday things like what we had for lunch or how our day went. We stopped talking about things that really mattered. He applied for a job at Stanford. I decided to go to law school. Later, I wanted a child, so I went off the pill and got pregnant."

"You did all of those things without telling each other?" Anne was amazed that her very vocal parents would do such a thing.

"We talked around it a lot. But yes, we basically made those decisions on our own."

"Why?" The pain of her parent's divorce still hurt Anne.

"If I knew that, I'd still be married," Jill said with a sad smile. "The problem started small, but before we knew it, it consumed our relationship. We tried to regain control, but it was too late. Once we'd lost the trust, it was impossible to get it back."

"Mom, I understand what you're saying about

communication, and I know it's important."

Jill took her daughter's hand. "Anne, last week we talked about you sharing your feelings about Simone with Maggie. Did you do that?"

"Not exactly," Anne replied evasively. "We just sort of worked it out."

"I see," Jill said slowly. "And are there other situations? Issues that are extremely important to you, but that you just haven't been able to share with Maggie, hoping that they'll just sort of work out?"

"Mom, I understand what you're saying. I really do. I know that Maggie and I have some stuff that we need to work through. But if I waited until everything was perfect, I'd never take this step. I'm committing myself to make this relationship work. I want to show her proof of that commitment."

"As long as you understand what you need to work on, and are willing to do everything in your power to do what needs to be done, I know you will have a wonderful marriage. You two are beautiful together, and I want you to both live happily ever after."

"But?" Anne said with a smirk.

"No 'buts' this time." Jill held up her hand. "Remember when I told you not to second-guess your love for Maggie? I told you not to let anyone talk you out of it. That includes your mom. I also told you to follow your heart. So, here's my only question: what does your heart say, Anne?"

She sat back and met Anne's eyes, which had already turned inward, considering her mother's words. Jill slowly stood. "Take as long as you need to answer. I'll see you later." Jill bent over and tenderly kissed her daughter on the top of the head.

"Thanks, Mom," Anne said softly. She cocked an ear to her heart and listened to what it had to say, making the biggest decision of her life.

Chapter
Fourteen

ANNE WAVED TO the guard as she hurried across the nearly empty parking lot. She struggled to hold on to her umbrella in the blustery wind, her pumps splashing in the unavoidable puddles.

Her court appearance had dragged through the afternoon, and then she'd met with her client for two hours, going over everything that had happened. Maria Ramirez wasn't a stupid woman, but the legal intricacies of custody cases overwhelmed even the brightest people.

Anne climbed into the car, throwing her dripping umbrella in the back and her briefcase on the passenger seat. She leaned her head against the headrest, taking a moment to think through her evening. Maggie was working a double shift so she could take a long weekend. That meant Anne needed to get herself food, and then get home and pack. They'd make an early start for Mendocino in the morning.

"Waking up Maggie after less than eight hours' sleep will be an interesting challenge," she muttered. She smiled, thinking about the smart-ass remark that Maggie would have made if she'd been present.

She peered at the rain pattering against the windshield. Mendocino would be just as wet, but that was perfect. They'd have major snuggle time in front of a roaring fire—for three days. *Life doesn't get much better than that.*

Chinese food sounded good, so she dug her cell phone out from her briefcase to place the order. She looked at the blank display on the phone and realized she hadn't turned it back on after getting out of court. She flicked it on and waited for the service to register. The message icon flashed, and with a little grin she dialed her phone mail. Maggie always called her periodically throughout her shift, and the messages always created a little ball of warmth deep inside.

"You have three new messages," the halting computer voice

reported. "Message one, received at 3:31 p.m."

"Hi, sweetie." Maggie sounded tired and definitely ready for some time off. "I just started my second shift and it's cold, wet, and miserable. Really makes me glad to be alive—not. Of course, I'll spend the rest of the day wondering about my Valentine's surprise. I know it involves going away. If it's somewhere dry and warm, you'll make all my dreams come true. Oh, and it'll be nice if you're there too. Love you."

Anne smiled at her lover's sarcasm. Maggie's crankiness would dissolve the minute she hit Mendo.

"Message two, received at 5:14 p.m.," the computer voice said.

"Hey, baby, it's me again. I forgot to say before that I hope your case went well. I'm sure it did, since you're the best lawyer in the world. Love you. Bye."

Anne smiled again.

"Message three, received at 6:36 p.m."

"Anne, it's Michelle."

It took a moment for Anne to connect the voice and the name. *Why is Moocher calling me?* And then her world stopped.

"Maggie's been...she's hurt. You need to come. We're at Berkeley General. The emergency room."

Anne couldn't breathe, couldn't move, couldn't think.

Finally, her lungs expanded, and she took a long, ragged breath. The rest of her senses focused slowly, and she shook her head, forcing her mind to work. She searched frantically for the car keys for a moment, then realized they were already in the ignition. She turned the key with a trembling hand and checked the clock. It was 7:15—more than half an hour since Moocher had called. She sped out of the lot, her tires squealing on the wet pavement. The guard glared at her, but she ignored him.

Anne drove frantically through the crowded streets of Oakland and Berkeley, weaving in and out of traffic. A few cars honked as she came perilously close to hitting them, but she didn't even glance their way. When she stopped at a red light she tried calling Moocher, but the call was forwarded to voice mail. Anne threw the phone on the passenger seat in frustration and peeled away when the light turned green. She felt a deep, bone-chilling cold, her body shivering and her teeth chattering uncontrollably.

She found a parking spot a block from the hospital. She didn't bother to grab her umbrella from the back seat, just ran down the sidewalk, ignoring the rain that soaked her hair and the pain of running in high-heeled shoes. She shoved through the automatic doors, not waiting until they opened fully, squinting in the sudden bright lights of the emergency room waiting area. She glanced around at the miserable-looking people sitting in blue plastic chairs. Several police officers stood in a huddled group, away from the waiting patients. She finally spotted Moocher, who stood next to a fellow officer. He was leaning toward her, talking in a hushed whisper. Anne hurried over to her lover's best friend and partner.

Moocher looked up as Anne approached. Her eyes were red and tear tracks marked her tired face. "Anne," she cried, tears springing to her eyes again. The officer who had been speaking to her moved away to give them some privacy.

"You said you'd take care of her," Anne said savagely. "You said nothing would happen to her. How the hell could you let this happen?"

"I'm sorry," Moocher said in an anguished whisper. She stood up straight, her hands to the side, as if to accept anything that Anne would decide to do to her. Anne looked at the open arms and saw the red stains on Moocher's uniform. Her stomach clenched violently when she realized the stains were her lover's blood. Moocher watched as Anne's face turned white and she reached out to catch the distraught woman as Anne's knees buckled. Moocher helped her into a chair and collapsed beside her, keeping her arms clutched around Anne's shoulders.

"I'm sorry," Moocher repeated. "I screwed up. I'm so sorry."

"Is she OK? Please tell me she's going to be OK."

"I don't know, they haven't said anything. She was talking to me in the ambulance, though. She kept asking for you."

Anne closed her eyes and tried to calm the maelstrom of thoughts and emotions that were sweeping through her mind. *Why wasn't I there for her? She needs me to protect her. I swore I'd never let her get hurt. I failed her. How could I have let this happen?*

"I'm sorry," she gasped, looking up at Moocher. "I shouldn't have said those things to you. I'm just so scared."

"It's all right. I know." Moocher let go of Anne and hugged herself, rocking slightly. "I'm scared, too."

"What happened?"

"It was so fast." A horrible, haunted look appeared on Moocher's face. "He was just a kid, just a sidewalk rat. He was smoking a joint and we went up to talk to him. We were just going to have a chat, you know, warn him. We walked toward him and he stood up. I turned away for a minute, to look at another kid, I guess—I don't know why. Maggie was just talking to him one minute and then...he had a knife, and before I turned back around, he stabbed her."

Anne's eyes closed. She felt the pain as if the knife had

entered her own body.

"He didn't move — he just smiled. For a minute, I was sure that I'd seen it wrong. Maggie just stood there with a confused look on her face, and he stood there smiling. Then she slowly fell. He took off and...there was so much blood."

Moocher wiped at the tears seeping from her eyes, and Anne felt her stomach clench again when she noticed the dried blood on Moocher's hands. She swallowed the bile that was rising in her throat.

"She's going to be OK," Moocher said, a look of determination settling on her face. "I know she is."

Anne put her arms around Moocher's shoulders and held her tightly. They sat there, holding on to each other, until finally a doctor approached the group.

"I assume you're all here with Officer Monahan? I'm Dr. Jakowski. Is there a family member here?"

Anne didn't move, knowing that Maggie had still not come out at work, but Moocher prodded her.

"I'm her life partner." Anne avoided the sideways glances from a few of the cops nearby. She stood, Moocher rising with her.

"Right, Ms...?"

"Doyle. Anne Doyle." Anne began to shiver again and clenched her chattering teeth. Moocher squeezed her hand, trying to offer what little comfort she could.

"Well, Ms. Doyle, let me tell you what's happening." He motioned for Anne and Moocher to retake their seats and sat down in an empty chair beside them. "Maggie was stabbed by a narrow serrated blade — probably a steak knife. The knife was deflected by a rib, which most likely saved her life. However, the knife did penetrate her abdomen and did some damage to her liver. She's bleeding internally, so we're going to have to take her into surgery and repair that."

"Will she be all right?" Moocher voiced the question that Anne wasn't able to utter.

"I can't tell you that. All surgery is risky, and this is a critical injury. But she is stable and responding well to treatment so far. Our surgeon is one of the best and has had a lot of success with this type of injury."

"What are her chances in terms of percentages?" Anne's voice cracked with fear.

"I don't like to give odds. I find that works in Las Vegas but not in medicine. I'd like to tell you that she'll be fine and will be able to walk out of here in a week or so. I can't do that, but you need to believe it anyway. Focus on it." He stood up. "I'll come by and talk to you when she's out of surgery."

"Thank you." Anne struggled to keep herself together, but tears were stinging her eyes. "Please take care of her."

"I will." The doctor smiled sympathetically. "That's one thing I can guarantee."

The doctor left, and Anne and Moocher leaned back in their chairs, settling in for the long wait.

Anne had never believed in the traditional concepts of an afterlife, but what she experienced for the next three hours was most assuredly Hell. Anything that some capricious deity chose to confront her with after her death would be nothing compared to the torment that ripped through her soul as she waited to hear whether Maggie would live or die.

Police officers came and went during the next few hours. Moocher spoke to several of them, and one or two even tried to say a word of comfort to Anne, but she simply nodded, unable to utter even the most basic words to reply. Her mind kept replaying an image — of Maggie lying in a pool of blood. She saw Maggie being stabbed, as if she'd witnessed the event herself. It played over and over in an endless loop.

At some point, a lieutenant arrived, and Moocher stood to greet him. He told them that the boy had been found and arrested. Moocher smiled down at Anne, who had remained seated. Anne tried to share her enthusiasm, but there was no room for any other emotion beyond the fear and guilt that consumed her.

Four hours passed before Dr. Jakowski re-entered the waiting room. As the doctor approached, Anne stood up quickly. She wasn't ready for the sudden movement, and black spots appeared in her vision. She swayed slightly and Moocher stood up beside her, grabbing her arm to hold her steady.

"She made it through the surgery and she's in the recovery room," the doctor said, flashing a tired smile. "As soon as she wakes up a little from the anesthesia, we'll move her into the ICU."

"Will she be OK?" Anne asked breathlessly.

"She's not completely out of the woods yet, but her prognosis is good. She lost a lot of blood, but the liver damage wasn't as bad as we had feared. We'll see how she does overnight, but I'm feeling a lot more confident than I was earlier."

"Thank you, Doctor." Tears sprang into Anne's eyes and spilled down her cheeks.

"No problem. A nurse will come out to take you to her when we've moved her. She may not be aware of you at all until morning, but don't worry, that's normal."

Anne nodded and watched the doctor walk away, his shoulders slumped with exhaustion. She felt Moocher hug her but refused to let herself hope until she saw Maggie — until she could feel her lover's heart beating, see her chest rising with breath, feel her warm skin.

Another long hour passed before the nurse finally came and walked them to the elevator. When they exited the elevator on the fourth floor, Anne looked immediately for Maggie. There were several glass-walled rooms in a semi-circle around the nurses' station, most with an occupant hooked up to a myriad of machines.

"Only one of you at a time, I'm afraid," the nurse said, turning to the two women.

Moocher nodded and sat down in a nearby chair. "Go ahead. I'll wait here."

Anne followed the nurse, who led her into a room. She stared at the occupant for a long time before realizing it was her love. Maggie looked so small and defenseless in the large bed, and her skin looked pale — almost translucent. She had tubes all over her body — an IV, a catheter, and a tube down her nose, which was taped to the side of her face. Anne approached carefully and stood by the bedside, afraid to touch her.

"You can hold her hand, but don't pull on it too much." The nurse looked at Anne with an understanding expression. "If you do, it might set off the machines. They're pretty sensitive. And talk to her. She's been in and out, but she can hear you."

Anne nodded faintly and sat in the visitor's chair, scooting it closer to the bed. She carefully picked up Maggie's small hand, stroking the back of it softly with her thumb. The nurse smiled and quietly departed.

"I love you, sweetheart." It was the one thing that she needed Maggie to understand above everything. *Please let her hear me. Please let her understand.*

Anne squeezed Maggie's hand and saw her eyelids begin to flutter, and then slowly open. The beautiful blue-green eyes were bloodshot and Maggie looked confused and frightened as she tried to focus on the strange world around her. Anne leaned down so that her face was closer, and she was pleased when Maggie's eyes locked on to her and the look of fear and confusion melted away.

"It's OK, baby, I'm right here." Anne squeezed Maggie's hand again. "You're going to be OK."

Maggie closed her eyes. Anne felt an almost imperceptible pressure on her hand as Maggie did her best to squeeze back.

The hand went slack again as Maggie drifted back to sleep.

Anne listened to the monitors as their steady beeps signaled the beats of her lover's heart. She watched Maggie's chest rise and fall as she took regular, steady breaths.

She's alive, she's alive, she's alive, she repeated to the rhythm of the machine.

And then the pain and the horror and the guilt came crashing down on her. She felt herself begin to collapse under the weight of it and stumbled out of the room, back to where Moocher sat waiting. When Moocher saw the distraught woman approach her, she feared the worst, and the blood drained from her face.

"She's OK," Anne reassured her. "She saw me. She's asleep."

"Thank God," Moocher whispered, letting her head fall into her hands.

Anne sat beside her, her breath coming in shallow gasps. The pain was crushing her and she had to escape it.

"I can't stay here." The words were an agonized whisper, but they echoed inside Anne's mind.

"What?" Moocher raised her face and peered at Anne in confusion.

"I can't do this." Anne tried to take a deep breath. Her eyes darted between Moocher and Maggie's room.

"Look, take a break." Moocher patted Anne's leg. "Go get something to eat, some coffee at least."

"No, you don't understand," Anne said, jumping to her feet. "I can't do this. I thought I could protect her. How could I have thought that? She would have been better off without me, without thinking that I could ever hope to do anything to keep her safe."

"Anne, I know this is a terrible, terrible thing. But it's not your fault." Moocher paused and seemed to be considering her own guilt. "Just calm down and suck it up. You have to be strong for Maggie."

"I can't," Anne said in a strangled whisper, pain etched across her face. "I have to go."

"What? No!" Moocher stood up and grabbed onto Anne's arm.

"When she wakes up, tell her I was here." Anne listened to her voice as if it belonged to someone else. She felt her mind shutting down as if curtains were being drawn. "I don't want her to think I abandoned her."

"That's exactly what you're doing," Moocher said desperately. "Please, Anne, don't do this."

"I'm not strong enough to deal with this. I was a fool to

think I could ever protect her. I have to go. I love her too much."

"You love her so much that you can't be with her?" Moocher said angrily. She took a deep breath. "Anne, that doesn't make any sense."

"I need to think this through." Anne looked again toward Maggie's room.

"Think it through, but don't do it alone," Moocher begged, clutching the arm that she still held. "Stay with her, and when she's better, talk to her about this. She'll make you understand this is not your fault."

Anne wanted to wake up from the nightmare—make everything all right again—but she couldn't. That inability consumed her. "I can't," she moaned.

"Please?"

"I can't!" Anne cried, ripping her arm from Moocher's grasp.

"Anne, if you leave her now, don't ever plan on coming back," Moocher said viciously. Her eyes grew icy as her anger took control. "You are going to destroy her, and I will never allow you to hurt her again. Do you understand?"

Anne looked into Moocher's brown eyes, seeing pain and anger and guilt reflected there. She wanted to say something, but she couldn't think. All she knew was that she needed to get out, get away. "I'm sorry," she managed in a strangled whisper.

She ran toward the stairwell, pausing in the doorway, but not looking back. She stumbled down the stairs, nearly falling when tears blurred her vision. As she descended, she thought about all of the people she'd failed—her grandfather, Simone, Katy. And now Maggie. She'd let each of them down. Failed them all.

She pushed open the door at the bottom of the stairs and rushed through the lobby and out the double doors, nearly colliding with an elderly woman in a wheel chair. The rain had stopped and the night was freezing, but Anne could feel the sweat prickle her forehead and drip between her shoulder blades. She drew in huge lungfuls of the icy air, leaning against the side of the building.

Tiring at last of the strange looks she was receiving, Anne forced her legs to move. She stumbled down the sidewalk toward her car. Her hands were numb from the cold, and she shoved them into the pockets of her coat.

When her left hand brushed against a small velvet jewelry box, she felt her soul shatter.

Chapter
Fifteen

"YOU SURE YOU'LL be OK?" Moocher bit her bottom lip uncertainly.

"I'll be fine, Moocher." Maggie rearranged herself in Moocher's bed, hissing in pain when she pulled her body the wrong way.

"I could call Roz and ask her if she could go after work."

They'd been talking about Moocher's trip to the grocery store for fifteen minutes. Maggie wanted Moocher to say, "I'm going to the store. Be back in a few," and then just go. But things weren't that simple anymore. She knew they never would be again.

"Moocher, please go. I'll be fine." Frustration sharpened Maggie's words and she regretted her tone. It wasn't Moocher's fault that even a trip to the grocery store had to be approached cautiously, like walking up to a stray dog in a dark alley.

"Well, if you're sure." Moocher's words were slow. It was obvious she was waiting for Maggie to change her mind, to say she wasn't quite ready to be left alone for the first time.

"I'm sure." Maggie somehow managed to make her words sound decisive and hid her trembling hands under the quilt.

"OK. I won't be long." Moocher moved to her desk and searched through the drawers. Maggie knew it was Moocher's attempt to give her one more opportunity to change her mind, but she watched her friend silently.

Moocher found a battered and torn envelope, which she looked at for a moment before laying on the desk. Her search continued until she found a pen. The first one didn't work, and after the second attempt she scribbled down her shopping list.

"Do you need anything?" Moocher asked, pen poised above the list.

"No." What Maggie needed was for Moocher to go. Her resolve was slowly eroding, like a snow fort on a warm winter's afternoon.

"Nothing you're craving? I've got the list of stuff you're allowed to eat and what you're not." Moocher searched around on the desk, and then held up a pink piece of paper they'd been given at the hospital.

"No thanks." It didn't matter what was on the list. Maggie had no appetite. Everything tasted of sawdust — dry and thick, sticking in her throat and congealing in her stomach.

"How about some ice cream?" Moocher tried to look excited, as if her emotions were contagious. "As long as you don't eat too much, I think it's OK."

"No, Moocher, just...get whatever you want."

Maggie saw pain flash in Moocher's eyes before she quickly turned away.

"OK," Moocher said quietly. She folded the envelope and shoved it in the back pocket of her jeans.

"Moocher?"

"Yeah?"

"Actually, I wouldn't mind some ginger ale." Maggie had to do something to take the pain from her friend's eyes. She really didn't want ginger ale, had never liked it, but it was the first thing on the approved food list.

"Right. Ginger ale." Moocher took the list from her pocket and picked up the pen. She carefully wrote the words down as if there was a chance she would forget.

"Thanks."

"No problem." Moocher smiled and shrugged, then picked up her cell phone. "Call me if you need anything."

"I will."

Moocher hesitated for just a moment. One more chance. But Maggie reached for a magazine to show that she was OK, that this was just a normal afternoon. Out of the corner of her eye she watched Moocher leave the room, then listened as her friend moved around the apartment. A drawer squeaked. That was Moocher retrieving her wallet. Keys jangled as they were removed from the hook in the kitchen. Boots made dull thumps against the living room carpet.

"Be back soon!"

The door thudded shut, the deadbolt clicking as Moocher locked it behind her.

Maggie's pounding heart filled the sudden silence. She was dismayed at how quickly the panic rose and engulfed her. She lay as still as possible, closing her eyes so that she couldn't watch her vision tunneling. She concentrated on breathing. In. Out. In. Out.

"Stop acting like a fucking freak!" she growled at herself.

Her frustrated outburst broke her concentration, and she struggled to get her focus back.

After a few more steady breaths, the yips of a small dog distracted her. She identified it as the neighbor's Chihuahua. She looked at the clock and confirmed that Mrs. Johnson would be taking it out for its three o'clock poo. And if it was three o'clock then —

"Mom! Can't I play X-Box now and do my homework after dinner?"

Tyler, the ten-year-old downstairs, had the same question for his mom every day after school. He was certainly tenacious. In the three days since Maggie had been listening, his mom never gave in to his request.

"I would have caved in by now," Maggie mused aloud.

She thought about being ten. She remembered running home to watch *Power Rangers*. Afterward, she and Sean would run around the back yard, pretending that they were long-lost Power Rangers, tragically separated from the other four. She sighed at the pleasant memory and realized that she was breathing normally again.

She looked down at the magazine that she'd pulled from the pile Moocher had bought for her. *Entertainment Weekly*. She found that its little chunks of fluff were just the right length to hold her attention.

"Ooh, a new reality show featuring supermodels, bug-eating, and a million dollars. Now that's original."

Maggie flipped the page and stared at an ad for a new SUV. The car was shown on a dirt road in a thick pine forest. Maggie peered at the photo. She felt as if she were walking on a path through the same dark, dank wood. Something was keeping pace with her, sometimes drawing so close that she could hear its footsteps, sometimes falling so far behind that she fooled herself into believing that it had gotten lost, given up the hunt.

She wanted to turn around and scream at it, grab it, shake it, tell it to go fuck itself. But it was stronger than she was. With less effort than it took to blow out a candle, it could rip her soul apart. So she kept walking through that forest. One foot in front of the other. Never looking behind. Dealing with the panic attacks that hit with sudden savage intensity, as if her mind was cramping from the effort of moving down that lonely path.

She turned the page, folding the ad down and concentrating on a review of a new animated film.

"A cat and a dog falling in love. Interspecies relationship. Slightly subversive for Disney. Of course, it's not same-sex. Make a movie about a princess falling in love with her lady-in-waiting—then I'll be interested."

Falling in love. She stumbled, feeling herself losing her balance, knowing that she was falling and knowing that it was going to hurt.

Brrring.

The ringing phone stopped her fall. Froze her in place, halfway to the ground.

Brrring.

It was her. Had to be. She was calling to say it was a mistake. Just a...mistake.

Brrring.

And she would explain and it would be OK. She would come back and they would face that thing in the woods together.

Brrring.

"I'm coming," she called, as if the caller could hear her. She struggled to move her legs from under the quilt and over the edge of the bed. That effort left her sweating and she took two large breaths before sitting up completely, pushing away from the pillows. She raised herself slowly but still saw stars and quickly swallowed the saliva that filled her mouth. She willed herself not to throw up.

Brrring.

"Don't hang up," she whispered desperately. She cursed the fact that Moocher didn't have a phone extension in the bedroom. She'd never make it to the living room in time. Sitting up had been hard. Standing was agony. Her legs held for exactly two seconds before collapsing like overcooked linguine.

Brrring.

Falling back to the bed jarred her abdomen, sending a searing blaze of pain along her body. Her head swam and she fought again to keep the contents of her stomach where they belonged.

The click of the answering machine penetrated the fog of pain in her head. She was too far away to make out the words, but she heard the greeting and then a woman's voice—she was sure of that if nothing else—leaving a long message after a shrill beep. There was a final click and then silence.

But this time the silence didn't panic Maggie. She slowly struggled back into the bed, shaking and sweating with the effort. She stared at the ceiling. Waiting. Hoping.

She woke some time later after dozing—her attempt at standing had left her exhausted. She cursed her weakness before realizing that she had been woken by the sound of a key in the front door's lock.

"There's a message on the machine!" she called before

Moocher was all the way in the apartment.

"All right, I'll get it."

Maggie heard the rustling of grocery bags, the front door closing, Moocher's footsteps moving through the living room into the kitchen.

"I couldn't get up to answer it!" Maggie shouted. Surely Moocher would check it before putting the groceries away.

"OK!"

Maggie listened to Moocher walk into the living room and fiddle with the machine. After only a few incomprehensible words, Moocher stopped the playback. Then walked into the bedroom.

"Just someone selling DSL," Moocher reported nonchalantly. "I got your ginger ale. And some mint chocolate chip ice cream, just in case you got in the mood for it."

"Thank you," Maggie whispered, feeling despair cascading through her mind. She fell with it, one word echoing in her mind as she tumbled into oblivion.

Why?

ANNE TORE OFF a strip of packing tape and pressed it against the box lid, smoothing it down with her palm. She picked up the black felt-tip pen and neatly printed "BOOKS" on the top and side. She glanced around the living room of the cottage, looking for anything she'd forgotten. She spied a CD under the player and picked it up. Not remembering whose it was, she threw it into the last box, then closed that one and taped it shut. She didn't stop her work or reply when she heard a soft knock at the cottage door. She frowned when the door opened anyway, and her mom entered.

"Need any help?" Jill asked, looking at the boxes.

"No." Anne wrote "CDs" on the box and then placed the cap back on the pen. She walked to the desk and put the pen in the top drawer. Then she lifted up a box and carried it outside.

Jill picked up a box and followed Anne outside.

"You don't need to do that," Anne said as she returned for another box. "But if you could be here later when Moocher comes to pick them up, I'd appreciate it. I'm sure she doesn't want to see me right now. Or ever."

"Why don't you try to talk to her?"

"And say what?" Anne was tired and numb. She felt the words come from her mouth, but felt as if someone else was speaking. "I tried to call. I left two messages which were never returned and Moocher hung up on me once. Which was probably a good thing, because I had nothing to say anyway."

"Then why did you call?"

"I don't know," Anne said dully.

"I think you do."

"Mother, don't do this. Not now. Please."

"Then when, Anne? When will you be ready to hear this?"

"Never!" Anne felt a surge of energy. "Maggie trusted me. She gave her soul to me. And I destroyed it."

"Oh, sweetheart, no." Jill's eyes shone with tears. "Maggie didn't give her soul to you. You and Maggie share the *same* soul. Don't you understand? Think about the times you were together. Think about what you felt—the warmth and strength and love. You two have something that most of us only dream about."

"We *had* something." Anne felt the numbing pain return. "But what we had is dead." She returned inside and brought out another box. It was light and her stomach clenched as she felt the soft toys tumble inside.

"Just make sure she's OK." Anne's voice was a strangled whisper. "And tell Moocher to take care of her."

"I will." Tears fell down Jill's face as she placed the final box on the pile.

Anne opened the garage and went inside, returning with a mountain bike. She placed the bike against the wall of the cottage, beside the boxes, then turned and walked down the driveway, feeling the other half of her soul fracture and fall away.

SOMETHING WOKE MAGGIE and for once it wasn't a nightmare. Whatever it had been—a car alarm or a slamming door—the sound was gone by the time Maggie was fully aware. She waited for the noise to return, then stretched and got out of bed, walking quietly to the kitchen so as not to wake Moocher. Though she was still staying in Moocher's apartment, her friend had been staying over at Roz's. This was the first night in a while that Moocher was home.

Maggie opened the fridge and blinked in the sudden light. She pulled out the milk carton and quickly closed the door. She preferred the kitchen lit only by the streetlight outside. It was enough to help her find the saucepan, pour the milk, and turn on the stove. She was pulling a mug from the cupboard when the soft pat of bare feet startled her.

"Hope there's enough for two." Moocher rubbed at her face and sat down at the little kitchen table in the corner.

"Of course." Maggie poured more milk into the saucepan.

She stirred the milk for a while, then poked a pinky in to test the heat. Satisfied, she poured the milk into two mugs, sat one down in front of her friend, and took the chair opposite, clutching her own warm mug.

"I figured you were sleeping over at Roz's to give me some space," Maggie said. "I was glad because I knew I was keeping you up all night with my nightmares." She paused, watching her friend, whose eyes were glued to her mug. "I should have realized it was because you were having nightmares of your own."

"Did I wake you up?" Moocher met Maggie's gaze, and then quickly looked down again. "I'm sorry."

"Hey, it's just pay-back. No problem." Maggie frowned when Moocher didn't respond. She took a sip of her milk and felt its warmth ease down into her stomach, warming her from inside. "So, talk to me."

"It's the middle of the night," Moocher said to her milk. "We should both drink up and get back into bed."

"Nice try. How about you tell me about your nightmare instead?"

"How about not?" Moocher pasted on a grin.

"Come on, I'm getting bored with mine. I'm sure yours are far more interesting."

"Doubt it." Moocher's grin disappeared.

"OK, you're going to make me guess, aren't you?" Maggie kept her tone light, but wasn't about to let go.

"Mags, let's forget this. Really. Let's just go to bed."

"No, no. This will be fun. It's like Twenty Questions. Here's my first guess—you're dreaming about drowning in a vat of chocolate sauce while all of your old girlfriends throw marshmallows at you."

Moocher didn't reply.

"OK, wait, I have another guess." It was hard to keep the tone light, but Maggie knew it was the best approach. "In your dream you're having sex with a really beautiful woman, but when you look down, the face between your legs is your third grade teacher—the nun with the hairy mole in the middle of her chin."

"This isn't a joke." Moocher's tone was so brittle it nearly crumbled into dust.

"OK, last guess." Maggie's voice became serious. "I'm really not the type of person who thinks that the world revolves around me, but I'm thinking that your nightmares are actually about...me."

Moocher stood up and walked to the kitchen sink, pouring her milk down the drain and placing her cup down forcefully.

"Don't walk away." Maggie's request was said in an even tone, but the plea echoed in the silent kitchen, the words resonating in both women's souls. Moocher walked back to the table and sat down.

"Talk to me," Maggie said softly. "Tell me about your dreams."

Moocher took a deep breath. She looked like she was going to refuse, but then said, "There's not much to tell. It's just what happened that day. We're talking to the kid, he makes the move, and I'm not fast enough. I can see the knife, but I can't reach him. I...I try, but..."

"That's not what happened." Maggie twisted her neck to look into Moocher's downcast eyes.

"What?" Moocher looked up sharply.

"That day. That's not what happened."

"Of course it is. Are you saying you weren't stabbed? I must really be psycho then, because I could swear my best friend was stabbed a few weeks ago."

"No, you're right. I was stabbed." The word was still hard to say and it tumbled awkwardly from Maggie's mouth. She ignored the feeling and focused on her friend. "But where does this 'I wasn't fast enough' crap come from? You didn't see the knife. I didn't see the knife. Until that knife was deep in my gut, there was no knife."

"You don't remember. That's what happens when people are seriously injured. They—"

"I do remember!" Maggie slapped her hand down, stopping Moocher. "Don't you do this. Please, don't you dare do this."

"I don't know what you mean."

"God, this is a mess." Maggie rubbed at her face feeling the sting of tears. She wiped them away, knowing it wasn't the time to break down. "What happened was *not* your fault. I was there and I remember. So unless you're going to tell me that you paid the kid to do it, it was not your fault."

"You don't understand."

"What don't I understand? Please, explain to me what I don't understand."

"I was supposed to take care of you," Moocher said in an agonized whisper, as if the words were torn from her throat.

"Oh, buddy, you did take care of me." Maggie grabbed hold of Moocher's hands. "From the first day you met me, you took care of me. It's just that bad things happen. I don't know why, but they happen. And the only good thing that can come out of this is to learn and grow stronger."

"It's so hard." Moocher clutched Maggie's hands.

"I know it is. But you've got to let go of your guilt. Please."

Moocher took a deep breath and let it out with a puff. "I'll try."

"That's all I ask." Maggie gave Moocher's hands a final squeeze before letting them go. "Now, you need to get some sleep. You have an early shift. We can talk more about this tomorrow."

"Not so fast, buckaroo." Moocher folded her arms across her chest and raised an eyebrow. "I think you're forgetting something. Since we're on the subject of nightmares, we might as well have a little chat about yours."

Maggie was swamped by the familiar feeling of doors slamming shut as her mind locked her emotions down. "They're a normal reaction to what happened," she said calmly. "They'll go away eventually."

"No they won't. Not unless you talk about them. To a professional or to me or to someone."

"I just need time." It was Maggie's turn to stare at her mug.

"It's been six weeks since you were stabbed." Moocher seemed to have as much trouble saying the word as Maggie had earlier. "Time is not going to make this go away."

"I hear what you're saying, and I'll just give it a few more weeks—"

"What are your dreams about?" Moocher interrupted.

"I told you before, they're boring. I'm sure you can imagine—"

"They're not about the stabbing, are they?"

"What?" Maggie's heartbeat raced. "Of course they are."

"You are the worst liar in the greater Bay Area, Maggie Monahan. Don't even try now. Tell me. What are your dreams about?"

"I can't...they're just..."

"They're about her, aren't they? That goddamn bitch."

"No, not exactly. I mean—"

"I should have called her back." Moocher wasn't listening. She stood up and paced through the kitchen. "I should have kicked the shit out of her."

"What do you mean, 'called her back'?" Suddenly, Maggie remembered phone calls and erased messages.

"She doesn't deserve to be living in the same world as you for what she did." Moocher continued to fume, ignoring Maggie's question.

"Moocher, stop." Maggie stood and grabbed onto Moocher's

arm before she could turn and march back across the kitchen. "Stop and tell me what you mean by 'called her back.' Did she call you? Did she call me?"

Moocher looked confused and then her eyes shifted guiltily.

"Oh, my God." Maggie felt dizzy and a buzz was beginning in her head. Her abdomen suddenly ached and she drew in a sharp breath. Moocher saw her distress and grabbed onto her, helping her back to a chair.

"Maggie, it's OK. Just sit down and breathe." Moocher rubbed Maggie's back. "It's OK."

Maggie took a few breaths and waited for her head to stop buzzing. "Tell me what she said. Please."

"It doesn't matter."

"Yes, it does. It does matter." Maggie looked at Moocher, feeling like she was adrift in the middle of a freezing ocean. "Why didn't you tell me?"

"You didn't need to hear her lame apology. What was she going to say? 'Sorry I walked out on you. Didn't mean to hurt you.' She knew what she was doing. That's one night I was there and you weren't. And I do remember, all too clearly, every second of what happened."

"You should have let me talk to her."

"No way!" Moocher stood and crossed her arms, standing back on her heels. "I did the right thing. You did not need to hear her bullshit."

"I appreciate that you were trying to protect me. I do. But it's my business."

"OK, let's call her." Moocher walked to the phone on the kitchen wall and held it out to Maggie. "Let's call her and wake her up. I wonder if she's having nightmares, too. Let's find out. And then let's ask her to explain why she walked out on you. We'll listen to her lame excuse and then we'll tell her to go fuck herself and then we'll get on with our lives. What a great idea."

"Moocher, put down the phone. This is not about Anne. This is about you and me."

Moocher held the phone, her eyes flashing defiantly.

"Please," Maggie whispered.

The simple word seemed to deflate Moocher. She put the phone back in the cradle on the wall and walked toward the table. "I'm sorry. I thought I was doing the right thing."

"Maybe it was the right thing for me not to talk to her, but I needed to make that decision myself." Maggie placed her head in her palms, feeling tired and weak. "I know you did what you did because you love me and you want to protect me. I'm really confused right now about what is right and wrong. Shit, I'm not

even sure what's up and what's down. But I do know that you
should have told me."

Moocher's eyes darkened, turning black in the gloom of the
kitchen. "I understand what you're saying." She sighed. "I'm
sorry. I promise I'll back you up. I'll do what you think is right."

"OK." Tears pricked the corners of Maggie's eyes. "I'll let
you know as soon as I figure that out."

As the tears began to fall down Maggie's cheeks, Moocher
knelt down beside the chair and pulled her friend into a hug. "I
think we've both failed at this figuring-out business. We need
help."

"Yeah," Maggie said, her voice breaking on a sob.

"It'll be OK. We'll get help, pal. It'll all be OK."

Maggie held onto the words like a lifeline and let herself be
pulled toward safety.

"WOULD YOU LIKE some iced tea?" Joanna Perkins moved
a Barbie doll off a chair so that Anne could sit down.

"No, thanks." Anne forced herself to smile. She wasn't in the
mood for social niceties, but she had to make an effort.

"I probably have some Kool-Aid made up as well," Joanna
said as she threw the doll into the toy box in the corner.

"Well, that's tempting, but I think I'll pass." The childhood
memories of Kool-Aid and Barbies took Anne's mind to a nicer
place. For a moment.

"Marc took the kids to a birthday party. It's nice to live in a
neighborhood with lots of kids, but it seems like there's a party
every weekend."

"I was hoping to see Katy. But I'm sure she's having more
fun at the party."

Joanna moved to the mantel where framed photos of the
family were lined up. Most of them featured a smiling Katy,
usually with her arm around Rashad, the Perkins' other foster
child. She picked up a picture and handed it to Anne. "Here's
the latest."

Anne gazed at the photo. The camera had captured the little
girl in the middle of a giggle. She was holding a stalk of celery
that a donkey was happily munching.

"It was taken at the little farm in Tilden Park a few weeks
ago," Joanna explained. "The kids love it there."

"I used to go there when I was a kid." Anne grinned at
another happy memory as she carefully placed the picture on the
coffee table.

"Katy in particular loves animals." Joanna took a seat on the sofa near Anne. "She told Marc the other day that she wants to be an animal doctor when she grows up. Of course she'll have to learn how to say 'veterinarian' first."

Anne chuckled politely, wishing they could get down to business. She needed this, needed to have something to focus on and take care of.

"I'm sure you have some idea of why I asked you to come over," Joanna said.

"Let me guess. It has something to do with Simone."

"You win the prize." Joanna grimaced.

Anne's eyes narrowed and she felt her muscles flex and her pulse quicken, as if she were preparing for battle. "How is the case coming along? I know your attorney is good. I've gone up against her several times in court."

"Yes, well —"

"Don't worry, Joanna," Anne interrupted in a take-charge tone, "there is no way in hell that I'm going to let Simone get custody of Katy. In fact, I'll do everything in my power to ensure she never even lays eyes on her."

"I don't think —"

"I know what you're going to say. I realize it isn't entirely ethical for me to represent you, so I know why you didn't come to me first. But I will be happy to help out your attorney. In fact, I'll call her tomorrow."

"Just stop a second." Joanna held up her hands. "I don't think you fully understand the situation."

"Sorry." Anne grinned sheepishly. "As you can see, I'm feeling a little passionate about this. Please, go ahead."

"I know that you feel strongly about Simone and ensuring that she not regain custody of Katy." Joanna paused and took a deep breath. Anne frowned in confusion as Joanna continued, "But Marc and I have decided to let Simone see *her daughter*." Anne didn't miss the emphasis on the words. "And, provided that everything goes well, we hope that some day Simone can have Katy back."

Anne sat very still, struggling to process the words. She finally shrugged in defeat and wrinkled her forehead. "I don't understand."

This isn't happening.

Joanne squeezed Anne's arm in mute comfort. "I know what you're thinking. I assure you that Katy is our only priority. We will protect her from Simone, and if this doesn't work out, Simone walks away never to return until Katy is an adult and makes her own decisions. Simone understands the conditions."

"Simone is very good at understanding," Anne said bitterly.

"But understanding and doing are two very different things."

"I hear you, Anne." Joanna nodded. "So we are going extremely slowly with this. All of her visits will be supervised for at least a year. We are keeping tabs on just about every aspect of Simone's life—her therapy, her Narcotics Anonymous meetings. She is drug-tested as part of her parole, and she has agreed to share the results with us. And Katy herself will see a child psychiatrist to talk about the situation. That will continue until we say otherwise."

Anne knew they had arranged for things that were rarely negotiated. The system didn't have the resources, and most of the time the participants didn't have the patience, or the desire, to truly do what was right for the children. It was a logical way to approach the situation. Unfortunately, emotions were a lot stronger than logic.

"She nearly killed Katy." Anne's voice held all of the horror of that afternoon. "You don't understand."

"I do understand." Joanne squeezed Anne's arm again. "I do."

"And you're giving her a second chance?"

Second chance. The words seemed to float in the room, like the scent of jasmine on a summer morning.

"Yes." Joanna nodded emphatically. "We're giving her a second chance."

"It's that simple, then?"

"Oh, no, it's far from simple." Joanna swallowed, obviously struggling to continue. "I love Katy as if she were my own. Marc and I had hoped to adopt her. We'd taken that for granted, found ourselves talking about little things—what she'll be like when she's a teenager, whether she'll be better at math or English, whether we'll buy her a car for her graduation. As if it was a foregone conclusion that she'd be with us forever, that she'd be our daughter. She's the fourth child we've fostered, but Katy is different. She's staked out pieces of our hearts, and when she leaves, she'll take those pieces with her. Saying goodbye to her will be the hardest thing I'll ever do."

Tears pooled in Joanna's eyes and Anne reached for a box of tissues, handing them over as the drops fell slowly down Joanna's cheeks.

Joanna wiped at the tears and then her nose before continuing. "But everyone deserves a second chance, Anne."

"We just don't always get one." Anne smiled bitterly.

"Oh, but we do," Joanna corrected. "It's just a matter of taking that second chance and holding on to it. Because if you waste it, there will be no more."

Anne felt cynicism fill her soul. *It is not that easy. But God, I wish it was.*

"I don't know if I believe that," she responded honestly.

"It's tough. I'm not always sure I believe it, either. But the more I see it happen, the easier it is to have faith. Just have faith, Anne. Believe in second chances."

Believe.

The word floated on the air and Anne watched it fly.

Chapter Sixteen

MAGGIE SAT ON a bench outside the courthouse, her face turned toward the sun. It had been a wet winter and now, as they were nearing May, the weather was finally starting to turn.

"OK, I'm done," Moocher called. "Let's go eat."

Maggie smiled tentatively. She stood up and followed Moocher toward the courthouse. As they reached the imposing glass doors of the building, Moocher stopped and pulled out her cell phone.

"Oops, almost forgot." Moocher moved away from Maggie. "I've got to make a phone call. Can you go ahead and get me a pastrami on rye? I'll meet you up there."

Maggie shuffled nervously toward Moocher. "Let's just forget it. We can go to that Greek place." She chewed on the nail of her index finger.

"Maggie, Roz told you, she's out of town." They both knew that "she" was Anne. "You'll be fine."

Moocher gently pulled her friend's hand away from her mouth. Maggie looked sheepishly at the wet, red finger. The habit of biting her nails had plagued her as a child. It had returned in the past few weeks—whenever she felt particularly insecure or frightened. Her therapist told her to work on it at her own pace. At this point in her treatment, it wasn't a high priority.

"I don't know..."

"Mags, it's 11:35. If you don't go right now, all of the courtrooms will break for lunch and we'll be in line for hours. Just go, get the food. I'll be up in fifteen minutes—tops."

Maggie nodded reluctantly and turned to go. She looked back once, and then forced herself to enter the building and cross the lobby to the elevator. She felt as if she was walking through deep sand, her steps dragging across the polished granite floor.

ANNE RUBBED AT the back of her neck, trying to ease the tension that lodged between her shoulders like a burning coal. Her head felt like a giant was squeezing it between his hands. She pulled out an aspirin bottle and popped the lid, shaking out the last two tablets.

Damn, I went through that bottle fast. I feel like I've had a headache forever.

No, not forever. Her mouth tightened into a grimace. *Just since Valentine's Day. Ten weeks.*

She walked to a drinking fountain in the hallway outside one of the courtrooms and swallowed the pills with some water.

The courtroom doors opened and her mom finally exited. "Ready to go eat?" Jill asked. "I'm free until two."

"Sure," Anne replied listlessly.

Jill's cell phone rang and she dug for it in her briefcase. "Hello?" She listened to the voice on the other end and then put her hand over the receiver. "Honey," she whispered, "I have to take this call. Can I meet you up there?"

Anne shrugged and nodded.

"Get me a garden salad and an iced tea," Jill requested, and then put the phone back to her ear.

MAGGIE LEANED AGAINST the back wall as the creaky old elevator car made its laborious way up to the fifth floor. Two people had gotten on with her on the first floor. On the second floor, two more got on, filling the small car. She felt her breathing quicken and tried to force herself to take slower, deeper breaths. *Claustrophobia — that's a new one. My therapist is going to love that.*

She leaned her head back against the polished wood and tried to think of wide-open spaces. When the bell pinged and the doors jerked open on the third floor, two of her fellow passengers got off, and she sighed in relief. Then she noticed two people waiting to get on. One of them was Anne.

Maggie's attempts at deep breathing failed completely. She began to pant and felt her heart convulse in her chest. It pounded so hard it felt like it was fighting its way out. She tried not to meet Anne's eyes, but she couldn't turn her gaze from the face she loved.

Anne's blue eyes were dull and gray, as if covered by fog. Her skin was gaunt and deep lines were etched in her face, a permanent legacy of her misery.

She looks so tired, Maggie thought, and then tried to quash her sympathy. *I shouldn't feel sorry for her after what she did to me.*

Anne entered the elevator and instantly spotted her love slumped in the back corner. Anne's breathing stopped as she squeezed into the crowded car. She wanted to turn around and get off, but a man was moving in behind her and she found herself trapped in the small space. Her eyes met Maggie's, and she gazed at the face that had never once left her thoughts since she'd first seen it.

Maggie's sea green eyes were sparkling with unshed tears. Dark purple smudges marred the skin below them. The few freckles sprinkled across her nose stood out starkly against her ashen skin.

She looks so tired. But she's alive; she's going to be OK.

Anne and Maggie tore their eyes from each other, looking down at the scuffed floor. The two women, simultaneously, thought about saying something to the other. But reasons for staying silent quickly clamored for attention.

I'm just not strong enough.

It's still too soon.

I don't have the words.

I'm giving you space.

The elevator bell pinged as it arrived on the fourth floor. One of the passengers got off, and just as the doors began to close, Maggie pushed her way across the car and out the doors. Once out, she took a moment to breathe. She felt a movement behind her and quickly walked down the hallway. She had to find the stairs and get out of the building.

Anne saw Maggie move and followed her off the elevator without thinking. When Maggie turned and walked quickly down the hall, Anne stopped and considered what she was doing.

She doesn't want to be around me. I should let her go. She watched as Maggie got further away, obviously heading toward the stairwell.

"Maggie, wait!" Anne finally shouted. The words echoed loudly in the hallway—or maybe that was her imagination.

Maggie stopped as if a hand had clutched the back of her shirt. She tried to keep walking, but the invisible hand held her firm. She was frozen in place and couldn't turn around. She began to sweat as she heard Anne's footsteps coming up behind her.

"Please wait." Anne's voice cracked as her throat constricted around the plea. As she neared Maggie, she could see tremors coursing through the smaller woman.

She wanted to reach out and take Maggie into her arms and make everything all right. She wanted that more than she wanted anything in the world. She reached her hand toward Maggie's shoulder, but then let it fall again, bitter tears filling her eyes.

Anne's heart broke as she watched her love continue to stand and not turn around. Maggie reminded her of a baby bird that had fallen from the nest—shaking from cold and terror, and lifting unformed wings in a vain attempt to fly away. "Maggie, can you talk to me?"

Still Maggie stood, not responding or moving. Anne looked around desperately and spotted an unoccupied conference room. It was available to visiting lawyers, and she had the key code. "Come in here?" she hesitantly asked.

Anne thought Maggie would refuse, but finally the smaller woman slowly turned. Her movements were stiff, like *the Wizard of Oz*'s Tin Man without his oilcan. Anne opened the door and waited until Maggie entered, then followed, closing and locking the door behind them.

Maggie crossed the room to the window and opened the blinds. The bright sunlight streaming in through the slats warmed her skin, and she closed her eyes, trying to draw energy from it.

Anne stayed near the door, giving Maggie all the space she could. The sunlight cast her love in a golden glow, but also revealed the extent of her ravaged body. Although Maggie's red-gold hair was clean and brushed, it was dull and limp. Anne could clearly see the vertebrae at the top of Maggie's spine where it extended beyond the collar of her T-shirt. Her jeans hung off her hips and bagged around her knees.

"I should hate you," Maggie said suddenly, not turning around.

"Yes, you should." Anne was surprised that her voice was so firm. She believed Maggie's words implicitly.

For another minute, Maggie stood silently, not following up the statement. Then, she slowly turned and faced Anne. "I've planned what I would say to you when we finally saw each other."

Anne felt her heart break at the sound of Maggie's voice. It was as dull and limp as her once-beautiful hair. "Go ahead." She let her arms fall to the sides. "Say what you need to say to me."

"When I pictured it, I always started by slapping you," Maggie continued, but didn't move from her place near the window.

"If you need to do that, then do it," Anne said tremulously.

"Well, that's just it." Maggie folded her arms across her chest. "Now that we're here, I realize that I don't need to do that." She felt confused and tried to make sense of her feelings. She stopped speaking again and looked inside herself. "There's only one thing that I need," she finally said, "one thing that I've needed ever since you — since I woke up in the hospital."

Anne had worked for ten weeks to close away the memory of that night. Despite her mom and Roz's best attempts to talk to her about it, she'd manage to build high, thick walls around the pain. Maggie's soft, stumbling words obliterated those barriers, hitting Anne harder than any physical blow. Her hands trembled, and she also crossed her arms.

"Whatever you need, I'll give it to you." Anne just wanted the nightmare to end; she wanted to atone for everything that she'd done.

"I need to know why," Maggie said starkly, looking directly into Anne's eyes.

"What I did was wrong." Anne drew in a tortured breath. "I am so, so sorry."

"I know that you regret what you did, but I don't need to hear your apologies." Maggie's voice became firmer as she realized what she did need. "I'm asking you to be honest with me. Please just tell me why you walked out, what you were thinking and feeling. I need to understand."

Prompted by the words, another memory assailed Anne. Her mom stood before her. They'd been talking about Simone. *Did you tell her your feelings?* her mom had asked.

And it is really as simple as that, isn't it?

Anne cleared her throat and unfolded her arms. "When we first started dating, you would look at me like you worshiped me. You treated me like your hero, and although I was uncomfortable with that at first, to be honest, I started to like it."

She lowered her eyes in shame, but forced herself to make eye contact again. "It was easy to fall into the role. I've done it most of my life. But most of my life I've also screwed up. Simone and Katy being the last in a long line of fuck-ups."

"What happened to Simone wasn't your fault," Maggie said softly.

"Trying to save Simone in the first place was my decision. And so was not being there for Katy. I know all of the arguments for why it wasn't my fault, but in my heart I couldn't stop thinking it was. When you came into my life, I had this overpowering fear that I would screw up again." Tears filled Anne's eyes. "I fought against it over the months, but it plagued my dreams and haunted my waking life."

Anne paused, trembling. She forced herself to steady before continuing. "When I saw you lying in the hospital, my nightmares became real. I had failed you just like I'd failed everyone else I'd ever loved. I felt as if I were drowning—the guilt and the anger flooded my soul."

"Who were you angry with?" Maggie asked, failing to keep her voice steady. Her arms were still crossed, and she hugged herself tighter.

"I was angry with myself for not protecting you—for thinking that I ever could," Anne answered quickly. Then she ran her fingers through her ebony hair and her face crumpled. "And I was angry with you—for expecting me to be your hero. I felt trapped in a vicious circle." She rubbed at her face in frustration, and then looked back at Maggie. "Now I realize that those feelings were from me, not from you. I had no right to be angry with you."

"You're wrong." Maggie held her hand up to stop Anne's protests. "I did want a hero and I let you play that role." She began to pace in front of the window, but maintained eye contact with Anne. "I knew you blamed yourself for Simone, knew you had taken on way too much responsibility for your grandfather, and I knew that you were terrified for my safety. But I never talked to you about it—really talked."

"I pushed you away whenever you tried."

"Yes, and I didn't push back. Then, after telling you about Patrick, I let you swear to protect me. It made me feel so safe. I didn't spare a moment to think about what it would do to you. The inevitable pain I was setting you up for."

"This wasn't your fault," Anne said firmly, shaking her head resolutely. "None of this was ever your fault."

Maggie's pacing took her to one end of the table and she continued walking, coming to stand before Anne. "It is *our* fault—yours and mine. If we don't acknowledge that, we can't move forward together."

Maggie watched as Anne reacted to the words, hope and fear dancing across Anne's face.

"Do you understand that it was *our* fault?" Maggie prompted. "That we share in the blame for this?"

"I agree that we both made mistakes in our relationship." Anne nodded as the truth settled into her mind. "But what I did that night was still my fault, not yours."

"You should have come back. You should have told me what you were feeling. We should have talked and sorted everything out."

"Yes." Anne nodded.

"But you didn't. There's nothing we can do to take that night back, to change what happened. All we can do is try to never let it happen again — never hide or ignore the thoughts that are terrorizing us."

Anne felt her heart flutter as she once again glimpsed the possibility of a future with Maggie. But fear grabbed her by the throat and extinguished the glimmer of hope. "I don't ever want to hurt you again," she gasped. The tears finally fell from her eyes, dripping in a line down her cheeks and falling off her jaw, darkening her silk blouse.

"You will." Maggie had to say the words, though she didn't want to. She watched Anne react to them, rearing back as if she'd been punched. "Anne, listen to me." Maggie tried to keep her voice calm. "We can't go on fearing that we'll hurt each other. We will. Sometimes we'll get angry and say hurtful things. We'll argue, we'll disagree, we'll bicker. But we'll apologize and make up. We'll love, we'll share, we'll discuss everything." She added firmly, "Everything."

"Yes." Anne's eyes reflected her sincerity.

"And we both need to understand that bad things happen," Maggie continued resolutely. "They're not your fault or mine. We can't let the fear of bad things happening rule our lives, we can't rely on the other person to protect us from them, and we can't take the responsibility for them if they do. Can you accept that?"

Tears still fell in steady drops down Anne's face. She looked like a lost little girl and Maggie fought the urge to pull her into a hug and tell her that everything would be all right. Anne had to reach that conclusion by herself.

"I'm scared," Anne finally gasped.

"I know, sweetheart." Maggie reached out and softly brushed the tears from Anne's face. Anne closed her eyes and leaned into the delicate touch.

"Think about how you've felt these last few weeks." Maggie grasped Anne's hand. "Shutting out everything — all of your feelings, thoughts, memories — anything that reminded you of what happened. Not letting anyone get close enough to say the words you needed to hear, that needed to be said. I know what it was like; I did the same thing."

"It was the only thing I could do to survive," Anne explained as she felt the soft hand squeeze hers.

"No, we weren't surviving," Maggie corrected, her jaw clenching with the determination to make Anne understand. "We weren't alive. When you don't feel, don't respond, don't see the world around you, you're dead. I don't want that anymore." Her eyes blazed with resolve. "I choose to live."

Anne was in awe of the smaller woman's courage. She

realized it was time to show a little bravery herself. She stepped forward and enveloped Maggie, pulling the smaller body toward her, wrapping one arm around her back and tangling the other in her hair. Maggie laid her head against Anne's chest and Anne nuzzled her red-gold hair, breathing in the scent that she had thought she'd never experience again.

Maggie fell into the embrace and wrapped her arms around Anne, clutching frantically as emotions bombarded her. She felt like she'd been wandering in a blizzard for days and had finally stumbled into a warm room. Someone put a blanket around her shoulders and led her to a comfortable chair in front of a roaring fire.

She had finally come home.

Maggie and Anne both sobbed, letting all of their misery and guilt and anger wash away with their tears.

"I want to live, too," Anne managed to gasp between her tears. Maggie squeezed her tighter. They stood that way for a long time, until the tears finally slowed and stopped.

"How did you get to be so wise?" Anne pulled Maggie's head back gently and tenderly wiped the remaining tears from her face.

"Well, I did have a little help," Maggie admitted with a small grin. "A very good friend and a very good therapist."

Anne smiled and picked up Maggie's hand. As she brought it to her lips for a kiss, she noticed the bitten nails. Maggie tried to pull her hand away, but Anne held it firmly, kissing each swollen, red finger.

"Old habit that seems to have returned," Maggie said ruefully. "Another thing my therapist and I need to work on. Although I think your kisses have already cured me."

"Then I'll just have to keep kissing you." Anne smiled. Maggie watched as the shadows cleared from the blue eyes.

"I can't believe this is happening," Maggie whispered. She trembled at the thought that she would wake up and find that it was all just a dream.

"It's real." With a finger under Maggie's chin, Anne tenderly tilted up the beautiful face. She softly kissed Maggie's forehead, feeling the tense lines relax under her lips. Then she kissed the dark smudges under each eye, tasting the salt of Maggie's tears. Finally, she met Maggie's lips.

The kiss brought a gentle warmth that settled into all of the cold places that lurked inside. The two women could almost hear a gentle click, as two pieces of the same soul were melded together once more.

"I've never been so terrified in my life," Anne whispered.

"But I can't let you go."

"I don't want you to let go. I still want you to be my hero."

Anne frowned in confusion, and Maggie brushed a finger over her lips. "I understand that I need to be my own hero. I need to face things on my own, learn to live in my own skin. You want to be a hero to me, without feeling that my life is dependent on you. Bottom line, we want to grow and become better people, right?"

"Of course," Anne replied firmly, running her fingertips lightly up and down Maggie's back.

"Then we'll grow together." Maggie drowned in the ocean of Anne's eyes. "I want to screw up and stumble, excel and run, and everything in between—but I want to do it by your side."

"So do I. " Anne clenched her jaw. "I still can't believe you forgive me."

"You made a mistake," Maggie replied solemnly. "You also did hundreds of wonderful things before that night. I made mistakes too, but hopefully did a few good things as well."

"Are we being graded on a curve?" A smile spread across Anne's face.

"I hope so," Maggie replied with an answering smile. "God, do I ever hope so."

Carrie, known online as zuke, began writing TV scripts at eight and forcing her friends to act them out. She lives and works in the San Francisco Bay Area with her husband and two rambunctious cats. When not writing, she is an IT consultant and avid cyclist.

Printed in the United States
33372LVS00005B/79-120